"Nicole, I—" Joshua stepped forward, realizing she was crying, and reached up to wipe the crystal drop away from her cheek.

"I'm sorry," he whispered, shamed that in all the months she'd been here, he'd never really considered what he'd asked of her.

"You don't have anything to be sorry for." She looked at him. A smile quivered across her lips.

"Then why are you crying? It must have been something I said."

"It wasn't that." She shook her head, pale hair flying around her shoulders. "It was just— everything."

"Huh?" He studied her, trying to understand.

"The emotion of the moment," she whispered. "I think I finally realized how proud you must feel sometimes. For a minute, it was almost as if your girls were my daughters, and we'd—" Her voice jerked to a stop. She blinked at him, a shocked look washing over her face.

LOIS RICHER

Sneaking a flashlight under the blankets, hiding in a thicket of Caragana bushes where no one could see, pushing books into socks to take to camp—those are just some of the things Lois Richer freely admits to in her pursuit of the written word.

"I'm a bookaholic. I can't do without stories," she confesses. "It's always been that way."

Her love of language evolved into writing her own stories. Today her passion is to create tales of personal struggle that lead to triumph over life's rocky road. For Lois, a happy ending is essential.

"In my stories, as in my own life, God has a way of making all things beautiful. Writing a love story is my way of reinforcing my faith in His ultimate goodness toward us—His precious children."

BLESSINGS

LOIS RICHER

Love Inspired.

Published by Steeple Hill Books

STEEPLE HILL BOOKS

Steeple
Hill®

ISBN 0-373-87233-X

BLESSINGS

Visit us at www.steeplehill.com

Printed in U.S.A.

I love the Lord because He listens to my prayers
for help. He paid attention to me so I will call
to Him for help as long as I live.
—*Psalms* 116:1-2

This book is for those people
in my own blessed community whose support,
kind words and gentle encouragement are
treasures a writer esteems most highly.

And for my boys, C and J, who now understand
glazed eyes, scribbles on bits of paper and
burnt lasagna are "normal" things for this mom.

And, as always, to my husband—
patient doesn't begin to describe you, dear.

Thanks.

Chapter One

"**W**hat have you done with my daughter?"

As fresh beginnings went, it stunk.

Barely an hour in a picturesque town with the unusual name of Blessing, Colorado, and already an irate father loomed.

"Where is she? And while you're at it, Arvilla, direct me to the unfeeling lout who ran over her. I'd like to press charges."

Blessing? They should have called it Catastrophe Corner!

Dr. Nicole Brandt gulped, fingers tightening on the stainless-steel kidney dish she was holding. The husky male voice continued its furious diatribe, though now it was muffled by the door Nicole's tiny patient quickly closed.

"That's my dad," the little girl whispered. "But don't worry, he's just scared. He always talks loud when he's scared." Tiny fingers curved around Nicole's lower arm, infusing warmth. "He's just pretending to be fierce."

He's doing a good job.

"Thanks, sweetie. I hope you're right." Nicole led the little tyke back to the table and lifted her onto it. "You'd better wait right here for him. Okay?"

The angel-wisp hair barely moved with the nod before they were interrupted.

"Ruth Ann?"

In a whoosh the door whacked back against the wall, knob thudding into the doorstop with a dull bump. A man stalked in, his long legs swallowing the considerable distance across E.R. room number two with ease. He stopped in front of the child, eyes searching her pale face, hand half-stretched as if he didn't dare touch.

"Are you all right, baby?" The words dragged out of him.

"I'm fine, Daddy. I hurt my arm." The little girl smiled sweetly from her perch on the examining table.

"You scared me to death, Ruth Ann Elizabeth." He closed his eyes, leaned back on his heels and lowered his voice. "To death."

"I'm sorry, Daddy." China-blue eyes big as saucers filled with mournful tears. "I didn't mean to do it. I never do. It just happened, Daddy."

Nicole smothered a smile as Ruth Ann's sad tears melted away and a cherubic look flew in to take their place.

"But it's okay now 'cause the lady fixed it." She held up her almost dry cast. "See? I got a cast."

"Huh?" The raven head jerked up from his chest, eyes flew open. He bent over her. "What did you say?"

Nicole stepped forward, wanting to reassure him. Her steps faltered as his enormous shoulders stiffened into a rigid line.

"What *lady* fixed it, Ruth Ann?" The words hissed out between clenched lips.

"This one." Nicole waited for him to face her, heart thudding when he did. "I fixed it."

Wow! Her eyes absorbed his chiseled good looks only until she realized they were marred by an angry frown. He had a right to be upset, Nicole reminded herself. No matter how gently you put it, his little daughter had been injured. Of course he was worried!

"Dr. Nicole Brandt, sir." She stuck out one hand, smiling. "I just happened to be in the area."

He didn't take her hand. Didn't even acknowledge it was there. Nicole let it drop to her side as his eyes completed their in-depth scrutiny of her blond hair, loosened now from its usual upsweep. With one assessing examination he took in her dusty green shirt, faded jeans and grubby, worn sneakers. Her moving clothes.

"You're the new doctor." It was not a question.

Nicole held on to her dignity by a thread.

"Yes, I am. I arrived this morning. I'm sorry about your daughter's arm. I happened to drive past the accident on my way from a tour of the hospital. The policeman had seen me here earlier. He said the ambulance was busy, but he thought it would be all right if I drove everyone here. Fortunately, the break was clean and easily set."

"You don't say?"

Something in the way he said that made Nicole choke back the rest of her rushed explanation. She examined his face more closely. His eyes glowed the same rich blue as his daughter's, but there were fine lines at the corners. Worry lines. And a harshness lay behind his eyes that Ruthie certainly didn't have, an icy bitterness that warned her of something he kept banked up, hidden from prying substitute doctors.

She swallowed and tried again. "The housekeeper—Mrs. Tyndall, isn't it?" His head jerked, once.

"Yes, well, she was there. I brought her and your other daughters with us to the hospital. Mrs. Tyndall assured me she was fully authorized to consent to treatment for Ruthie, and since the nurses didn't object, I decided—"

"*You* decided?"

To say he smiled was to overstate that grim uplift of his mouth. So...arrogant. As if he questioned not just her brains, but her ability.

Nicole shrugged the thought away. It was a small-town thing, that's all. Once she was established in the clinic, had the local guy's blessing, they'd come to accept her.

She hoped.

"Excuse me? You were saying?" One black eyebrow flicked up at her in silent demand.

"Yes. Sorry." Nicole flushed, the hot red stain burning her cheeks, then plunging down her neck. She summoned her courage.

"I was going to say that *I decided* it was best to treat your daughter quickly, get the arm into a cast as soon as possible. Since we did have permission." She smiled at Ruthie, wishing her father would lighten up. "Kids this age are pretty active."

"I'm well aware of the antics of children this age." His eyes frosted over to a glacial chill. "You may remember that I have three of them."

"Oh." Actually he might have ten for all Nicole knew. No doubt he thought the nurses had already told her. "Yes, of course, Mr.—?" She glanced up, wondering if he'd ignore the hint, as before.

"Darling," he finished smoothly. "Joshua Darling. And it's Doctor."

"Ah. I see." Oh, no! Nicole prayed for courage. This

was the man she'd be working with? Her heart did a nosedive straight to her toes. *Good one, Nici. Alienate him first thing. Excellent beginning.*

She forced herself to smile.

"It's nice to finally meet you, Dr. Darling."

His dubious look cast doubt on her statement. "I'd like to see the X rays. Now."

"Yes, of course." She turned to find the nurse who'd hovered while she set the arm, but there was no one else in the room. "I'm sorry, I don't know where she's taken them."

"Arvilla!" Dr. Darling barked the word out loudly enough that the whole hospital could have heard.

"Yes, Doctor. I'm here." The short, bustling woman handed him a big brown envelope. "I suspected you'd want to see these, so I didn't file them—yet."

He snapped the pictures out of the envelope and onto the light screen, peering at the outline for several minutes before he turned his glare on the petite nurse.

"You didn't *suspect* I'd want to set my own daughter's arm?" His blue eyes dared the nurse to flinch. "You know that nobody treats my family but me."

"You were out of town, Joshua. At the clinic. We didn't know when you'd be back. Ruthie had a simple fracture. Since Dr. Brandt has already been approved by our board and the forms have all been processed, I saw no reason she shouldn't go ahead and help your daughter."

"Really?" Dr. Darling glared for two seconds longer, then returned his gaze to the pictures.

Arvilla looked small, but Nicole just knew she was one of those people with a mighty spirit. She could tell it from the way the nurse refused to back down. That thought cheered her immeasurably when her own knees threatened to buckle under his icy regard.

"She was hurt, Joshua," Arvilla whispered. "And we could help her. Isn't that exactly what you would have wanted us to do?"

He sighed then, tiredly, as if he'd had one too many emergencies today. A large capable hand raked through his hair before he gathered the little girl in his arms and hugged her against his chest. His words whispered out over the angel-fair ringlets.

"I'm sorry, Arvilla. Of course you did what's best for Ruth Ann. I know that. It's just that I remembered—"

To Nicole's surprise, Arvilla stretched one chubby arm up and patted the forbidding doctor on the back of his football shoulders, forestalling whatever he'd been about to say.

"I know, Dr. Darling," she murmured, her eyes kind as they met his. "I understand. And this little monkey is fine, thanks to your new partner. That's the important thing, isn't it?"

"Yes, it is." He glanced over Ruthie's head, his blue eyes meeting Nicole's.

The ice didn't exactly melt, but Nicole thought there was a Chinook in the offing.

"Thank you for helping my daughter." He set the child down.

"You're welcome." She glanced from doctor to nurse, unsure of how she should proceed. "I'm sorry if I did something wrong."

But Joshua Darling ignored her to kneel on the floor in front of his child.

"What happened, honey? How did you break your arm?"

The little girl fidgeted, her eyes avoiding his until at

last she met his scrutiny. "Riding the scooter," she mumbled.

"In the street?"

He stayed exactly where he was, but Nicole saw the tightness grip his body, felt the tension surge into the room.

"Just on the edge." Ruthie's eyes dropped and her bottom lip trembled. "I was showing Roz and Rach how to do a trick an' it bounced on the curb and flew up. I couldn't stop it fast enough." The words tumbled out helter-skelter.

"I'm afraid the scooter is a write-off," Nicole admitted with a rueful smile. "Perhaps I could help her choose a new one?"

"That won't be necessary." Joshua Darling never even looked at Nicole. "When something is ruined because we broke the rules, we can only blame ourselves. Isn't that right, Ruth Ann?"

"Uh-huh." She sniffed back a sob, dashing one dirt-smeared fist across her cheek. "I'm really sorry, Daddy."

"Sorry that you broke it, or sorry that you got caught?" He let her think about it for a minute. "You're Rosalyn's older sister, Ruth Ann. She looks up to you. What if she tries to copy you next time and a car comes along? She could be very badly hurt. Being a big sister who disobeys is dangerous. Do you understand?"

Ruthie sniffed, her flaxen head bobbing up and down once in silent agreement. "I won't ever do it again, Daddy. Promise."

"Good. Now Arvilla will take you to Mrs. Tyndall and the other girls. Tell Mrs. Tyndall I said you can all go home in a taxi. We'll talk about your punishment later."

"Yes, Daddy."

"Good." He kissed the top of her shiny blond head and received a hug in return. "Off you go."

As the child left the room with the nurse, Nicole watched Dr. Darling rise to his feet. He looked haggard, defeated. His shoulders slumped under the tired tweed of his jacket.

Nicole simply stood, watched and waited.

At last he remembered her, his eyes sliding up to meet hers. At that moment a mask slid over his face, concealing the worry and fear she thought she'd glimpsed. In one second he went from concerned father to the doctor in charge.

"Dr. Brandt, I am truly glad you've arrived, though I apologize for the circumstances. I shouldn't have barked at you so rudely. Please accept my excuse of absolute fear and allow me to begin again. I'm Joshua Darling." At last he thrust out his hand.

"It's very nice to meet you." Nicole shook it, assessing the firm grip. It was the kind of grip you could depend on. "I was actually looking for my new home when I ran into your daughter."

Uh-oh, bad choice of words. His lips pinched in a grim line as he frowned at her.

"This is Thursday. Surely you realize that you don't actually start the job until Monday?"

"Oh, I realize that was the arrangement you and Professor Adams came to, but I didn't want to leave everything till the last minute. I thought I'd get settled in, take a look around the hospital, see the town this weekend and be all ready for work Monday morning." *I also had to get out of the city before my father could change my mind.*

Dr. Darling nodded as if her reasons were perfectly normal. He checked his watch, then beckoned.

"Follow me. I have a few scripts to write, then I'll show you where Aunt Winifred lives, though I can't fathom how you could miss the place. Not after the detailed description I gave your professor."

Now might not be the time to admit she hadn't exactly been looking at the house numbers. Nicole had a hunch Dr. Darling was already suspicious of her abilities, so he'd hardly understand she'd been caught up in the homey scene of kids playing on big green lawns, of dogs barking and porch swings swaying in the April breezes. He probably took all of that for granted, living in a place called Blessing.

Once he'd signed the appropriate paperwork, Nicole trailed behind Dr. Darling out of the hospital and across to the doctor's parking area. He stopped beside a nondescript beige four-door station wagon that looked as if it had seen many miles of tough country road.

"I'm assuming you have your car with you?"

She nodded, pointed to the red sports car her father had given her last winter. The contrast between it and his couldn't have been greater. Joshua Darling's eyes widened in disbelief.

"You got them all in that?" he squeaked. "Even Mrs. Tyndall?"

Nicole subdued her smile, nodded.

"It wasn't easy, but then, we didn't have far to go."

"Thank heavens." He grimaced at the folded-back roof. "Not exactly meant for kids. It might be best to ride with me for now. That way I can point out a few landmarks on the way. I'll bring you back later to collect…that." He jerked a thumb at her car. "I have to come back for rounds, anyway."

"Fine."

So he didn't like sports cars. Or maybe it was the color. That was a switch. In Boston the medical residents had tried to bribe her to go out with them just so they could drive it.

Nicole shrugged and told herself she didn't much care either way, as long as it got her where she wanted to go. It was just a car, not an indication of her personality. In fact, she would willingly have tossed the keys back at her father, returned the expensive vehicle in a second, for a chance to hear him say the words she'd longed for all these years.

But Shane Brandt had never said he loved her, not since her mother's death twenty-four years ago.

Dr. Darling tugged open the door on the passenger side of his car and Nicole climbed in. He got in the other side, then started the motor.

"I guess we'll start with the main part of town. That brick building is the office. We're open Monday to Friday, nine to five. Receptionist, one lab tech and a nurse. Closed for holidays and weekends. Town hall, recreation center, library, church." He rattled off the information, waving a hand here and there as they rolled along at a sedate twenty-one miles per hour.

"Those are apartments for seniors. Out of fashion though it may be, we still occasionally make house calls there."

He seemed to be waiting for her to comment, but Nicole only nodded, scanning the pretty town curiously.

"This is the oldest part of Blessing, as you can see by the houses here."

"It's lovely." Nicole gaped at the huge wraparound porches and burgeoning flower beds that perched on vast green lawns like the backdrop in some whimsical fairy tale.

"Most of them have been kept up pretty well. Some are historic sites." He waved a hand toward a small blue lake. "The newer architectural wonders in Blessing are over there. They don't take near the same amount of upkeep, have normal heating bills and enjoy a great view."

"Oh, but these old houses are chock-full of character. They're charming."

Except for the one on the far end. It looked... neglected? No, that wasn't exactly the word. The paint was fine. It was more the shaggy lawn and unplanted flower beds that seemed out of place here in never-never land.

Nicole ignored it and focused instead on the maple-lined streets. "The town is lovely."

"Yes, it is. This one is Aunt Winifred's home. It's way too big for her, of course, but as the self-appointed matriarch of Blessing, she feels compelled to maintain her place in the history of the town. Besides—" he grinned, his lips curving with affection "—she grew up in this mausoleum and won't hear of leaving it."

Nicole swallowed, stunned by his good looks when he let go of that forbidding reserve. "I can understand why she doesn't want to leave," she murmured, glancing at the house, which she'd admired earlier.

He pulled up to the curb and stopped the car.

"Come on. I'm sure she's home. It's Thursday afternoon, after all."

Whatever that meant.

Nicole climbed out of the car and followed him through the white picket gate and up a sidewalk flanked by hordes of sunny daffodils waving in the gentle breeze.

The house was a masterpiece of pure Victoriana. It was the same house she'd been ogling just before Ruthie had clashed with the pavement. So how come this woman— their aunt?—hadn't offered to help?

They climbed five sparkling-white steps bounded by climbing shrubs and huge clay pots with dark purple pansies peeking out, to arrive at a brilliant red door.

"She's a bit eccentric, but she has a good heart. This door is about the only thing she's changed in the place." Dr. Darling rapped the brass knocker with authority, then twisted the handle to open the door.

"Aunt Winifred? It's me."

A woman bustled into the foyer, wiping her hands on an immense white apron as she did. She had to be over sixty, but she was obviously not living in the past. Her soft fawn-colored hair lay in short, stylish waves about her face. She wore a periwinkle-blue blouse tucked into matching slacks, pure white sneakers and a smile as big as all outdoors.

"Joshua! My dear, how are you?" She hugged him exuberantly, as if she hadn't seen him in months. "Come in. I'm glad I made it back before you arrived. Thursday afternoons are supposed to be my time off, and I usually go shopping. But it's so busy in the afternoons that buying groceries always takes longer than I expect." She frowned, brushed his hair back off his forehead. "You look tired, dear. What have those girls been up to now?"

"More of the same, I'm afraid. Ruth Ann broke her arm today."

"Mercy!" The older woman tut-tutted her dismay, but her eyes were on Nicole. "I'm sorry I wasn't here to help."

One mystery solved.

"Aunt Winifred, this is Dr. Nicole Brandt. She's going

to be working with me. And staying with you, if the deal's still on.''

"Of course it's on. How lovely you are, dear. Your hair is quite gorgeous. I always did say blondes have more fun." Miss Winifred winked as she shook Nicole's hand firmly. "I'm going to love having company here. This big old house rattles with just me in it."

"You could move out, you know. Those new condos on the hill are much smaller." Joshua glanced around, grimacing. "There's too much work here for you."

"Nonsense! This place has been standing since Matthais Blessing first built it in 1874. The Blessings have always lived here. Besides, what would I do without my gardens? Come."

She led them out to a screened porch that sat at the back of the house. Here, too, flowers dotted the deck and the yard beyond in a riot of color.

Nicole cleared her throat. "Excuse me, I don't think I understood. You mean you're one of the original founders of this town?" She glanced at Joshua. *What about the "aunt" relationship?*

"We're not related by blood," Joshua muttered.

"Actually, I'm not an *original,* either." Miss Winifred fluffed her hair, preening just a little. "I am the last of the direct descendants, however."

"Yes, of course. Er, that's what I meant. Sorry." Nicole winced at her tactless words. "You must be very proud that the town has done so well. It looks like a lovely place to live."

"It is, rather. We have our problems, but we manage. I've never wanted to live anywhere else." Miss Winifred set a pitcher of iced tea on the table, then fetched three glasses. "Joshua did tell me where you were from, but I'm afraid I've forgotten."

"Boston." Nicole let it go at that. There was no point in explaining. People seldom understood.

"But how wonderful! I lived in Boston when my father sent me to finishing school." Miss Winifred smiled. "He thought it was important for me to be trained in society. Of course, people don't worry about that anymore, but it was a big thing then."

"My father sent me to Lucerne to be 'finished.'" Nicole regretted saying it the moment the words left her lips. It sounded pompous, as if she were bragging.

But Miss Winifred merely nodded, her eyes far away. "A lovely place. I always wanted to visit Switzerland."

"Yes, it is special. But so is this." Nicole took a sip of the drink, eyes widening at the flavor. "Your tea is wonderful."

"Raspberry juice, dear. Gives it a hint of fruit flavor without overpowering." Miss Winifred sat down opposite Joshua. "Boston's elegant in the springtime, too, of course."

"Yes. I've loved it there. But a change will be nice."

Up to now Joshua hadn't said anything. Suddenly he cleared his throat.

"I understand that Blessing is just a short stop on your path," he said quietly, as if testing Nicole.

Don't be so touchy! He's probably worried that you'll take off at a moment's notice.

"Well, Professor Adams did say you wanted a temporary doctor," Nicole reminded him. "I believe that was the arrangement with your first candidate, though I understand he never actually showed up?"

"No, he backed out at the last minute." His face tightened, lips pinched in a tight white line.

"I see. Well, I can't commit to staying permanently,

but I'm willing to help out for six months or so, less if you don't need me anymore.''

"That's fine. I shouldn't think it would take much longer than six months to find a new partner,'' he mumbled, obviously considering the shortness of her visit a blessing.

"But, Joshua, six months isn't long at all! I had hopes Nicole might enjoy it here and want to settle down.'' The older woman seemed disturbed by this news, as if she hadn't known her houseguest wouldn't be a permanent resident of the town.

"Oh, I'm sure I shall enjoy every minute, Miss Winifred.'' Nicole glanced around. "Especially in this wonderful home. You can just feel the history, can't you?''

"Besides, Aunt Winifred, in six months she won't have a chance to tire of the scenery before she heads back to Boston. Isn't that right, Ms. Brandt?''

Nicole blinked. Was he afraid she'd stick around too long?

"I thought you were a doctor?'' Miss Winifred fiddled with the condensation on her glass, forehead furrowed. "I understood you were fully qualified to work with my nephew.''

"Yes, I am.''

"Then why on earth wouldn't you want her to stay, Joshua? A lovely young woman like this would be a boon to our town.'' Miss Winifred studied him curiously. "Certainly the single men will think so.''

She had the same vivid eyes as Dr. Darling, Nicole noted, vaguely surprised by the discovery. Hadn't he said they weren't blood relatives?

His sigh was audible.

"I told you all this before, Aunt Win. Remember? I'm looking for a partner, someone permanent, like I had before...." Joshua Darling's voice died away. His eyes seemed to lose their shine and harden. Clearly he detested explaining.

"Yes, but..."

Nicole jumped into the awkward moment.

"I'm afraid I wouldn't be able to stay anyway, Miss Winifred."

"Oh. Why, dear?" Miss Winifred looked faintly troubled by the words. "Are you engaged?"

"Oh, no. Nothing like that." Nicole could just imagine her father's response to that. "I'm waiting for a spot to open up so I can take some advanced surgical training. A professor of mine thought I should use this time to make sure I won't regret my decision not to stay in general practice."

"I see." Miss Winifred seemed disturbed by this news. "That's too bad."

"No, it's good for us, Aunt Win. It gives me a little more leeway to find a new partner. It's an important decision and I don't want to rush it, but I can't spend every waking moment at the office or the clinic. I've got to spend some time with the girls, too. Especially now that they're growing so fast. This way some of the pressure will be off."

By the look of his face as he raked a hand through his black hair, Nicole thought Dr. Darling needed a break. His head tilted back. He leaned against the wicker chair and closed his eyes, weariness evident in the etched lines on his face.

Nicole felt a rush of sympathy for him. She actually knew very little of his history except that he was a single parent and his partner had left rather abruptly.

"I was told that you run satellite clinics as well as your regular office. How do you manage that and the office hours?'' Perhaps there was more than one way she could help.

''It isn't easy. For the past month I've done the clinics every other week. On those days I open the office here in Blessing from five in the evening until nine, after I return from the satellites. Today's one of those days.''

No wonder he was tired!

''I could go with you tonight, if you like. Just to give you a hand. Surely with two of us, things would go faster?''

He sat up with a jerk, suddenly wide awake.

''That's, er, very kind of you. But no, I think I can manage for the rest of this week.''

''But why—'' She stopped, surprised by the stern look on his face.

''Look, Dr. Brandt. It's very important to me that my office operates on a certain routine, within prearranged parameters. I don't make sudden changes and I don't adjust anything unless I'm certain it will be either cost-effective or serve my patients better. I've managed to keep my practice very successful by following a precise organizational method, and I would like, as much as is possible, for you to adhere to that schedule.''

''Well, yes, of course.'' Nicole blinked. *What on earth have I gotten into?* ''I was just offering to help.''

''Which I appreciate.'' He drained his glass and stood, peering down at her. ''But I think you've done enough today. Ruth Ann's arm was above and beyond the call of duty.''

''It was just a cast!''

Nicole hated to have him towering over her, so she stood and faced him. Something strange was at work here. She just wished she knew what it was. Then she saw the little nerve ticking just under his jaw, and real-

ized there were many things her new boss wasn't saying.
Perhaps it was better to back off now, and find out what
was behind all this from his ''aunt.''

''If that's your wish, Dr. Darling, it's perfectly fine by
me. If you change your mind, just let me know. Otherwise I'll see you in the office Monday morning at eight.''

He blinked, then nodded.

''I hope you won't mind if I catch a ride back with
you. My car's still at the hospital.''

''Yes, of course. And I still have rounds.'' He bent to
press a kiss against Miss Winifred's white powdered
cheek. ''You're sure you want to do this? It won't be too
much?''

She laughed, a light musical trill.

''I'll love it. Nicole, you come on back and we'll get
you settled in. Then we'll have a chat—just us girls.''

That laugh was infectious. Nicole found herself grinning as she climbed into Dr. Darling's car and waved at
the tiny figure surrounded by flowers.

''Your aunt's quite a woman,'' she murmured, retracing the route with her eyes as they traveled.

''Yes, she is. I hope you'll enjoy it there, but if you
feel the need to be on your own, she'll understand. She
possesses a very strong intuition where people are concerned.''

''You sound as if you expect the worst.'' Nicole stared
at his frown and decided to bite the bullet. ''Perhaps it
might be better if you just said outright what it is that's
bothering you about my presence here, Dr. Darling.''

''Perhaps you're right.'' He slid into his spot at the
hospital, switched off the engine and turned to face her.
''I hope you won't find this offensive.''

''I'll manage. Please speak freely.'' She blinked at the
relief that flooded his face. What on earth—

"The position you are filling was only ever meant to be temporary." He swallowed, his Adam's apple bobbing up and down. "No matter how much you like it in Blessing, no matter what my aunt says, I am not looking to you as a permanent partner."

"I thought we'd settled all this," she sputtered, more than a little surprised by the vehemence of his words. "I intend to return to school."

"Good. Because when I take a partner, I intend for that person to be perfectly suited to my practice. I've spent years devising certain strategies that have proven themselves over time. I have no need or desire to change my approach. Whomever I take on will have to accept my ways and get used to them."

"I see." She unlatched the door, then twisted to look up at him. "In fact, you're looking for the perfect partner."

"Yes, exactly."

"And apparently you believe that person is not me." She shrugged. "Well, don't worry, Dr. Darling. It doesn't sound like my kind of thing at all." She took a breath, then let out the words she knew she'd regret. "Actually, what you're describing doesn't sound like a partnership at all. More like a dictatorship."

He didn't seem offended.

"Maybe it is. Whatever you want to call it, that's what I intend to have. I hope you're willing to stay under these conditions, knowing you won't be a permanent fixture in town."

Well, really! Could he be any more blunt?

Nicole climbed out of the car, her mind racing with all the things she wanted to say. But only one thing was really important.

She slammed the door, then leaned down to speak through the open window.

"I'm a doctor, just like you, Dr. Darling. My patients always come first. After that, I'll do my best to follow your, er, dictates. See you Monday."

As she walked across the pavement to her car, Nicole had to force herself not to dig in her heels. She was so mad!

Cranky, rude, sourpuss—the names bubbled up. Those three sweet, innocent little girls were his daughters? How could such a thing be possible? He was so…cold.

"Welcome to Blessing," she muttered to herself as she got into her car. She drove out of the lot and took the first right turn back to Miss Winifred's, plotting her conversation as she went.

Miss Winifred. Yes, I do believe I'll take you up on your offer of that talk. But I think our main topic of discussion had better be Dr. Joshua Darling.

Nicole pulled up in front of the gorgeous house and switched off her car. All around the sound of children's laughter permeated the air.

"Yes, indeedy. By the time Monday morning comes around, I ought to be well prepared to deal with Dr. Joshua Darling." She flicked the trunk lock open and climbed out, preparing to carry her cases inside.

"For my first question—how in the world have the good folks of Blessing allowed a crusty grouch like him to retain the name Darling?"

As beginnings went, maybe that wasn't a bad place to start.

Chapter Two

Monday morning, armed with determination, her black bag and a prayer for patience, Dr. Nicole Brandt thrust back her shoulders and walked into the offices of Joshua Darling, M.D.

Did I really need this detour on the road to surgery, God?

Since she'd been asking the same question for days now, she didn't wait for an answer, but sucked up her courage and smiled at the woman behind the desk as she saluted.

"Dr. Nicole Brandt. Reporting for duty."

The nurse grinned, sharing the joke as she tossed off a slightly lopsided salute in return.

"Penny Zane, Dr. Brandt. And this is Carole Court, our resident lab tech. Edwina Jessop, our receptionist, only comes in for afternoons. You'll meet her later. We've been expecting you."

"Uh-oh. That sounds ominous. Who squealed on me?" Nicole pulled her lips into a pout of complaint.

"Ruthie. We saw the cast." Penny's eyes sparkled

with mischief. "Don't ever tell her a secret. She'll spill it every time, usually at the worst possible moment."

"I'll remember that." Nicole grinned. "She is a sweetie, though, isn't she? All that wispy fair hair makes me think of a little cherub."

Carole and Penny shared a look.

"What did I say?" Nicole didn't understand the flicker of understanding that passed between them. Was there something wrong with Ruthie?

"Dr. Brandt. I'm glad you could make it." Joshua stood in the doorway, his expression stern. "I'm assuming that you've already met my staff and signed the appropriate forms, so we'll get started."

He waited a moment, then lifted one black eyebrow in a query that silently spoke volumes. Nicole stifled her sigh and nodded.

"Yes, of course, Dr. Darling."

"I'll take your bag and put it in your office while you have a look around, Dr. Brandt." Penny whisked the article out of Nicole's hands, her lips barely moving as she leaned closer to whisper, "We'll do the sign-up later."

"Thank you, Penny." Nicole offered her a huge grin of gratitude.

"No problem. If you need anything, just let me know. Technically Dr. Darling is the boss, but I'm really in charge of this place." She tossed Joshua an impudent grin that was not returned, then sauntered down the hall. Carole followed her.

"Your staff seem very nice," Nicole murmured, searching for some way to open the discussion.

"They do a good job."

That wasn't what she meant, but Nicole let it go. He directed her to a small gloomy room.

"This is your office. Penny or Carole will leave the patient's file here." He continued on with a litany of instructions that delineated each and every action she was expected to perform during office hours. "Any questions?"

Nicole blinked.

Questions? She had a ton of them, and most began with why. He had a system, that much was clear. But was it a system that worked as efficiently as it could? Not so far as she could see. Changes rippled through her brain one after the other and she opened her mouth to suggest a few.

But one glimpse at Joshua Darling's face had her clamping her lips together without uttering a single word. Now was not the time. She was the new kid on the block, hadn't even seen a single patient, excluding Ruthie. Prudence would be wise.

"I asked if you had any questions, Dr. Brandt."

"Yes, I heard you." She swallowed, her eyes trailing around the dull, barren little office.

At least I can change some things in here. It is my office, after all.

"And your answer is?" He shifted from one foot to the other, impatient to begin his own work.

"I think perhaps it would be best if we dealt with my questions as they arise. I'm sure there will be some, but let's not anticipate them."

"I've found anticipation helps circumvent a number of problems. It makes you prepared, Dr. Brandt." He stood there, a dubious look on his face. "You're sure you can handle this? We're fully booked up for the entire week. If it gets too much for you, I'd like to know as soon as possible."

He thought she was going to leave him high and dry.

The revelation shocked her. Did he really assume she was such a poor doctor that she'd hightail it out the moment life got complicated? Then he had no idea of Nicole Brandt's durability. She didn't run out when things got tough. Not ever.

Pride and determination coursed through her veins. Compared to the rest of her life, this job in Blessing would be a piece of cake.

"I'll be fine, Dr. Darling. I'm used to being busy. I promise you I won't collapse under the strain."

He wasted several more seconds peering at her as if he couldn't ascertain whether or not she was serious. Then he shrugged.

"Fine. I'll admit I'm rather relieved to hear that, Dr. Brandt."

"Feel free to call me Nicole." She grinned. "After all, in a town this small, everyone must know everyone else's business. Surely first names wouldn't be out of place?"

"I prefer to retain a degree of formality in the office, Dr. Brandt. It engenders patient trust." His eyes flashed an unspoken warning.

The words slipped out before she could control them.

"Are you saying that your patients don't trust you unless you call them by their surnames?"

As a joke, it fell flat.

His whole body stiffened.

"My patients think of me as their doctor, their physician. When they walk through those doors, they expect me to treat their diseases." His lips pinched white. "What they believe or chatter about outside of this office is none of my concern. Now, if you've nothing else, your first patient is waiting."

Dr. Joshua Darling turned on his heel and left the room.

"Ouch!" Nicole flopped down on the edge of her desk, her eyes wide with shock. "Why do I feel as if he doesn't really want me here?"

"Because he doesn't." Penny slipped through the door and whipped it closed behind her. "I mean, he does want your help. He can't possibly function without it anymore. But he hates change and lately he's had to deal with a lot of that."

"Miss Winifred told me about his wife. How sad."

"It was horrible, of course. Cancer always is. But that was only the beginning." Penny straightened a tilting stack of files and opened the first one on the desk. "Sign here."

"You mean about his partner leaving for South America?" Nicole took the hint and moved to sit while she scrawled her name across the papers presented. "Yes, I can understand how difficult that must have been."

"He never said a word, of course, but I think he felt abandoned. They'd been quite close. Then, when you add all of that to his problems at home. Well." She threw up her hands. "I guess it's no wonder he gets a little testy now and then. The next one, too, please."

"At home?" Nicole signed. "What's wrong at home?"

Penny chuckled. "Stick around, Doc. You'll understand after a few days. Those little cherubs you saw can wreak a lot of havoc. We're trying to make allowances for him."

And that, Nicole guessed as the nurse scurried out of the room, was blatantly obvious. She knew from Miss Winifred that Dr. Darling's wife had died of cancer almost two years ago. But he was a doctor—he'd seen death before. Of course, it was far worse when it was someone you loved, but he had his daughters. Surely he was learning to cope?

"Your patient is in examining room two, Dr. Brandt. May I show you the way?" He stood in the doorway, watching her.

"No, thanks. I just need a second or two more with this file. I promise I won't knock your schedule off too far." She smiled, then glanced back down at the case history.

"See that you don't."

Nicole made a face at his back, then snatched up the file and stalked toward the room. Tonight she was going to give Professor Adams a call and beg, bully, even bribe him to push up her place on the waiting list. She'd made up her mind, and coming here had only reinforced it.

General practice was not her forte. Hadn't she always known that? She wasn't good with people. She was a loner, used to dealing with her own idiosyncrasies. But when it came to reading others, she'd always been a flop. Wasn't that why surgery seemed so perfect? Technique was number one with surgeons. People skills came a distant second when you were removing an appendix.

But that's not the only reason you've chosen it, is it?

Nicole paused, her hand on the doorknob.

You think your father will finally love you for yourself if you can do the one thing your mother never achieved.

Sometimes being a loner wasn't so great, especially when you talked to yourself—and yourself talked back.

Thrusting that little voice to the back of her mind, Nicole opened the door and breezed inside the treatment room, a smile pasted on her face.

"Hi, I'm Dr. Brandt. How can I help you today?"

* * *

Twenty past five and she still had three patients to see!

"I'm really glad to have met you. I think you'll find that medication will take care of your rash with no problem. Okay?"

Nicole tried to hurry the woman, but to no avail. To tell the truth, she'd rather enjoyed the garrulous Millicent Maple. Her words shed new light on Dr. Darling and his rambunctious daughters.

"I'm sorry to babble on so, doctor. But you promise you'll stop by our bake sale on Friday? We're featuring quilts, too."

"I'll try my hardest." Nicole waffled her fingers in a wave and scurried out the door.

Maybe he wouldn't notice. Maybe he was tied up with his own chatty granny, catching up on all the latest Blessing news.

"You're behind, Dr. Brandt."

She almost groaned. Instead, Nicole fixed a saccharine-sweet smile on her lips and turned around.

"Yes, I am, Dr. Darling. Since every patient is new, it does take some time to go through the case histories. I'm sure you can understand that. Excuse me." She opened the door and walked inside, determined to meet each need without watching the clock.

At ten after seven Nicole sat down to finish her files. At twenty after eight, with Penny's help, she managed to get the whole lot off her desk.

"There we go. All ready to start fresh and clean tomorrow."

Penny grinned, but her next words were cut off.

"Dr. Brandt, why have you kept my staff overtime?" Nicole twisted to face him, her face burning.

"Just a moment, please, Dr. Darling." She turned to

Penny. "Thanks so much for all your help. I'm really sorry I've kept you so long, but I don't know what I'd have done without you."

"Not a problem. Actually, I enjoyed it. Good night." Penny lifted the stack of files, grinned at Dr. Darling and sauntered out of the room.

Nicole closed the door behind her.

"Now, Dr. Darling. What was it you wanted to talk about?"

"Your lack of organization," he muttered, staring at the mess she'd made of her office.

"I am not disorganized—I am new in this town. I am trying my best to do a good job here, but I will not sacrifice time with my patients to satisfy your need for a timetable. I'm sure that, given time, your 'quotas' will be met." She got up, pulled on her jacket and lifted her purse. "Now, if that's all, I've had a very long day. I'd like to get home."

She was too tired and too frustrated to wait for his assent. She walked out of her office, out of the building and down the street toward Miss Winifred's.

It really was a glorious evening. The sun was just beginning its descent and the spring air had cooled off enough to bring a quickness to her step. It felt good to stride along, stretching muscles that had been tense for far too long. Her stomach rumbled as she walked, reminding her that lunch had been a long time ago and rather puny at that.

Once on "her" street, as Nicole had begun to think of it, the tension slipped away as she strolled under awnings of newly budded maples, drawing in the scent of crocus, hyacinth and daffodils that blossomed in every yard but the last.

She paused for a moment at the gate to Miss Winifred's to stare at the house just down the street, across the way. The Darlings lived there. She should have guessed it that first day, but it had taken Miss Winifred to point it out. There were bicycles strewn across the driveway. Bright pink balls, a green plastic doll carriage and a child's yellow jacket spilled across the still-shaggy grass.

But there were no flowers in the window boxes or tumbling out of the big urns that sat beside the front porch.

"Hey, it's her!" Ruthie barreled out the front door and down the steps of her house, clad in a flowered pink nightgown and a pair of fuzzy slippers. "Hi, Doc! Remember me?"

"How could I forget?" Nicole grinned. "Hi, Ruthie. How's the arm?"

"Oh, it's all right. I hafta get this cast cut off pretty soon, though. Our class is going to take swimming lessons!"

"Hmm. That sounds like fun, but you'll have to wear it until your arm is healed." Nicole listened as the little girl chattered about her life.

"Ruthie? You'd better get your butt in here before Dad gets home." An older version of Ruthie stood on the doorstep, glaring at her sister.

"Do you remember? That's Rachel. She thinks she's the boss, but she isn't. She's only one year older than me, and I'm six."

"Ruthie!"

"Just a minute," Ruthie yelled over her shoulder. She leaned closer to Nicole, her face screwed up in concern. "Quick! What am I supposed to call you? I can't just say doctor all the time, can I?" Ruthie's blue eyes darkened as she considered. "You did mean it when you said we'd be friends?"

It had been a ploy, something to get the child to trust her while she treated the arm. Nicole had never had sisters, never been around young children. She knew diddle about being their friend.

But something in this sprite's eyes made her want to be Ruthie's friend.

"Ruthie, I'm warning you!"

"I'm coming." Dejected, Ruthie turned toward the house, slippers flopping as she walked.

"It's Nicole. You can call me Nicole, Ruthie. And yes, I'd like to be your friend. If you want to."

"Good." Ruthie's smile transformed her face as she raced back, ignoring her sister's angry squeal. Her head tipped to one side. "But Nicole is what everyone calls you. You should have a special name, a friend name." Her face tilted up, curiosity evident in the big blue eyes. "Don't you have one?"

"A special name?" No one had ever called her anything but Nicole. Except her mother, she suddenly remembered. So long ago, when they'd snuggled together and read stories. That's where Nici had come from.

"You could call me Nici," she murmured. "My mother used to call me that."

"Does she still?"

"She's dead. She died when I was a little girl."

"Hey," Ruthie crowed, eyes blazing. "Just like me! My mom died, too. She always called me Ruthie. Now there's just me an' Rachel and Roz." She lowered her voice, checked over one shoulder. "Sometimes I call her Rosie. An' there's my dad, of course. He sometimes calls me Ruth Ann. I like Ruthie better."

"Then Ruthie it is."

They grinned at each other like coconspirators. The

low rumble of an engine drew Ruthie's attention. She gulped, then offered a watery smile.

"Whoops! It's my dad. I gotta go."

She scurried toward the house, turning when she reached the top stair to smile and lift her hand. Her voice rang through the air as clear as a bell.

"See you tomorrow, Nici." Then Ruthie slipped into her house.

"Good night, Ruthie. See you tomorrow." Nicole waited just long enough to watch Dr. Darling try to steer into his littered driveway.

Then she turned and quickly walked through the gate and up to her temporary home, determined not to be there when he bawled those darling girls out for leaving their toys in his way.

The red door opened before she got there.

"My dear, what a long day you've had!" Miss Winifred ushered her inside. "Come along, I've got a bowl of chili just waiting for you, and some of my fresh kaiser rolls to go with it."

"Sounds perfect." Nicole shed her coat and bag at the entrance, then followed her hostess through to the kitchen. "Smells good, too."

She sat down obediently, whispered a quick grace and sampled the big fluffy roll.

"These are wonderful! Did you have a good day at your bakery?"

Nicole knew for a fact that her hostess had risen before four this morning in order to get a head start, and yet Miss Winifred looked as fresh as she always did.

"Yes, thank you, dear. We had a lovely time. Furly Bowes, she's my assistant, you know. Well, Furly got there long before me, had all the breads nicely rising. We had our cases filled before nine. I do love it when that happens. Folks appreciate a full selection.''

Miss Winifred walked over to the counter and returned with a plain white box with red script running across one corner. Nicole read it surreptitiously. ''Blessing Bakery—made with love.''

''I brought you one of my specialties.''

''Oh, you shouldn't have! Not when I'm such a pushover for anything baked.'' Nicole savored the last spoonful of chili with a smile. ''We used to have a housekeeper who made shortbread at Christmas. It literally melted in your mouth.''

Now, where had that come from? The people of Blessing, Colorado, didn't need to know the details of her pathetic past. Nicole lifted the lid of the small square box.

''Oh! It's a big cookie.''

''One of my love cookies. I only make them when I feel the Lord gives me a special message to pass on.'' She sat down across from Nicole, her eyes sparkling. ''Go ahead, read it.''

With gentle fingers lest she damage the flaky, heart-shaped cookie, Nicole lifted it out of the box. Vivid red icing spelled out a message.

''All sunshine makes a desert.'' Puzzled, she looked across at Miss Winifred. ''It's very nice.''

''Oh, it's not just nice, dear. Those are words to live by. Problems come to us for a reason and help us appreciate the good times far more than we would have without them. Here, let me pour you some tea to go with that.'' She tipped her cornflower teapot, allowing the fragrant aroma of black currents to waft through the room.

''This tea is like nectar.'' Nicole sipped again, then broke off a tiny corner of the cookie and ate it. ''Your cookies are delicious, too, Miss Winifred. I promise I'll think about your words.''

''Thank you.'' The older woman fiddled with her cup, her forehead wrinkled. Finally she looked up at Nicole. ''I haven't been completely honest with you, dear, and I'm afraid that's caused you some hurt.''

''What do you mean?''

''Today was difficult, wasn't it?''

Nicole quickly glanced away. She had no desire to answer.

''I knew it would be.''

''How could you know?'' Nicole kept nibbling, working her way around the icing words.

''If nothing else, I can see it on your face. You're worn out. It's partly the newness of the job, of course, but I believe it goes deeper than that. My nephew is not an easy man to deal with lately. He's had too many surprises to render him totally accepting of his situation.''

''What do you mean?''

Miss Winifred sighed heavily, her eyes shiny with unshed tears.

''Joshua loved his wife and family. He loved his work. The inroads he made into giving this community quality care and providing for his family's future drove him. Then suddenly that future was ripped away. He's hurting, confused and discouraged. He feels he's lost control of everything, that nothing is happening the way he wants. To Joshua, control is everything.''

''I don't suppose losing his wife or his partner was easy.'' A rush of sympathy washed over her. It had to be difficult managing under these circumstances, trying to keep everything together.

''No, it wasn't. It tore apart everything he'd believed was true. Now he's floundering.''

"He's more than competent as a doctor. He gives first-rate care to everyone he sees," Nicole reassured the older woman.

"Medically, yes. He does his job very well. But he remains aloof from it, outside his patients' problems. He can't let himself get involved, you see. And that's a big problem."

"It is?" What else was a doctor supposed to do, for heaven's sake?

"Yes, dear. You see, over the past eight years this town has grown used to running to Joshua. They've seen him handle situations they never believed could be solved. They've grown to trust him with their lives, their children, everything. He's served on town council, the school board—oh, a host of things."

"I'm glad." What else could she say? She, who'd never been deeply involved in anyone else's life, though she'd longed to.

"But now he's opted out."

"Excuse me?" Nicole lifted her head to stare at her hostess. "What do you mean, opted out?"

Miss Winifred shrugged.

"Joshua doesn't get involved. Oh, he diagnoses whatever's wrong, just as he always has. He hands out the required prescriptions, deals with the injuries that need treating, repairs the wounds as best he can. But emotionally, he doesn't get involved."

"But—" Nicole stopped the words. What in the world could Miss Winifred mean? That Joshua was still mourning? Wasn't that natural for a man who'd lost a beloved wife?

In a second Nicole's mind flashed back to her own mother's death and her father's grief-stricken state.

Surely this little baker woman couldn't be suggesting that Joshua Darling—

"He's locked himself into a rigid need for control." Miss Winifred shook her head sadly. "My sister would have known what to say, how to get him to refocus. I've tried, but…" Her voice trailed away, sadness filling its soft tones.

"Your sister?" Nicole was getting lost.

"Joshua's mother. She was such a bright, vivacious woman. She always wanted children, but they weren't able to have any. They adopted Joshua when he was nine. He was a sober, determined little fellow even then, but Honey, my sister, could coax the joy out of him with just a word or a touch."

"What happened to her?"

"She and my brother-in-law holidayed in Florida after they got it into their heads to be sailors. They were celebrating their eighteenth anniversary. A gale damaged their boat. They were lost at sea. Joshua was twelve then. I took him in, raised him. They'd have wanted that."

"I'm sorry." Nicole laid her hand over the smooth white fingers.

"Oh, don't be. Honey never did anything if she couldn't do it wholeheartedly. That's why I know she'd know exactly how to deal with Joshua. Unfortunately, I don't."

There wasn't anything Nicole could say. She wasn't exactly sure what the problem was, but even if she understood completely, Dr. Darling would hardly accept any personal advice she had to offer. He'd made that more than clear.

"That's why I was so hopeful when I knew you were coming. I believe God sent you here specifically to meet our need, Nicole." The blue eyes flashed with intensity.

"I think He intends to use you to help Joshua reenter life."

Dread—stark, utter dread—rolled over Nicole, swamping her.

"Miss Winifred, I'm very glad I could come to Blessing, and if I can help out at the office, then I'm glad to do so. But I don't think you should look for anything more." She gulped, then took a sip of tea, her throat bone-dry. "Believe me, I'm not anybody's answer to prayer."

"Oh, sweetheart, my faith isn't just in you. It's in God." The blue eyes glowed with inner fire. "Someone has to show Joshua that we don't control the future. Someone has to help him understand that following all his rules and laws isn't going to protect him from life."

Miss Winifred got up from the table, rinsed out the teapot and dried it carefully. She set it inside her cabinet, closed the door quietly, then turned and faced Nicole, her intense scrutiny unnerving.

"I believe that someone is you. Good night, dear."

"Good night." The words tumbled out of their own accord, which was a good thing because Nicole couldn't organize her thoughts at all as she climbed the stairs to her room.

Help Joshua Darling?

Her own world had now spun totally out of control, the surgical training she'd so carefully planned delayed by circumstances she couldn't alter.

Nicole felt the burn down to her soul. She couldn't even get her own father to see her as anything more than a mere replacement for her mother.

How in the world was she supposed to help a man who already had all the answers he wanted?

Chapter Three

"Rosalyn Alyssa Darling, stop that caterwauling. You're not suffering from any life-threatening injury. If you will race through the house, you will get hurt. I've told you that before."

Joshua almost groaned right along with Rosie when his youngest daughter sent up another heartrending sob that tugged at his heart. He felt totally helpless. Giving in to his emotions, he gently gathered his baby's compact little body into his arms and cuddled her close, soothing her sobs as he always had.

"Kiss?" She tilted her chin up for his cure.

"Kiss," he agreed, dabbing his lips against the alabaster skin and holding them there. She was so delicate, so precious. And such a fireball.

Three seconds after the kiss, she wiggled out of his arms to hurtle herself down the stairs in hot pursuit of her oldest sister.

"Rachel, help Rosie get dressed, will you? Please?"

Another Sunday morning, another two hours of sheer bedlam. Sometimes he wondered why he bothered drag-

ging them all to church. But he knew the answer. Kyla.
She'd insisted from the moment Rachel had come into
the world that her children would know God in a personal way.

As if anyone could know God like that.

He stuffed the regrets down and concentrated on getting his tie straight. *Wouldn't want anyone to think anything was wrong in the Darling house.*

Joshua offered a wry smile to his reflected image,
twitching the tie into place as he did. Sheer pride, he
owned. Such a stupid quality to hang on to. As if everyone in town didn't already know something was wrong
at the Darlings'. It was evident the moment you looked
at the house, never mind what it looked like inside.

Why— He stopped himself, refusing to let the words
gain hold in his brain. What difference did it make why
it had happened? It had. The point he needed to concentrate on was managing what was left of his future. No
matter what happened, the blame could not be laid at his
door.

Not again. He'd do everything he had to, to make sure
of that.

Control. Sure, steady, unblinking control. That would
get him through.

"Uh, Dad? I think you better come down here. Like—
now."

Joshua groaned. What had they done this time?

He took the steps three at a time, ignoring the puddle
of clothes left at the bottom.

"Rachel? Where are you?"

"In the kitchen."

He burst into the room, expecting flames. What he saw
made him just as nervous. Nicole Brandt stood inside the
door, a white ceramic dish balanced in her hands. Her

ash-blond hair fell in a shining curtain around her shoulders. She wore a navy dress with perfectly tailored lapels and a trim white belt. The merest little wisp of a blue hat sat on top of her head. It looked ridiculous.

She looked gorgeous.

Apparently his daughters thought so, too. They stood in rapt attention, mouths gaping. To her credit, the beautiful doctor didn't bat an eyelash at the unwanted attention.

"Good morning, Dr. Darling. Miss Winifred asked me to deliver this. She said that if you put it in the oven now, at three hundred degrees, it will be ready to eat when church is over." She held out the dish.

"Oh. That's very kind of her. Thank you." Joshua stuffed the dish into the oven and set the temperature. "But why didn't you use the front door? Surely it's closer?"

A funny looked washed over her model-perfect features. Chagrin, maybe? No, sheepishness, that was it. She licked her lips, fiddled with the white leather strap over her shoulder, then peeped up at him through her lashes.

"I would have," she murmured. "But there's an elephant on your step."

Ruth Ann burst into delighted giggles, Rachel chuckled and even Rosalyn grinned.

"There's no elephant!" He forced himself not to smile.

"Well, it's not exactly an elephant." She temporized. "But it's huge and gray and has slobber dribbling all over its face." Her disgust was obvious.

"Ladybug!" The girls turned and raced to the front door.

Joshua beat them to it.

"No way," he said firmly, locking the door and setting

the chain for good measure. "I do not want that animal traipsing through this house. Mrs. Tyndall can't keep up with the cleaning as it is."

"But— Dad!"

"Yes?" He raised his eyebrow at Rachel and saw her wilt.

"Nothing." One by one the children drifted away to continue their preparations for church, leaving him alone with *her*.

"So now you can understand why I thought it best to use the back entrance." Nicole Brandt flicked her eyes up to stare into his. "I hope that's not a problem? Your dog is, er, rather large."

He knew she wanted to add something to that. Probably a remark about the beast's filth. He hastened to correct her.

"Of course I understand. And, no, it's not a problem at all." He glanced around, checking. What else? Oh, yes. The dog. "Ladybug does not belong to us, thank heavens. She simply visits frequently because my daughters insist on feeding her table scraps. I'll phone her owners."

He made the call quickly, stating his case in a cool, crisp tone. Why didn't people leave animals that size on the farm? Or tie them up if they had to keep them in town?

"I'm sure they'll pick her up soon."

"I hope so." She turned to peer out a side window. "It's enormous. Why would anyone call it Ladybug?"

"If you find the answer to that, I'd really like to know about it." He walked back toward the kitchen, speaking over his shoulder as he went. "It's a mystery to me. Have a seat if you're staying."

"Hmm." She sat, long, slim legs crossed delicately.

''Will you button my dress up? Please?'' Rosalyn held up her favorite fluffy blue dress.

Joshua stifled his groan. It was several sizes too small. He should have given it away ages ago, but Ruth Ann clung to that dress like a lifesaver.

''Not that one, honey,'' he murmured, and lifted up a freshly pressed cotton one Mrs. Tyndall had ironed yesterday. ''It's too small, remember? Try this.''

''I like this one.'' Her bottom lip jutted out in that stubborn thrust she used to get her own way.

Joshua prepared himself for battle. But before he could speak a word, *she* intervened.

''I'd love to help you, Rosalyn. You're such a big girl, aren't you? How old?'' Nicole waited for the requisite number of fingers. ''Four? And you still fit into this?'' She pretended to squeeze it over the little girl's head. ''Oh, dear.''

''What's the matter?'' Ruthie balanced in the doorway like a stork, one shoe on her foot, the other clutched in her hand.

''Her head's too big.''

Joshua almost smiled as Nicole pretended to twist the dress this way and that, her fingers pressing down on Rosie's scalp.

''Way too big. It just won't fit.'' She glanced up at him suddenly, her eyes glowing. ''I think we'll have to operate, Dr. Darling.''

''Operate?'' Rachel turned from her stance by the window to stare at Nicole. ''On what?''

''On the dress, of course. How else can we get a too-big head into a too-small dress? We may have to operate on the arms, too. They look pretty tiny.'' Once more she tried to draw him into the game. ''Don't you think so, Dr. Darling?''

"Hmm. Asking for a second opinion, Dr. Brandt?" He allowed his eyes to indicate his view of this silly game.

"Oh, I think so. Don't you? When a case is as serious as this I always—" She stopped speaking abruptly.

Joshua forced himself to stop staring into her eyes and figure out what she was doing. He glanced down. Rosie had tossed the favorite dress onto a nearby chair and now began to struggle into the cotton one he'd presented.

"Don't op'rate on my dress," she demanded, glaring up at Nicole.

"We were just teasing, honey. It's your dress, and I wouldn't dream of damaging it." Nicole swept a soothing hand across blond frizz that never quite lay down no matter how often Joshua combed it. "It's a special dress, isn't it?"

"Uh-huh. My mommy made it for me."

"Really?" Nicole got up and rescued the tired blue fabric from the chair. "Then we must take very good care of it. One day you can help your little girl into it and tell her about how your mama made this specially."

A lump came into Joshua's throat as he watched her slim fingers smooth the fabric into neat folds until the dress was a small square.

"There. Now you can put it in your treasures box."

"She don't got one."

"Doesn't have," Joshua corrected automatically. The girls ignored him, their eyes fixed on Nicole.

"She can start one. It's never too late."

"Can I get one, Dad?"

"Me, too?"

"Me, three?"

The woman never even let him get a word in!

"I have an idea. I moved some of my stuff into Miss

Winifred's and I have a whole bunch of boxes. After church perhaps you could each come over and choose one, if your father thinks it would be all right.''

He almost made a face at the thought of more clutter in those messy bedrooms. But just in time, Joshua caught the yearning looks on little faces and knew he had to agree.

''I suppose it would be all right. If you promise to keep them put away.''

Naturally they all solemnly promised. As if!

''Fine.'' He twitched his tie into place. ''Now let's get moving. Church will be starting in twenty minutes.''

Joshua let them dash off to retrieve whatever it was little girls took to church. When they were gone, he turned back to face his guest.

''If you'll excuse us—''

''Actually, that's another reason I'm here. Miss Winifred left ages ago, but before she did, she ordered me over here to catch a ride with you.'' She smiled weakly, as if the last thing she wanted was to ride in his vehicle.

He didn't blame her. He'd rather ride in that red sports car of hers any day. Her words sank in.

''Aunt Win's not going? Why not? Is she ill?'' Joshua rapped the questions out automatically. ''Perhaps I'd better take a look.''

''She's fine. I told you she's already left.''

The words halted him. He replaced his bag, closed the closet door, then turned around.

''But why—''

''She had to get to church early. Apparently they decided to hold an impromptu choir rehearsal this morning and she wanted to be there. I wasn't ready, so she told me about the casserole and said to ride with you.'' She frowned at his lack of response. "I could have walked if I'd known how to get there."

"In those shoes?" He eyed her shapely ankles, the narrow heels and shook his head. "Hardly. What happened to your car?"

Her face grew very pink. "I locked the car keys in. I don't know how. It's never happened before. I was certain I'd left them in my pocket."

Joshua's radar went on alert.

"You don't have a spare?"

"That's the really strange part. I'm positive they were on my nightstand last night, but this morning they're sitting on the car seat—inside the car. And of course I'd put the roof up. It's really odd." Her cheeks remained a bright pink. "I feel like a fool. Miss Winifred said no one would be available to help me until Monday."

"Yes, that is weird." Dismay fizzled up Joshua's spine as a twinkle of doubt surfaced in his mind about those keys. Not again! He'd warned her about matchmaking before. Surely Aunt Win wouldn't try to pair him up with Dr. Brandt?

But in his heart of hearts Joshua knew his aunt would dare that and more if she thought it would help heave him out of what she considered the pit of his despair.

"Dr. Darling?"

Joshua sighed. It was pointless to hope for a way out. This was a small town where everyone knew everyone else. If he didn't offer to take her, they'd all be talking about him. Again.

"You'd better call me by my given name," he muttered at last. "Since we're neighbors."

"All right." She tilted the blue hat forward, just a millimeter. "If you agree to do the same."

He hesitated. But what could he say? "Fine."

"Dr. Darling, have I done something to offend you?"

One shoe dangled from his finger as he fought for control and a way to avoid the question.

"Why do you say that?"

"Ah, a true debater. Answer a question by asking another question." She nodded, a knowing light glimmering in her eyes. "I'll bet you get away with that a lot."

"Obviously not enough." He slipped his other shoe on and tied it slowly, taking his time while his mind whirred. Nothing. "I'll stand by my question—why do you ask?"

"Because of your attitude, of course." She sat perched on the edge of her chair not two feet from where he stood.

"My attitude?" Joshua frowned. She said it as if he'd been rude. There was nothing wrong with his attitude. "What attitude?"

She sighed. "Never mind. I know a block when I see one."

"Dr. Brandt—Nicole. I have no idea what you're talking about. I don't have an attitude or a—a block, as you put it, about you or anyone else. All I want is a short-term assistant who can function within the parameters I've set out without causing additional stress."

"Do you realize that in the past week you've reminded me at least three times, every single day, that I am not a permanent fixture in your office?" She leaned forward, eyes blazing in her beautiful face.

That spark of anger alerted Joshua; he knew he'd gone too far. He stayed exactly where he was and did her the courtesy of quietly listening, though it cost him dearly.

"Hear this, Dr. Darling. I am not staying. I will not be hanging on to your coattails, prevailing upon you to keep me when my six months are over, not even if you beg me on bended knee.''

As if that would happen!

But Joshua got the drift. She was mad. The air around her sizzled, and her blond hair flickered through the air just like the girls' hair did when there was too much static. He almost smiled.

Big mistake.

''Don't you laugh at me! I have plans for my future, Dr. Darling, big plans. And they do not include working for, with, or beside you after my term here has been served. There's no way I'm prepared to give up my dream of surgery and remain secluded in this little town, meting out care to my patients in parsimonious ten-minute intervals. Not one chance in a thousand.''

Like you.

Joshua heard everything she didn't say. He knew she'd seen past his pretense of doctorly concern to the cad he was beneath. He'd been going through the motions of caring for his patients, and she knew it! The thought galled him, but he couldn't acknowledge it—not here and not now. He just couldn't.

''I'm glad to hear that, Dr. Brandt, because as you know, I intend to find the perfect partner.'' This time he left the remainder unsaid. ''Girls! It's time to leave. Now.''

They came from all corners of the house, black patent Mary Jane shoes tapping overhead, across the oak floors in a cacophony of scurrying steps. One by one, the girls bounded down the stairs and presented themselves in the front hall.

Joshua gulped at the sight.

They had on hats. Strange, gaudy-looking straw boaters that had originally arrived as Easter bonnets from

Aunt Win, and had subsequently been decorated with fuzzy chicks of various rainbow colors, tiny bird's nests and pussy willows.

He thought Rachel's was almost decent, covered as it was by tiny pink bows and rosebuds. Until he saw the gaping hole at the back and remembered that Ladybug had sampled it. Straw stuck out, tattered and broken.

Deliberately Joshua moved on to Ruth Ann. She was artistic, creative. Surely—but no, her hat had obviously suffered from her one-handed state. The pretty blue ribbons that had once rippled down her back now hung wrinkled and dingy, their ends frayed. Her motif was chicks. Little puffy bits no bigger than Joshua's pinkie rimmed the brim, peeping down into her face, their stick feet barely secured to the straw.

But it was his baby, his smallest angel, who'd gone all out to imitate their guest. Yards and yards of filmy white cloth not unlike the bathroom curtain swathed her hat, bent the brim so that it drooped down and created a beehive effect that swayed whenever she moved. A bit of the fabric draped over the front of Rosalyn's hat, completely shielding her eyes and all but the very tip of her little pink nose. The entire concoction was held in place with a thousand safety pins that glittered and shone in the sunlight.

"Don't worry, Dad. I helped her with the pins," Rachel informed him with an artless smile.

"Thank you, dear." Joshua never knew where the words came from. He only knew that his girls had worked feverishly to attain the same fashion statement as Nicole, and failed miserably.

He also knew that anything he said now would be wrong, so he clamped his lips shut, held open the front door and motioned them all outside.

"Thank goodness Ladybug's gone."

"Yeah, she would have wrecked our hats." Ruthie led the way to the car, eased her way in, then turned to help Rosie.

Rachel followed in a stately saunter that threatened to trip them all up if they didn't get out of her way.

Dr. Nicole Brandt stood beside him watching the procession, a smile twitching at her lips. Finally she looked at him. He was shocked by the merry twinkle dancing in her eyes.

"You did very well, Dr. Darling," she whispered. "Now keep a stiff upper lip and everything will be just fine."

"Easy for you to stay." He didn't bother to hide his pained expression. He waited for her to walk out the door, then went to close it. Her hand on his arm stopped him.

"Dr. Darling?"

"Yes?" He frowned. What did she want now? Hadn't she wreaked enough havoc in his life?

"About the casserole."

"I put it in the oven and set the temperature, as you said." He tried to close the door again, but her delicately sandaled foot prevented that. "What?"

"You have to turn the oven on," she whispered.

Her eyes met his in one quick glance, then she went sashaying down his walk as if she belonged there in her pencil-slim dress, fancy high heels and that ridiculous hat.

Joshua turned his back on them all and went inside to switch on the oven. He knew that—he did! It had simply slipped his mind...with so much else going on.

Discomfited by his own forgetfulness in front of his new doctor, he stomped back outside, slammed the door closed so hard the window creaked, and snapped the dead bolt home with his key.

"I love Sundays," Nicole sang out as soon as he was in the car. "It's so much fun to gather together and hear Bible stories. I always imagine what it must have been like in those olden days. I love it."

"Me, too."

Agreement with Dr. Brandt's sentiments echoed through his car twice more. What was he raising—parrots?

Joshua kept his mouth clamped shut and concentrated on getting them all to church without disaster. Once there, he chose a parking spot as far from the door as possible in hopes that the wind would take care of the hat problem for him. Unfortunately, the day was totally calm and the hats remained firmly attached to his daughters' heads.

The girls raced across the lot as fast as they could manage, calling to their friends as they went.

"I don't think it's fitting to take those, er, creations, into the house of God," he muttered, staring up at the gigantic cross that sat atop the church.

"Why on earth not? They worked so hard making them. You should be proud." Nicole frowned at him fiercely. "Every single time those girls go out of their way to make something special like this, you should be bursting your buttons with pride."

"Their mother would kill me."

Dr. Brandt's eyes grew cool, frosty. The tension between them grew until he could feel the ice crackling.

"I doubt that very much. I think she'd be very proud. But even if it were true, their mother isn't here. They are. And so are you. They need to know you love them, no matter what."

What had caused such anger? he wondered. It came from nowhere. One minute she was smiling like a movie star, the next growling at him as fiercely protective as a mother cub.

"I do love them." Why was he defending himself?

"Have you told them that lately?" She glared.

Joshua stalked away, a spurt of anger burning inside. What right had she to judge? She didn't have three kids dependent on her. She was free as a bird.

"You can run, but you can't hide." The whisper came from behind his left shoulder.

"I'm not running. I just thought I might sneak into the back pew before anybody figured out the three in those ridiculous getups are my daughters."

Her hand on his arm prevented him from entering the sanctuary. He looked from it to her eyes, and flinched at the challenge he saw there.

"'Man looks on the outward appearance,'" she whispered. "'But God looks on the heart.' And I can tell you right now, Dr. Darling, that those three girls with their funny hats have the purest little hearts in this entire building."

She stepped past him, walked through the doorway and disappeared inside.

Joshua grimaced at her invisible back. Dr. Nicole Brandt would make a good surgeon. She cut right to the quick without messing about.

The problem was, her condemnation burned all the way to his soul.

Chapter Four

"It's not that I want to leave you alone, dear." Winifred inclined her head, her eyes darting around the foyer packed full with those departing after the service. "It's just that Furly and I always go out for lunch on Sunday. The poor thing has no family, you know. She depends on me and I don't want to cancel our date. Silly of me to have forgotten it, really."

"I'll be fine." The words slipped out automatically, though Nicole couldn't help wondering why the woman hadn't said something about this lunch date earlier.

"No, you—I know! Why don't you share lunch with Joshua and the girls? I'm sure they'd enjoy seeing a new face at the table." She looked delighted with her idea.

Nicole wanted to run.

"Miss Blessing, there's no need for that. Really. I'll just make a sandwich. I've got a new text I'd like to study anyway." No way was she going back inside that house with the grouch.

"You can't!" The words burst out, loud enough to attract attention.

"I beg your pardon?" Nicole stared, amazed that this calm, competent woman seemed so frazzled.

"I—I haven't any bread. Or buns. I forgot to bring some home yesterday. And there's no meat. Sandwiches need meat." She turned, caught sight of her nephew and waved him over. "Joshua, yoo-hoo."

He came willingly enough, until he spotted Nicole.

"Is something wrong, Aunt Win?"

"No." Nicole pressed her heels into the floor and refused to look at him.

"Yes," Winifred said at the exact same moment. "I have a lunch date with Furly and there's not a thing in the house for Nicole to eat."

"Nothing to eat? At your house?" Skepticism marred Dr. Darling's good looks.

"Not a thing, dear. I've been a little preoccupied lately and I guess…" She let the sentence trail away.

"You're feeling all right, aren't you?" He raised a hand, as if to check her temperature. "Nothing bothering you?"

Winifred backed up.

"I'm fine, dear." She smiled at him. "I just wanted to ask you if Nicole could share that casserole I sent over for you and the girls. It's not nice for her to have to eat all alone."

Nicole held her breath, suppressing the laugh that bubbled up as distaste flooded Dr. Darling's expressive eyes.

"But—why doesn't she go with you and Furly?"

"Oh, I couldn't do that, dear." Winifred rushed into speech, words tumbling out at a furious pace. "Furly has something rather important that she wants to confide in me, you see. I don't think she'd open up with someone else around."

Oh, to be wanted. Nicole felt like a tennis ball being shunted back and forth, from one court to the other.

"Couldn't she tell you at work tomorrow? You two are alone there for hours."

"No, Joshua." The older woman's voice firmed. "I think it's best if Nicole eats with you. There's plenty of that casserole for one more to share." Winifred leaned forward and pressed her lips to his cheek. "Thank you, dear." Then she sailed away, majestically nodding to the left and right at various friends.

Joshua glared at her back, his mouth twisting into a grim line.

"Listen, I'll look after myself. There's no need for me to impose on you, other than accepting a ride back." Nicole almost laughed at the chagrin that washed over his face.

"Of course you'll ride back with us, and eat lunch, too." His glance roved the parking lot in front of the church. "We'll leave as soon as I find the girls." He turned away to locate his children.

Nicole reached out and stopped him with a hand on his arm. He looked down at her hand, then up into her face.

"Problem?"

"Just because she said it doesn't mean we have to obey. I'll be fine. I'll catch a ride with you, but that's all. You just enjoy your afternoon off, with your daughters."

His lips tightened, but he said nothing more until they were driving home.

"I'm afraid I have to insist you eat with us, Dr. Brandt. My aunt expects it. Afterward you may feel free to leave whenever you wish."

She tried to get out of it up until the moment he turned into his drive.

"I will not change my mind, Dr. Brandt."

"Oh, for goodness' sake!" Exasperated, she climbed out of the car. "You've really got to get over this rigid adherence to rules." She stomped down his driveway toward Miss Winifred's.

"Where are you going?"

"To change my clothes. I'll be back in three minutes. We can eat, and then you'll be free of me."

In actual fact, it took Nicole more than five minutes because she made a detour through Winifred Blessing's kitchen. While it was true that there were no buns or bread hidden away, there was a box with the familiar red Blessing Bakery script. Inside were six featherlight croissants that would have made yummy sandwiches. Nicole snatched the box on her way out.

"Two can play this game, Winifred," she muttered, retracing her steps across the road.

Ruthie opened the front door before she got there.

"I changed, too." She scrutinized Nicole's favorite jeans with a curious look. "You got holes in your pants."

"I know. It's because I wear them so often. They're my favorite. Don't you have favorite clothes you like to wear?"

The little girl shifted. The door opened wider to reveal her father.

"Don't ask that," he warned. One glance took in the disreputable jeans. "Hers aren't in quite that bad a condition, however."

Nicole was not in the mood to endure another word of censure. She thrust the box of croissants at him.

"These are for lunch. Compliments of your aunt." She glanced down as Ruthie's hand twined into hers.

"Wanna help me set the table?"

"Sure." It was better than staring at Joshua Darling, Nicole decided. He'd changed, too. The suit and tie replaced by khaki cords and a tan shirt, he looked every inch the respectable family doctor. Not one hair was out of place.

Sheer perversity made Nicole say it. "Are you going to help us with the treasure boxes?"

"Uh—I beg your pardon?" He walked toward the kitchen, as if he could get away from her.

Nicole followed right behind, tugging Ruthie with her.

"You remember, Daddy. We're going to make treasure boxes so we can keep our special things in them." Ruthie dragged open a drawer and began hauling out cutlery.

"Oh. Boxes. Yes. Right." He plopped the croissants onto a plate and set them on the table, then turned to find the butter.

Nicole countered every step he took with her own as she searched for plates, cups, napkins. His impatience at the constant run-ins grew until he finally demanded she sit down and let him work in peace.

"I could make a salad," she offered, and pulled the ingredients from the fridge.

"I don't like radishes." Ruthie frowned, watching carefully as Nicole kept slicing thin red pieces into the lettuce. "An' me and Rach don't like those green things, either."

"You're kidding?" Nicole slipped a bit of celery into her mouth and crunched on it. "This is my second-favorite food. It's even better when you put cream cheese on it."

"Show me."

Nicole dressed several celery sticks. Ruthie picked up one and let it graze her lips. After a minute she took a bite, nodded and took another one.

"See? I told you." Nicole divided up some raw carrots and stuck them around the side of the bowl. "You never know if you don't try it."

"As a rule, I do not think that is a plan for living for my daughters." Joshua Darling stood, arms akimbo, watching them. "But in this case, I accede."

"Because it's vegetables, you mean? But there are lots of things about living that have to be experienced. You can't hide out from life." She stared at him, wondering what had caused that dark cloud at the back of his eyes.

"I wasn't suggesting you should hide. Merely exercise caution and reason." He turned and left. Moments later the other two girls came rushing to the table.

They joined hands and repeated a charming grace together, then Dr. Darling began dishing out the casserole, which wafted yummy clouds of fragrant chicken through the air.

Once the others had seen Ruthie take an assortment of the salad ingredients, they began to help themselves, as well. Soon they were all happily chewing on celery.

"How are we going to decorate our boxes?" Rachel asked, her mouth full.

Nicole set down her fork. "How would you like to decorate them? It's entirely up to you."

"What should we do, Daddy?" All three turned to Dr. Darling for advice, their little faces hopeful.

He glanced up from his plate, eyes wide.

"I, uh, I'm sure whatever you decide will be very nice," he finally managed. "Dr.—Nicole will help you."

"But we want you to help us, too, Daddy." Ruthie's

big eyes begged him. "It's Sunday today. You don't have to do more work today, do you, Daddy? You worked yesterday and Mrs. Tyndall had to take us to her house. We missed our picnic, Daddy."

"Yeah. And you didn't even see me do my special song in the school play because you had clinic that night." Rachel took up the chant.

Nicole risked a look at Dr. Darling. What she saw there sent her head bowing, her eyes on her plate. Hurt? Frustration? She pretended to sip her juice, wishing for all the world that she'd stayed at Winifred's.

"Children, you know that I'm the only doctor in town right now."

So what am I? Nicole fumed. Chopped liver?

"When someone gets hurt, I have to help them. I don't want to miss things, but sometimes I must. You wouldn't want Mrs. McGregor to sit at home in pain when I could help her, would you?"

"I hurted," Rosalyn announced. She held up her leg with its tiny bandage.

"I know, sweetie." Dr. Darling leaned over and pressed a kiss on the injured area. "But that was weeks ago. It's all better now."

"Hurts," the child insisted, and held up her arms for a cuddle.

"Let's finish our lunch now." After comforting his youngest, Joshua Darling settled back in his seat and resumed eating. So did everyone else. But there was no conversation.

Once the meal was finished, the girls happily cleared the table, storing the soiled dishes in the dishwasher. When the last glass toppled inside, Ruthie slammed the door shut, then danced over beside Nicole.

"Can we start now?"

"Start?" Nicole glanced from father to child.

"Our boxes." Ruthie hopped from one foot to the other.

Wishing she could disappear, but loath to break her promise, Nicole finally nodded. "First we'll have to get the boxes from Miss Blessing's."

With Ruthie clasping her hand on one side and Rosalyn on the other, Nicole started toward the front door.

"I'll be there in a minute." Rachel stood by her father at the sink, waiting, tea towel in hand, to dry Winifred's dish once he'd finished washing it.

"Okay." Nicole led the other two to the front door. Once there, she realized she'd left her purse behind. She told the two girls to wait outside, then started back toward the kitchen.

"But it'd be just for a little while, just an hour this afternoon, Dad. You don't have to help us, but if you were there, we could talk to you. I want to tell you about our spelling bee. I want you to listen." Rachel's voice rang with desperation.

"Rachel, you know there's nothing I'd rather do than play with you. But I've got a lot of—"

"Paperwork. I know." Rachel sighed loudly. "You've always got paperwork."

"Rachel, it's my—"

"Your job," she finished, her voice rising. "Well, sometimes I wish it wasn't. Sometimes I wish you were a plumber. Avis Arnold's father takes off every Saturday and every Sunday. They do things together, go places." Her voice dropped. "Like we used to do with Mom. I wish she was here now. At least she'd have time to listen to me."

Before Nicole could leave, Rachel burst out of the kitchen, brushed past her and flung herself through the open front door. A second later her father followed, then stopped short when he saw Nicole.

"I'm sorry. I—I didn't mean to eavesdrop. I came back for my purse." She snatched up the item and walked back through the house. "I needed my keys."

He never said a word, never gave a sign that he'd heard one word of her halting apology. Instead, he turned and walked back into the kitchen, shoulders slumped, hands drooping at his sides.

Wake up! Nicole wanted to scream at him. *They'll soon be gone and you can work all you want. You won't ever get back this opportunity.* All the hurt feelings she'd felt during her own childhood flooded back with heart-rending clarity.

But there was one tiny difference between Joshua Darling and her father, Nicole admitted as she walked across the road, the girls chattering by her side.

Deep down inside, Joshua Darling loved his children.

She had never heard those words from her father's lips.

"You're sure you want to do this?" Penny Zane's whispered question drew Nicole's attention from the file she'd been studying.

"I'm sure. We're snowed under. I have nothing to do in the evenings. If you can take it for a week or two, we could clear up the backlog."

"Give him a breather now and then, you mean?" Penny grinned. "I'm up for it. That overtime money you talked about will go a long way to paying for my new fridge and stove. And Carole is squeezing every cent to cover that wedding she wants."

"You won't tell him?" As a plan, Nicole was very

aware that her idea lacked in a number of areas. Not the least of which was the secrecy factor.

"Are you kidding? If he finds out, we're blaming it all on you. He'll skin you alive," she warned. "He can't stand anyone tampering with his system."

"What's he going to do—fire me? Then he'd be worse off than before." Nicole shrugged. "Don't worry about it, Penny. I'll be fine. If worse comes to worst, I'll just go back to school a little earlier than I'd planned. Or something." She held up the file she was holding. "This was on my desk. I didn't see this patient."

Penny leaned over, read the name. "Mr. De Witt. You're right. Sorry. Carole must have slipped up. That's Dr. Darling's patient. Has a lot of pain. Dr. Darling can't seem to find anything that works."

"Yes, I noted that when I read it." Nicole juggled the idea, then made her decision. "Next time he books, would you have Edwina send him to me? I'd like to take a look. I have an idea."

"You would? Sure." Penny flipped the chart closed and tucked it under her arm. "He's back in next week, actually. Checkup. She squeezed him in, so I can move him easily enough."

"Subtlety, Penny. With a lot of subtlety." Nicole grinned at the nurse's tipped-up nose.

"Aren't I always?" she quipped. Then she walked out the door.

"Isn't she always what?" Dr. Darling stood in the doorway, his face curious.

"Subtle." Nicole scanned her list, then tucked it into her pocket. "Are you off now?"

He snorted. "Hardly. I've got that pharmaceutical rep to see."

"He's gone."

"Gone?" Joshua frowned at her.

"Yes." Nicole nodded. "About two hours ago, I think. Had some pressing business at home. Kid's piano recital, I think he said." She met his curious stare with a bland smile. "I took the samples he left and the information kit and put them in the lab for you to look over."

"You did?"

"Uh-huh." She made a nice neat stack out of her finished files and laid them in her basket.

"Oh. Uh, thanks. Well, then, I'm off to that house call on Morgan."

"I did that, too." She stood, picked up her purse and walked toward him. "While you were with that screaming kid. I needed the break, so I left."

"But your patient?" He frowned, obviously ready to lecture her.

"Canceled. Worked out well, don't you think?" She stood waiting in the hallway, hoping he'd take the hint. "I don't think there's anything else this afternoon, so you might as well head home, just as I intend to."

"Are you trying to get rid of me, Dr. Brandt?" he demanded, his forehead pleating in an angry frown.

Yes! her brain screamed.

"Why would I do that?" she asked meekly. "It's your office, after all. I'm just the substitute, not the partner. I have no right to tell you to do anything." *Go home!* She pulled the door to and locked it. Then she walked down the hall. At the end of it, she stopped, looked back, saw him staring after her.

"Oh, by the way," she said quietly. "The lock on my office door broke. I took the liberty of having it replaced. See you." Having said it, she scurried from the building lest he stop her and ask for the key.

One look at the stack of files behind her desk and he'd know she was up to something.

"I'm glad you like these evening hours, Mr. Wilson. Dr. Darling needs the time with his family, but I'm happy to see anyone who wants to come to these clinics." Nicole waited until the grocery-store owner had left, made a notation in his file, then added it to the pile on her desk.

"You're still running behind." Penny leaned against the counter, one leg crossed over the other. "Mr. Wilson was in there for twenty-two minutes."

"I know. But it was worth it. I learned a little more about Blessing and he finally believes I know what I'm talking about. Good deal all around." Nicole glanced around, fully expecting to see Joshua come striding down the hall. "No problems?"

"None. Carole's already gone. I've locked up. Let's go."

"Yes." When she'd come up with the idea of seeing patients after Joshua had left, Nicole hadn't realized how draining it would be. Now her day was nonstop, but she loved it. The patients were becoming friends, and that was something she'd never experienced before.

She stood outside the back door, waiting for Penny to set the alarm. Car lights swept over them.

"Aunt Win said there were lights on down here. Anything wrong?" Joshua Darling climbed out of his car.

"Nothing wrong, Doc. Just that your partner forgot her keys, so I came down to let her in. She's kind of a ditz about this alarm, you know." Penny turned to wink at Nicole.

"She's not my—"

"I have to go. My show will be on in eight minutes.

Bye." Penny waved a hand, then started jogging toward her home.

"Partner," Joshua finished, staring after her. "I never knew she was so addicted to television."

"She's not addicted. She just has a favorite she doesn't want to miss." Nicole studied his wrinkled shirt and dusty pants. "What have you been doing?"

Dr. Darling made a face. "Girls' club."

"So you were studying…dusting?" Nicole couldn't help chuckling at his disgusted grimace.

"They insisted I attend so they could demonstrate the skills they'd learned. Rachel's apparently been helping Mrs. Tyndall vacuum. Tonight, during her demonstration, the machine broke. I happened to be sitting in the line of fire when the bag disintegrated."

"Oh." Nicole tried desperately to control the gurgle of laughter, but it would not be suppressed. She peeked up at him, prayed the gloom of the evening would hide her expression and started laughing.

"It's not polite to laugh at another's misfortune," he chided, but something in his eyes told her he wasn't offended.

"Sorry, but I have this mental picture." She giggled again.

"Go ahead, laugh. I have to get home. Aunt Win is trying to put the girls to bed and I know exactly how that will turn out."

Nicole frowned. "What do you mean? How could it turn out?"

"Surely you've noticed that Aunt Win believes in bedtime snacks?" He seemed surprised by her negative response. "Haven't you seen plates of food left on the counter after you've eaten dinner?"

"Yes, but I assumed they were for her. She's always bustling around—she must use a lot of energy."

He grinned. "You have no idea about life with Aunt Win, so it's up to me to broaden your education. Get in, Dr. Brandt. You are about to witness Aunt Win feeding the starving masses." He held his car door open for her.

"I usually walk after work," she muttered, but climbed in anyway.

"This isn't after work." He started the car and steered down the street.

Nicole pinched her lips together. She'd almost blown it that time. They couldn't keep the evening clinics a secret forever, of course. But after almost three weeks of secrecy, she was excited about them and determined not to stop, no matter what Dr. Darling said. Two nights a week were nothing to her and she enjoyed the experiences it provided. After all, she was here to learn.

"You're very quiet. What's wrong?"

Nicole frowned. "Why should something be wrong?"

"Because you usually have some pearl of wisdom to offer whenever we have three minutes alone. You and my aunt share that trait." He peered through the windshield at the bike on the driveway and groaned loudly before parking on the street. "Nothing to say, Dr. Brandt?"

"Quite a lot, Dr. Darling. But I've decided to give you the night off." She climbed out of the car, ignoring his gasp of surprise.

"Thank you, I think." One black eyebrow tilted upward. "You're too kind."

"I know."

He bent, lifted the bike and set it in the bike rack beside the house. "I wonder how many times I'll have to remind them before they actually learn to put their stuff away?''

''Fair warning, Doc. I could change my mind and tell you what I think about fathers who complain about kids' toys being in the way.'' She grinned, delighted to see she'd stopped any retort he might have made.

''Hmph'' seemed to be the best he could manage.

''What is it you wanted me to see?''

''Right this way.'' He led the way inside the house, placed one finger in front of his lips and pointed toward the kitchen.

Nicole preceded him, looked inside and gaped.

Three angelic little girls and their guardian angel/great-aunt sat around the kitchen table, scooping up spoonfuls of ice cream covered in sauces, nuts, whipped cream and cherries. Ruthie saw her first.

''Hey, Nici, we're having a night lunch. Want some?'' She held out a spoon of the melting sugary stuff.

''I, uh, I have an allergy to milk products, Ruthie. But thanks anyway.'' Conscious of Joshua's lean body close behind and his snort of disbelief, she stepped into the room, took a chair and placed it beside the little girl. ''What's in there?'' she asked curiously, seating herself.

''Everything.''

''The girls have good appetites,'' Miss Winifred murmured, licking her own spoon. ''We've almost finished off this container.''

''Yes, well, I think that's enough sugar for tonight, girls. We'll cover your bowls and maybe you can eat the rest tomorrow. Okay?''

Brows lowered on three sticky faces, but one look at Joshua's unsmiling face sent them scrambling for plastic wrap. The bowls were tucked carefully into the freezer.

''Wash, and brush your teeth thoroughly,'' he called

as they raced up the stairs. "If you're quick, you can come back and say good-night."

They were so quick, Nicole feared for their teeth.

"Good night, Nici." Ruthie squeezed her arms around Nicole's waist and hung on, her eyes tightly closed.

Though it was a new sensation, Nicole decided she liked it. Here at last was unconditional love. She loosened the girl's arms, bent and hugged her properly, brushing a kiss against the top of her head.

"Good night, Ruthie. Sleep well."

The other two awaited their turn, so she hugged them both and wished them good-night, then watched as they moved to Winifred for her blessing. In a flash they were scooting out the door, bumping up the stairs.

"Hey, what about me?" Dr. Darling frowned at Nicole as if she were to blame for this lapse in affection. "What about my hug?"

"Don't look at me," she muttered, then hoped he hadn't heard.

"I wasn't." He had.

Ruthie tore down the steps again, her face crinkled in a smile. "C'mon, Daddy. You only get a hug and a kiss if you tuck us in and listen to our prayers. You know the rule."

"I'm supposed to be the one who makes the rules around here," he muttered as he climbed the stairs.

"Thank God for those three sprites." Miss Blessing began clearing the table. "I don't know what his life would be like without them."

Nicole chose not to answer. It was none of her business anyway. She was just a temporary partner, a stand-in at his office.

But maybe, just maybe, if she did her job well, kept the office running as smoothly as possible, he would see how much his three daughters needed him right here.

Was that why God had sent her here?

Chapter Five

"Good grief, we must have had every mother in town in here. Have you ever seen so many bee stings in one week?" Carole huffed out a sigh of relief, leaned back in her chair and groaned as the clock chimed six.

"No," Nicole agreed, her head throbbing. "And I don't want to again. That was too much. What is there, a wasp convention in town? That last one in the eye was awful."

"Very ugly," Carole agreed. "I phoned the town office, asked them to send someone to check out the playground, since that's where most of them were stung. Quite the birthday party." She rolled her eyes. "Turns out there were several wasp nests, one right under the slides. They'll remove them tonight."

"Hello, dears." Winifred Blessing breezed through the door, looking robust and frustratingly cheerful. "Working late again, I see."

Guilt immediately overwhelmed Nicole at the reprimand she felt was implied.

"Dr. Darling is working late, too," she explained in

self-defense. "We've had so many patients, we've been squeezing them in wherever we can." She saw one eyebrow tilt. "Bee stings," she explained. "Or hornets, or whatever they are. That's what has us behind. I hope you haven't been stung?"

"I wasn't criticizing, dear. I know how busy you've been. And I never get stung. But even if I did, it wouldn't bother me. I won't get sick. It's part of the Blessing heritage." Suddenly Winifred frowned. "You say Joshua is still here?" She shook her head. "But it's Mrs. Tyndall's night off. He should have been home an hour ago!"

"I'm going, Aunt Win. I'm going. Just a few odds and ends to clear up. She won't mind if I'm a bit late." Joshua smiled at his aunt, then returned to the file he was holding. "Carole, make a note to book Mrs. Fiddler for blood work, will you? I've indicated what I want."

"Yes, Doctor." Carole took the file, added it to the pile already loading down her desk. "I'll do it on Monday, first thing."

"Joshua, go home. Immediately."

Nicole had never seen Miss Winifred so angry.

"Is something wrong?" He looked confused by her order. "The girls?" His forehead furrowed, his body stiffened.

"The girls will be without a caregiver if you don't get yourself home immediately. I'm surprised Mrs. Tyndall hasn't phoned."

"Actually she has." Carole caught his frown and hurried to explain. "I did pass the messages on to you, Doctor."

Joshua's forehead wrinkled as he tried to remember. "Did you? I guess I forgot. I've only got another half hour—"

Miss Blessing shook her head. "You have no time at all. In fact, I'll be surprised if the woman doesn't quit the moment you arrive."

"Quit?" He stared. "Why would she quit?"

Winifred removed his stethoscope, lifted the lab coat from his shoulders and edged him toward the door.

"Her daughter is scheduled for a C-section tomorrow morning, remember? Mrs. Tyndall was supposed to be at her house in Leamington by six to look after the kids while Annie and George went to the hospital. They must be frantic." She held open the door and motioned. "You get home right now and let that poor woman have some time with her family."

Surprisingly, Joshua complied, murmuring meekly, "Yes, Aunt Win."

"And don't fuss about dinner. Nicole and I will be over as soon as we're done here. I put something in the oven." She shooed him out the door and slammed it behind him. "Poor Edna."

Nicole's headache kicked up a notch. She'd dealt with, or rather tried to avoid, Joshua Darling all day long. She had no desire to go to his house tonight and be subjected to more suggestions about how she should be doing her job differently. She'd been in Blessing almost three months and she was doing as well as anyone could with someone peering over their shoulder all the time.

"Miss Blessing…Winifred," she amended, at that lady's glower. "I'd like to help you out tonight, truly, but I'm very tired. I've got this headache, and I just want to lie down."

"Lie down? Tired?" Winifred looked scandalized. "I've been up since four, child. Done a full day's work, and then some. The remedy is not to lie down—it's to change the conditions. I expect you're tense. Dealing with bawling children all day long would give anyone a headache. Am I right?'' She looked to Carole for confirmation, then nodded. ''Thought so. When did you last eat?'' she demanded, and when Nicole didn't immediately answer, turned back to Carole.

''I brought my lunch today. Ate it between calls. I don't think Nicole's eaten anything.'' Carole made a face at Nicole, as if to say she couldn't help blabbing.

''Ah-ha. Exactly my point. Your weakness and headache stem from malnourishment. A doctor should know better. Come along, dear.'' Winifred tut-tutted, then wrapped her arm through Nicole's and marched her to the door. ''We'll get you home, you can have a quick shower and you'll feel good as new.''

''My purse,'' Nicole heard herself protest weakly, and she saw Carole scurry to her office. She returned seconds later, thrust the bag into Nicole's outstretched hand and grinned.

''Anything else?'' she asked, her eyes twinkling with fun.

''No, thank you, Carole. You've been a great help. Now, you get on home yourself. You deserve a good break.''

''Thank you, Miss Blessing. I believe I will. Good night.''

There were several choice remarks Nicole wanted to make, but with Miss Winifred's arm threaded through hers, marching her along as if in the army, it was all Nicole could do to keep up, wishing that just this once she'd weakened and brought her car to work.

Even so, she had to admit that by the time they made it to Miss Blessing's big white house, she did feel better. Her headache had lessened to a bearable level and some of the kinks in her body had loosened.

"Away you go, Nicole. Into the shower. Turn it on massage. I find that a great help." Winifred nodded, then bustled into the kitchen, listing items on her fingers as she went.

There was no way out. Nicole showered, changed and walked back downstairs ten minutes later, dread dragging at her heels.

Loaded down with food from Miss Blessing's kitchen, she walked across the street and managed to tap one elbow against the door, Winifred trailing behind.

"Nici!" Ruthie stood in the doorway grinning from ear to ear. "Hi, Auntie Win. Did you bring something yummy?"

"Lasagne, garlic bread, a salad, some fruit Jell-o and a bit of cake for dessert." Winifred eased past Nicole, jerked her head in the general direction of the kitchen. "Come along. Ruthie, you could carry this bag for me."

Ruthie took the bag and marched forward. Nicole was about to follow when she caught a glimpse of Joshua at the top of the stairs. He stood there staring down at her, a strange look covering his handsome face.

"Hi," she murmured, bracing herself for a reprimand. Instead he smiled, his blue eyes snapping with something she couldn't define.

"Couldn't get away, could you?" He started down the steps, but his eyes never left her face. "I must say I'm delighted."

"You're delighted?" The very idea made her frown. "Why?" When he smiled like that, Joshua Darling made the knees go weak.

"Because for most of my life Aunt Win has been or- dering me around. It's particularly satisfying to watch her focus her talents on someone else for a change." He remained on the last riser, watching her.

"Why are you two just standing here?" Winifred bustled into the room, grabbed Nicole by the arm and tugged. "Come along, dear. You, too, Joshua. I've decided it will make a nice change to eat outside, on the deck. The girls are waiting."

"Yes, Aunt Win," he murmured obediently as he lifted the box out of Nicole's arms. He winked at Nicole, and grinned from ear to ear. "We're coming right now." He waited for her to precede him. "See what I mean."

"You don't have to look so smug," she muttered, keeping her voice low enough that Miss Winifred wouldn't hear. "Just remember that I'm not your permanent partner. I'm halfway through my time here. Soon her focus will be back on you."

The smile drooped a little.

"By the way," she added, holding the screen door open for him, "how is the search going?"

"Search?" He set the box down on the edge of the table and began unloading it.

"The perfect partner. Have you found one yet?" Something suspicious fluttered through his eyes. "Have you even begun?"

"I've hardly had time," he defended, making a great production about uncovering the salad and setting the cake on top of a side table. "You must admit, it's been hectic."

"Yes, but you want to get rid of me, don't you?" She rearranged some of the dishes and began pouring juice for the girls. "Remember, I can't stay indefinitely. As soon as a spot opens up—"

"You're gone." He nodded. "You've told me two hundred times, at least."

"Who's gone?" Ruthie plopped down at the table,

brushing away a fine sheen of sweat that covered her forehead. "I'm hot."

"Chasing your sisters around the yard will do that." Joshua called to his daughters and seated them, then held Miss Blessing's chair.

Nicole took the opportunity to slip into her own chair. Rachel murmured grace and then Joshua began serving the lasagne.

"Who's gone?" Ruthie repeated, her mouth full.

Sensing a reprimand was on the way, Nicole spoke quickly. "I am. In another three months."

As if caught in some crazy time warp, the entire group froze, forks halfway to their mouths, cups raised. All except Dr. Darling. He ignored them all, munching on a piece of steaming garlic bread.

"But you can't go!" Ruthie wailed. "You just got here. Besides, you're my best friend."

Nicole smiled, brushed her hand over the untidy braids.

"Thank you, Ruthie. That's very kind of you. You're my best friend, too." She served herself a little Jell-o, not because she wanted it, but because she needed a minute to organize her words.

"Honey, you know that Dr. Brandt is just a temporary replacement."

Nicole clamped her lips together, fuming silently. Why did he have to sound so happy about it?

"She came to help us out for a little while, but she's not going to stay in Blessing. She has to go back to school."

"Why? Did she fail or something?" Ruthie fixed her big blue eyes on Nicole. "Didn't you study enough?"

"I didn't fail anything, Ruthie. I just want to take

some more training. I couldn't get into the school right away, so I came here to work until there's a spot for me.''

''But we don't want you to go!'' Rachel's plaintive wail drew a frown from her father. ''You make things fun. Like our mom used to.''

Dead silence reigned. All eyes swerved toward Joshua, whose face drained of color, though he kept his head tilted down. Nicole knew he was furious, and that he blamed her for this intrusion into his personal life. But right now she didn't care about that. She was more concerned with the three little girls, who looked as if she'd abandoned them.

''We have had fun, haven't we?'' She smiled at them, ached to pull their glossy heads to her and hug for all she was worth.

It was a strange feeling for someone like her to have, someone who didn't know anything about love. But she wanted to know. She wanted to experience the purely giddy sense of knowing that someone would care for you no matter what you did. If only her father could see—

Nicole pushed the past away and searched for words.

''We'll have lots more fun times. There are a ton of things we can do together. Let's think about that, plan something special.''

Their sad faces stared at her for several moments. Then they looked at each other, trying to do as she asked.

''We could have a bike ride and go fishing in the lake,'' Rachel finally whispered. ''We haven't done that in ever so long.''

''That sounds like fun.'' Nicole risked a sideways glance at Joshua, found his gaze focused on his daughters, watching as their small faces came alive with interest.

"Go camping." Rosalyn blurted the words out, then grinned. "Campfires."

Suddenly the ideas burst forth, fast and furious. But Joshua simply sat there, part of their group, yet separate, as if he didn't quite know how to fit in, what to do with their suggestions. Nicole's heart ached for him. How had he let the special times go? Was it up to her to help him get them back, to rebuild the family bonds that had weakened since his wife's death? Was that why she was here?

"I think the fishing idea is great," she told them, already seeing herself reclining on a beach while this little family fished together, laughing and teasing each other about the one that got away. Surely fishing was something a man could do with his children without losing face?

"What kind of hooks do you use?" She glanced at Joshua. Perhaps if she asked him questions directly, he'd get into the spirit and begin to take part.

Instead the girls smothered giggles, their eyes sparkling with excitement.

"What's so funny?" Nicole frowned at their glee.

"Doesn't much matter about the hooks, Nici," Ruthie informed her with a grin. "We use worms to fish."

"Oh." Nicole tried to control her shudder of distaste. "I don't think I'd be very good at it, after all. Maybe fishing's something you should do with your father."

"You can't leave Blessing without at least trying your luck with a pole," Winifred encouraged. "Tomorrow's Saturday. I think it would be nice if you all went fishing. Joshua, you could show Nicole how to put the worm on the hook."

"Uh, no, thanks," said Nicole. "I have something planned for tomorrow." She refused to feel guilty at the disappointment flooding three eager faces. "Maybe another time."

"Tomorrow sounds good." Joshua resumed eating, some of the color coming back into his face. "You girls get to bed early tonight so we can get up before the birds, and I'll take you fishing. There are a lot of things we can learn at the lake."

Winifred leaned closer to Nicole, her voice low as the girls reminded their father of all the equipment they'd need.

"You can read those musty old books anytime," the older woman hissed. "A little fresh air, some sunshine, that's just what you need."

"But—"

"The girls need you, dear. If I know my nephew, and I do, fishing will turn into a forced biology lesson that will only engender lectures and tears. Joshua's forgotten how to relax and just enjoy the girls. He's too concerned about their education, their health, all the things he's losing control over. Help him make this a fun outing for all of them. Please?"

Nicole sighed. Winifred wasn't playing fair, and she knew it. How could anyone deny themselves the opportunity to spend time with those three adorable minxes, even if it meant holding a fishing rod with a worm on it? She couldn't. Still, she had to draw the line somewhere, and that line stopped just short of threading worms onto a hook.

"All right. I'll go fishing. But that's all. No dinner afterward. No story time, no throwing me together with *him*." Unfortunately everyone had stopped talking and the last words emerged rather loudly into the silence. It was obvious that Joshua had heard. His mouth pinched together, and his shoulders jerked to their usual rigid stance.

"I don't think you have to worry about any more matchmaking, Dr. Brandt. My aunt knows better, don't you, Aunt Win?" His dark glare dared the older woman to deny it.

Winifred reached over, patted his hand and smiled.

"Now, dear, don't get so upset. I just want Nicole to see some of our beautiful countryside while she's here, and she can give you a hand with the girls while she's doing it. The two of you can forget about all those patients and just relax." She smiled that winsome smile that said she would ignore any objections. "Now then, does anyone want cake?"

As Nicole sipped her coffee, she watched Winifred and Joshua exchange glances. She shifted uncomfortably in her seat, wishing she'd stayed in the shower, and out of this family meal. She was getting too involved, and she knew it. So did Miss Winifred, though she pretended otherwise.

"All right, girls. If you're finished your meal, you can carry your dishes into the kitchen. Then perhaps your father will throw a few balls so you can practice batting. Your coaches told me you need to work on your softball skills." In one fell swoop, Miss Winifred had them all organized.

Nicole cleared away the rest of the dishes, loaded the dishwasher and washed the containers too big to fit into it. Every so often she glanced outside, almost mesmerized by the laughing man and his three giggling girls.

"Look at him. When he relaxes, Joshua is a completely different man. Tender, caring," Miss Winifred murmured, standing just behind Nicole. "He needs to do this more often. If he'd just let go and enjoy them, let them see that he loves them no matter how many rules they break, they'd be so much more secure.''

"I don't think Dr. Darling requires my help with those girls, not now and not tomorrow." Nicole rinsed the counter, folded the dishcloth and stepped away. "He seems to be managing just fine."

"For now." She nodded. "He's too tired to maintain his usual posture tonight. It's easier to just relax. But come tomorrow, he'll be back to his usual form. You're the only one I've ever seen who refuses to let him bully her, who challenges him to really think about his actions. Joshua needs more of that."

"Not from me, he doesn't." Nicole poured herself another cup of coffee and moved to sit outside on the deck. "I can't get too involved, Miss Blessing. I don't want them to fuss when I go, and I will be going," she warned.

"I know." Winifred sighed, her face sad. "It's just— I suppose I'll have to pray some more," she whispered.

Pray for what? Nicole wanted to demand. But she said nothing, her eyes on the dark-haired man now sitting cross-legged on the grass, tickling his daughters.

Why, Dad? Why couldn't you have loved me like that?

"I don't like worms."

"What?" Joshua Darling stared at her. "You're a doctor, you're heading into surgery. You're going to touch a lot worse than worms!"

"I'll be wearing gloves," she muttered, hiding one hand behind her back when he held out the wiggling thing.

"You want me to find you a pair of surgical gloves so you can fish?" He hooted with laughter. "Dr. Brandt, I would never have believed it. You're a sissy!"

"Am not!" She glared at him, incensed that he'd try to show her up in front of the girls.

"Sure you are. You're afraid of a teensy little worm." He huffed his disgust, threaded the worm on her hook, then dropped the line in the water. "Here." He held out her rod.

"Thanks." Nicole grabbed it and hung on for dear life, praying the fish would avoid her worm.

"As I recall, you were the one who thought fishing would be such a delightful excursion for the girls." His voice mocked her squeamishness.

"I didn't say *I* would be fishing," she muttered. "I assumed I'd be able to sit on the shore, read a book or something, while everyone else was throwing their lines in."

"Casting," he corrected. "When you're fishing, it's called casting."

"Whatever." She turned the little handle, her eyes on the dragonfly flitting over the water. She imagined what it would be like to be free to skim across the water, touching down here and there, fluttering away when danger got too close.

"You have to keep winding or the hook will snag on something." He watched her turn the little handle at top speed and shook his head. "Too fast. A fish could never keep up with that."

"You fish your way and I'll fish mine," she told him, winding even faster.

The hook burst free of the water, flew in toward shore. Nicole watched in horror as the big juicy worm plopped right onto her shirt.

"Gross!" She jerked the rod out and the hook spun through the air to splat against the smooth water.

"Hey!" Ruthie twisted to glare at her. "If you splash like that, you scare the fish."

"I'll just move downstream a little. That way I won't bother anyone." Fully conscious of Joshua Darling's knowing smirk, Nicole marched fifty feet away, turned her back and threw—no, cast—the line the way he'd taught her. She wound slowly for a few minutes, watching the silver minnows that swam near shore. Then her rod made a screeching noise and she couldn't get it to wind any farther.

"Drat! Now they'll think I'm a complete incompetent." She looked over her shoulder, found the others busy with their own fishing. Good. She jerked hard on the rod and watched in amazement as the spool unwound and fishing line spun out across the water.

"Oh, for Pete's sake." She chewed on her bottom lip as she rewound the excess line. Then there was a tug, and it began feeding out again. What to do? If she carried the rod with her toward Joshua, it would feed out even more line. She frowned, trying to figure out the next step in this fishing expedition.

"Having problems?" He stood two feet away, behind her, his eyes crinkling at her frustration.

"It's caught on something. I can't get it wound up. Every time I try, it undoes again."

He looked from her face to the water. "Wind slowly," he ordered, moving to the edge to watch.

"I've *been* winding slowly. It doesn't help." She wound and wound, then felt the line jerk before it zipped free again. "You see. There's something wrong with this fishing pole."

"There's nothing wrong, Nicole." His eyes sparkled with something very close to fun. "You just caught a fish."

She stared at him, mentally noting that he'd finally called her by her first name without any hesitation.

"I don't want to catch a fish," she whispered.

His eyes opened very wide. "You don't?"

She shook her head.

"Then why did you come fishing?"

"I'm beginning to ask myself that question." She stared at the rod in her hands. "How do I get my hook back?"

"Keep winding slowly. When it pulls back, you let it go a little, easing it in toward shore. The fish will tire and we'll catch it." At her jerk of surprise, he reached out, his hands covering hers. "Careful, you almost lost the rod."

"Dr. Darling, I don't want to *catch* it! I don't even like fish very much, except to watch them swimming in the water." She made a face at the rod that had started everything. "Couldn't we just let it go?"

He shrugged. "I suppose. If you want." His face told her what he thought of that. "But first you have to get the fish in here, so you can get the hook out."

"The hook with the worm?" she asked carefully.

He barely managed to conceal his laughter. "Uh-huh."

"Oh." Nicole did some fast thinking. "I'll baby-sit for nothing, anytime you want, if you will please remove the hook from my fish."

Joshua Darling stared at her, speechless.

"Well?" She was getting sick of winding this thing. Wasn't the fish tired?

"You are a very unusual woman," he muttered.

"Now you notice." The line zipped away again. Nicole sighed, kept winding. "Will you do it?"

He nodded. "An offer I can't refuse. All right. Try and ease it in to shore, preferably near me."

She eased as best she could, but the fish had other ideas. It flipped and swam and pulled until her arms ached in their sockets.

"I hate fishing," she muttered, turning to the side to direct the fish on shore as she pulled back on the rod. "Just to prove who's boss, I should—oh!" The fish, obviously giving up, flew through the air and landed directly in front of Joshua Darling, splashing him in the process.

"Wow! It's a big one. Ruthie, come here."

Ruthie flew across the sand, her eyes huge. "You caught a fish, Nici," she whispered, awestruck.

"I know." Nicole glared at the pale white scales, felt her stomach twitch. She fought to control her emotions, knowing he would only laugh at her squeamishness.

"Can you get my camera, honey?" Joshua squatted down, his hands gently working to free the hook from the fish's mouth. "I think Nicole should have a picture of her fish before I let it go."

"Let it go?" Ruthie stared. "I thought you told Auntie Win we'd be eating fish for sup—oh." She saw the glare on her father's face and ran off to get the camera.

"He bit hard," Joshua murmured. "It's in fairly deep."

"Will it live if you let it go?" Nicole glared at the rod, wishing she'd dropped it into the water before the fish had come along. She watched as the poor slimy thing flopped around in the shallows, its tail flapping madly.

"I think so." He glanced up, frowned at her, then looked for Ruthie. "Got it?"

"Uh-huh." The little girl motioned to Nicole. "You squat down by Daddy, put your hand on top of his so it looks like you're holding the fish.'' She adjusted the viewfinder, then frowned. ''You have to smile, Nici. A big smile.''

''As if I'm enjoying this?'' Nicole kept her voice low, so only Joshua could hear.

''Exactly. Just remember—fishing was your idea.'' His hand, despite the cool water, lay warm under hers. ''Got it, Ruthie?''

''I jiggled. I better take another one. Don't move now. Smile, Daddy.''

Joshua felt his mouth move in obedience to his daughter's command, but in truth, he couldn't have stopped staring at Nicole if his life had depended upon it. His attention homed in on the clouds filling *her* eyes and suddenly he realized what was wrong.

It wasn't that she didn't like fish or worms—it was the act of killing something that was alive that bothered her. A woman like her, confident, self-assured and smart, was bothered by something like a fish? It seemed incongruous with what he knew of her. And yet—he knew it was true.

''That's enough, Ruthie,'' he murmured. He lifted his hand, watching as Nicole stroked one finger a hairbreadth above the fish. ''If we're going to let him go, it had better be now. Okay?'' he asked her.

She nodded. ''Yes. Please.''

Joshua eased the fish through the water, loosening his fingers inch by inch until it finally whipped its tail to the left and swam away.

''Will it live?'' she whispered, peering up at him, her face devoid of makeup, bare inches from his.

He nodded.

''Oh, thank goodness.'' She squeezed his hand, her

thousand-watt smile flashing out. "I don't know what I'd have done if you hadn't been here."

He didn't know what to say to that, didn't know how to respond. She was offering friendship, a common ground to share. Part of him wanted to let go of all the constraints that had bound him to the course of life he'd chosen two years ago and enjoy her company. But the other part choked with fear. He had three children who depended on him, that nagging little voice reminded. Duty, obligation, responsibility. Nothing could get in the way of that, nothing could be allowed to sidetrack him.

Besides, Nicole Brandt was halfway through the required six months. If he didn't get into action, she'd be gone and he'd be as badly off, or worse. The whole point of her presence was to give him a chance to recruit a partner. He needed to focus on that, not think about befriending her.

"It wasn't anything." Joshua jerked to his feet, almost bumping heads with her as he stood.

"Oh!" She blinked, then also rose, stepped away from him. "Well...thanks anyway."

He nodded, walked back to his own rod, picked it up and cast as if his life depended on it. Nicole Brandt had a way of making him forget things he should be concentrating on and daydreaming about things that could never be a part of his life, and he didn't like it, Joshua decided. It was dangerous.

He'd learned his lesson the hard way. He wouldn't forget it now. It was better to stick to business, focus on what had to be done. Alone.

But as he stared over the water, part of him wondered what it would be like to forget about duty—just for a little while.

Chapter Six

"Dr. Darling? I understand you asked to speak to me." Nicole juggled the files she held in one hand, while she tried to cradle the phone in the other and sign Carole's paper at the same time.

"Yes, I did."

The silence lengthened, then stretched into oblivion. She wanted to wait for him, to be patient and polite, but she didn't have the time. She had to get on with it or she'd be here till midnight.

"Dr. Darling?"

"Yes, I'm here."

"Well?"

He sighed, then began to speak.

"I have a patient here who has just had what I'm certain is a heart attack. I have him stabilized, but I don't want to leave him just yet and he refuses to go in the ambulance. If I can, I'd like to bring him back with me, check him in and get him settled."

Carole beckoned madly from the doorway. Nicole

could hear a child squealing at the top of her lungs and knew she was needed.

"Fine. Do what you think is best." She almost hung up, but something in his tone stopped her. "Dr. Darling?"

"The thing is, it's Mrs. Tyndall's night off and she promised to baby-sit the new grandchild. I don't want to ask her to stay and deprive her of that. I'd ask Aunt Win, but I can't reach her. For some reason, Furly doesn't seem to know where she is."

"I'll look after your daughters. No problem." Ha! She felt like a fool saying it. What did she know about caring for children, after all? But still, this was an emergency. "Is that all you need?" she asked, conscious of Carole's rising impatience.

"Well, yes, but I had a few suggestions I thought I should give before—"

Nicole cut him off. "Look, Joshua, I'm up to my ears today. Right now there's a kid needing stitches who's screaming her head off and the waiting room is full to overflowing. I've got to go. I'll look after the girls until you get back, okay?"

"Yes, I suppose that's the best we can do."

Her indignation rose like mercury in the sun.

"The best we can do?" She whooshed her breath out, began to count to ten, but stopped at two, unable to stem her fury. "I'm trying to help you out, Joshua Darling, just as I have been for the past four and a half months." The angry words grated out, weariness at this silly unspoken feud blazing into an inferno.

"Obviously I've done something wrong again. I offered to baby-sit whenever you wanted and I stand by my offer. If you don't want my help, fine. Get someone else. But make your decision now, because I can't waste any more time with your dithering. I need every moment I can get to deal with *your* patients." It was a snarky thing to say, and she regretted it immediately, but Nicole was so tired of being found wanting.

"I'm sorry to have troubled you." The words crackled across the airwaves, frigid in tone. "That arrangement will be fine. I'll try not to be too long. I'm sure you have other plans. Thank you, Doctor."

"No, thank you, Doctor," she murmured sweetly, then gently replaced the phone. "Thank you for nothing," she muttered, furious that he could still get to her like this.

"Do you want to talk about it?" Carole asked, one eye on the waiting room.

"No, thank you. There's nothing good I could say, so it's better to remain silent." Nicole handed her the finished files, started for the door, then checked herself, grinning at Carole. "Thanks for pinch-hitting, Carole. Penny's overloaded."

"No problem. I'm used to helping out."

"Well, I appreciate it. Now, where exactly am I headed?" she asked.

"Westward ho—toward the screams." Carole chuckled.

Due to a mother's hysteria, the afternoon clinic lasted far longer than it should have. Nicole raced through her paperwork, conscious of the time that flew past.

"These are the responses to that ad Dr. Darling ran six weeks ago." Penny looked at the file, then shrugged. "I don't know what to do with them. He hasn't looked through any of them. Some of these people have been calling, leaving messages, some have asked to have their names removed, some want to know more."

"Six weeks?" Nicole shook her head. "It doesn't sound like Dr. Darling believes this perfect partner he touts is to be found. Which makes sense—nobody's perfect. Not even him.'' She thought for a moment, tapped one finger against her bottom lip. ''You know, I have a hunch he's avoiding making this decision, Penny. However, I think you'd better make some appointments for interviews. If he refuses to see them, I'll do it. I'd feel responsible if I left here without someone else to step in for me, but there's no way I'm willing to opt out of my surgical training.''

Which wasn't exactly true. In fact, given a choice…

''Can you do double duty next Friday?'' Penny closed her eyes for a moment, thought over the schedule. ''He could do the interviews in the afternoon and fume about it all weekend.'' Her eyes sparkled with teasing lights. ''Maybe he'll be over it by Monday.''

Nicole didn't deign to comment on the likelihood of that. She simply nodded and continued charting. Then there were rounds at the hospital. By the time she walked up the path to the Darling home, it was ten minutes after seven.

''I'm getting better,'' she congratulated herself. ''Maybe by the time I leave, I'll have this ten-minute-appointment thing licked.''

Her brain simply scoffed.

''Nici!'' Ruthie stood in the doorway, her eyes wide with delight. ''I didn't know you were coming over tonight.''

''Actually, neither did I.'' She greeted Mrs. Tyndall, asked about the new baby. ''Their father got held up at the clinic and I said I'd step in.''

''All right! Hey, Rach, guess what?'' Ruthie went tearing up the stairs.

''They do love to have you here,'' Mrs. Tyndall murmured. She explained about the casserole she'd left

warming in the oven. "The girls had a snack earlier, but
I think they're hungry now. I always keep a little back
for Dr. Darling. If I don't set it in front of him, he doesn't
eat, just opens that briefcase and starts working. It's not
healthy, even if he is a doctor."

"I'll keep a plate for him," Nicole assured her, then
watched as the older woman left.

Supper was a riot of girl chatter, each sister anxious
to share their day. It was as if they'd kept everything
bottled up for too long, and now they just had to let it
out.

"I'm sorry if we're talking too much," Rachel apol-
ogized, her cheeks bright pink. "Daddy calls us chatter-
boxes. He doesn't like it when we talk too much."

Nicole's heart ached for the girls who tried so hard
not to overtax their daddy.

"I like it when you tell me about your day. But sometimes it is good to have silence, just to listen." She
tweaked Rosalyn's nose when the little girl frowned in
confusion. "I expect your dad gets tired sometimes, and
just needs to relax for a minute."

"We try not to bother him when he first comes
home," Rachel whispered. "That's what Mommy used
to do. She'd tell him to relax for a few minutes and she'd
take us all into her room and read a story." Tears trembled on the tips of her lashes. "I wish she was here
now."

"I know you do." There was nothing Nicole could do
but offer her shoulder and hug the little girl close. "But
it doesn't matter how tired your daddy gets, he'll always
love you. You know that, don't you?"

"I guess so." Rachel blinked, looked to Ruthie for the
right words.

"Sometimes it's scary." Ruthie's chin jutted out as if she knew she shouldn't have said it.

"Scary? Why?" Nicole frowned. It was obvious something was bothering them, that something preyed on their minds. Maybe it was none of her business, but wasn't it better that she settle their worries than let this continue? "You can tell me, Ruthie," she coaxed. "I won't scold."

"Well." Ruthie peeked up at her, then, catching Nicole's glance, slid her eyes away. "Sometimes when we go to bed, Daddy isn't home."

"And sometimes when we wake up, he isn't here." The words seemed to spill out of Rachel.

Nicole nodded. "I know. He has to go to the hospital sometimes, doesn't he?" She watched the fair heads nod. "Is that what bothers you? But there's always someone here with you, isn't there?"

"Yes. Mrs. Tyndall comes back or Auntie Win comes over."

It was clear the problem lay deeper. Nicole thought for a moment, decided to keep probing. Clearly, something was wrong.

"Are you afraid of the dark?" she asked softly.

"Rosie is. Sometimes." Ruthie fiddled with her napkin. "But we have night-lights, so that's okay. We just turn them on."

"Then what's the matter?"

The girls looked at each other, eyes transmitting an unspoken message. Then they looked at her. It was Rachel who finally explained.

"What if he doesn't come back, Nici?"

"What do you mean?" She stared into the three worried faces, puzzled by the words.

"Mommy went away. What if Daddy goes away, too?

Then what will we do?'' Ruthie's fingers scrunched up the paper napkin into a ball. ''Where would we go?''

''To Auntie Win, I guess.'' Rachel nodded. ''She's our relative.''

Nicole could hardly believe what she'd heard.

''Girls, your father isn't going away. He's going to come home here, check to make sure you're asleep and tickle you awake in the morning.''

''He is?'' Rosalyn's eyes grew huge. ''He didn't tickle me this morning.''

Nicole had to smile at that. They were so literal. And afraid. She'd have to be careful here.

''Your mommy went away because she was sick. Her body was tired and she couldn't be here anymore, so she went home to God. She didn't want to go, but she didn't want to be sick anymore, either. She loved you very much and she knew if she left your daddy here, he'd take very good care of you.''

''But what if he can't?'' Rachel frowned, her whole face screwed up. ''What if he gets sick, too?''

''Does your daddy look sick?'' Nicole asked, watching their faces while she prayed for wisdom. ''I'm a doctor. How about we discuss this case? Is he tired all the time? Does he have to lie on the couch? Doesn't he get out of bed in the morning?''

''That's silly.'' Ruthie shook her head. ''Our daddy is strong. He even gives us piggyback rides. Sometimes.''

Nicole could tell that wasn't a recent memory. Her heart ached for the hurting family. In a tiny repressed corner of her heart she understood exactly what these children felt. They weren't totally secure in their father's love. They needed him to be there more often, to ease their fears and assure them that he would never leave them. How she wished Joshua could hear this discussion!

"Daddy must be strong. Mrs. Tyndall says people depend on him. You can't depend on somebody if they're not strong."

"You're absolutely right, Rachel." Nicole brushed the fair hair back, pressed a kiss to her forehead. "Your daddy is very strong. That's why people come to him and ask him to help make them better. That's why he works so hard, even when you guys are sleeping. Because he wants to help people, and because he's strong and he knows what to do."

"Like you," Ruthie exclaimed. "You knew how to fix my arm."

"Yes, and I'm glad I did."

"So maybe you could stay and then Daddy wouldn't have to go away so much. Maybe he could read us stories at night, every night, like when Mommy was here." Ruthie's voice brimmed with hope. "Maybe if you were the doctor boss, Daddy could be the helper. Then you could go see the sick people at night."

"I'm sorry, honey. I wish that were possible. But your daddy is the boss here. He's the one people go to with questions. I'm just here to help out for a while." She tried to soften the words. "But, girls, it doesn't matter how often your daddy goes to help someone else, he always, always comes home to you. Doesn't he?"

They nodded, blond heads glistening.

"And that's the most important thing." Not wanting to dwell on the topic any longer, and uncertain of whether she'd allayed their fears or simply drawn them off target, Nicole encouraged the girls to help her clear the table and load the dishwasher. Then they hurried outside to play a rousing game of soccer.

Tired out by the activity, they didn't protest when she proclaimed it bath time. Later, snuggled up in Rosalyn's bed, they looked like three miniature angels. A lump swelled in her throat as Nicole accepted the storybook they handed her and began to read.

"Daddy should be home pretty soon. He'll be glad we cleaned up the kitchen. Daddy doesn't like to come home to a mess." Rachel yawned, her eyelids drooping. "We've been trying to be really quiet when Daddy's home so we don't bother him."

They were protecting him in the hope that he wouldn't leave them. It was so sad, and yet, Nicole knew, so typical. She winced at her own memories of tiptoeing around the house so she wouldn't disturb her father, so that he wouldn't send her away because she was a bother, a walking reminder of the woman he'd loved and lost.

"Rachel, I wish I could make you understand how much your daddy loves you, that he doesn't really care about noise or mess or any of those things, as long as you girls are safe and happy." A sudden thought flickered through her mind. "Why don't you talk to him about it when he comes home?"

Something very like fear blanched their faces.

"Oh, no. It's okay, Nici. Really. We know our dad is a good doctor and we're really proud of him, but we don't want to cause a fuss. Daddy hates fusses." Rachel nudged Ruthie, her eyes transmitting an unspoken message.

Like obedient soldiers the two eldest hugged their little sister, then moved to their own beds, where they huddled under the covers and closed their eyes.

"Good night girls," Nicole whispered, tucking each one in, brushing back the fair strands to graze her lips across their cheeks. "Sweet dreams."

"Good night, Nici." It was repeated twice more.

Nicole wandered downstairs and picked up the medical journal she'd been reading earlier. She glanced through the pages, desultorily noting the descriptions. Something snagged her attention and she returned to it, reread it carefully.

"Mr. De Witt," she whispered, a light clicking on inside her brain.

She sorted through the symptoms, tried to remember what was in the file. Could Joshua Darling's diagnosis be wrong? And if it was, did she have the temerity to tell him?

"Dr. Brandt—Nicole. I hope I haven't kept you too long?"

As if summoned, he now stood before her, black bag in one hand, jacket slung over the other. His face was in shadow so that she couldn't read the expression on his face.

"Are the girls in bed?"

Nicole nodded. Now there were two things he needed to know, and she didn't want to tell him either one.

"Have you read this article?" she asked, holding up the journal.

"Haven't had time yet." He flopped down in the big easy chair across from her and let his head droop back. "There never seems to be enough time for reading anything but storybooks. Why?"

"N-nothing." He peered at her. "Well, it's just that I thought you might be interested in what they have to say in relation to Mr. De Witt." She described the article's findings, but was interrupted partway through.

"That's not Dermot's problem. I've done the tests and his heart seems rock solid. Anyway, he's my patient, not yours. You have no right to question my diagnosis."

"I wasn't! His file was accidentally in with one of

mine.'' She clamped her lips shut, wishing she'd kept silent.

"I'll speak to Edwina."

"No, don't do that. It wasn't her mistake." She saw the way his jaw clenched and knew he would do it in spite of her protest. "She tries very hard to adhere to your precise schedule, but life has a way of interfering in spite of our best efforts." She glanced down, made up her mind. "Still, I do think you should look at this. It says—"

"Not tonight." The words slipped out between gritted teeth, his eyes fierce as they met hers. "I'll look later."

"I'm sorry." She sat silent for a moment, then laid the booklet on a nearby table. "Your patient?"

He shook his head. "He made it to the hospital, but that's all."

"I'm sorry." Feeling like a malfunctioning CD, repeating the same thing over and over, Nicole sought for another subject. "I kept a plate for you. Would you like it now?"

"I'm not hungry." He sighed. "Thanks."

"Something to drink, then?"

He shook his head, his voice harsh in the stillness. "Don't fuss, okay?"

"I'm not fussing. I'm merely asking if you'd like a drink. I'm sure you're tired and I was trying to help out, but it seems that whatever I do is wrong. It's no wonder the girls are so confused."

He paid attention to that. Suddenly Joshua Darling was bolt upright in his seat, his face drawn into harsh lines that warned her to back off.

"You are speaking about my daughters?" he grated, one eyebrow tilted in that annoying way. "What is it you feel *my* children are confused about, Dr. Brandt?"

"You." She ignored the ice emanating from him and threw down the gauntlet. "I understand that you're committed to your career, Joshua. So do the girls. They understand it so well, they're going out of their way not to bother you with their fears."

"But they bothered you?"

She hated that sneering tone, but Nicole refused to budge until she'd had her say.

"They let a few things slip tonight and I encouraged them to talk." She took a deep breath. "They're afraid you're going to go and never come back. They're worried you'll leave them, as their mother did, and they don't know what will happen to them."

"How dare you!"

"How dare I?" She couldn't believe he'd said it. "How dare I what? Be concerned for them, care about them, want to help? How dare I believe that a patient who hasn't responded to your treatment might find something else effective? How dare I notice that you're alienating everyone around you because you put timetables and schedules and money before people? How dare I suggest you haven't got your priorities straight, that you aren't even trying to find my replacement in spite of six great applicants?" She paused, lowered her voice and pinned him with her eyes.

"Or, Dr. Darling, do you mean how dare I presume to listen to what you refuse to hear—that your sweet, darling daughters are afraid that one day you'll forget about them and bury yourself in your work completely?"

He flinched, his face ashen, his hands fisted on the arms of his chair.

Nicole stood, knowing she'd said too much, cut too deep. As a surgeon-to-be, she needed practice at getting to the heart of the matter.

"I think you'd better leave now." His voice emerged flat, emotionless.

"I apologize," she murmured, though he gave no sign that her diatribe had even dented his armor. "I wanted to ask you to speak to them, to reassure them. I didn't mean to lose it like that."

He stood, towering above her, scant inches away, and yet distant.

"Why apologize? I'm sure you believe in what you're saying." He walked toward the front door, gripped the doorknob. "Thank you for standing in tonight. You may consider the debt repaid."

"But you won't be asking again." She picked up her purse and walked toward him. "I'm sorry. I care about those girls. I was trying to help them. And you. I was hoping you'd understand that some simple reassurances would destroy their fear of abandonment."

"I repeat, I have no intention of abandoning my daughters!" The words hissed out at her, daring her to say more.

"I know that." Nicole nodded, stepped past him onto the doorstep. "But maybe you should tell *them*," she whispered. "Good night." Then she turned and walked away, waiting for the door to slam behind her.

It never did.

Instead, she felt his hand on her arm, turning her to face him. His eyes blazed with anger.

"Would you mind telling me what it is that makes you such an expert on children, Dr. Brandt? I thought your particular field was surgery."

"I'm not an expert." Nicole weighed how much to tell him, then decided. She'd gone too far. There was no point in backing down if she wanted to save those girls some of the pain she'd gone through.

"My mother died when I was a little girl," she told him softly. "I've spent the better part of my life walking a tightrope, wondering if my father doesn't want me around because he doesn't love me, or if it's simply because I remind him too much of a woman he loved. And here I am, at my age, still pushing myself, still trying to win his admiration, if not his love. Pathetic, isn't it?" She met his stare.

"I didn't mean—"

"The truth is, Dr. Darling, that I can't bear the thought that those three girls might go through the same thing."

Twisting her arm free, she turned her back and walked away as the tears coursed down her cheeks.

Chapter Seven

"If that's the way you truly feel, Joshua, perhaps it's better if I leave. Permanently. Consider today my last day."

Joshua Darling clamped his lips together and watched as the best office nurse/manager he'd ever had turned her back on him to hide the tears he knew glossed her eyes. Why couldn't he do anything right lately?

"Can't we discuss this, Penny?" he asked quietly.

"What's the point? You've already made up your mind. Apparently you feel I've chosen sides against you. I haven't, you know. I've simply been doing my level best to keep this place going." She twisted to face him, her jaw jutting forward. "Nicole was trying to help, too. She thought evening clinics would lighten your load, and she was right. She was also right about streamlining the way we handle the billings. It's saved me hours of overtime and we get paid sooner. But you disagree. Fine. It's your office."

"The cost—"

Penny turned redder than he'd ever seen her. She

marched up to him, raised one hand and began counting off.

"First, the extra hours didn't cost you a dime. Nicole paid me out of her own pocket. And I doubt she claimed one red cent from you. Second, streamlining our billing methods has saved you far more than it cost. If you'd bothered to look at my notes, you'd see that. Third, Mr. De Witt was not getting better and you know it. I know that's what you hate the most, the fact that I let her see him."

Her voice was rising, growing progressively louder in the empty waiting room. Joshua hated confrontations, but wasn't it his duty to keep things under control? Why couldn't they see that? Accept it?

"Penny, you and Dr. Brandt—"

"All right! Yes, I colluded with her and had the lab run those tests—which was a good thing. She was right! Now maybe we can help him. Isn't that why we're here?" Her eyes dared him to deny it.

He swallowed the gall that filled his stomach at the thought of Dermot De Witt. The man was a friend, a good friend. Why couldn't Joshua admit the truth, agree that his treatment wasn't working? Why had it taken someone from the outside? Was he losing even the most basic ability to care for his patients?

His head jerked up as Penny continued.

"And fourth, you can blame me for making booking mistakes all you want, but the truth is that your patients are flocking to Nicole because she truly listens to what they have to say. She *wants* to hear about their families, their work, their *petty little woes.*"

He flinched as the echo of his own words rang through the empty office.

Penny's eyes clouded, and she reached out her hand, touched his arm.

"What happened, Joshua? You used to care passionately about these people. They knew you were there for them and they respected you for that commitment. You bent over backward to make sure their interests were served. They looked to you as a community leader and you never let them down or made them feel they were imposing." She frowned. "But lately, it's as if the only thing you care about is the money they bring in."

He stepped backward, staggered by her words. "No!"

"I'm sorry, but it's time for the truth. You've got to let go of this need to control everyone. What is so wrong with delegating? Not life-and-death decisions, but simple things that you shouldn't be bothering with. If you don't, you'll burn out." She sighed, pulled a hand through her perfectly coiffed hair. "Nicole won't be here much longer. She never planned to stay beyond six months. How could she, in good conscience, walk away knowing there was no one to take her place? She had me set up those interviews because she isn't that uncaring."

Like you.

The condemnation hit him in the gut, drained him of any response. Anger, acid rich and fiery hot, burned inside, eating up the reserve restraint he'd been so careful to maintain.

She was to blame. She'd turned them all against him, even Aunt Win. His cheeks burned at the reprimand implicit in his aunt's words from last night. *Nicole is a good doctor, Joshua. Whether you like it or not. In fact, I suspect she'd love to stay in general practice, but you've made that very difficult, harping on her departure all the time. I know how strongly she speaks of surgery and the training she'll take, but sometimes I wonder if surgery is what she really wants, or if she's doing it for some other reason.*

Nicole's sad words from two weeks ago came back to haunt him. Did this push for surgery have something to do with the father she believed didn't love her?

Penny's quiet voice halted his thoughts.

"I like you, Joshua. I think you're a wonderful doctor who has had to deal with a whole lot at once. But you've changed and, I'm sorry, but I'm not comfortable with what's happening here. Take the weekend. Decide what you want. If you think we can still work together, I'll be happy to come back. But be warned, I'm going to want some changes. We can't go on as we have been. I'm not a child and I will not be treated as such. I've earned more than that, don't you think?"

Penny nodded at him, picked up her handbag, then walked out, her shoes tapping against the cement like tiny nails hammered home.

He was a failure.

She hadn't said it in so many words, but that's what she'd implied. Somehow, despite his best efforts, the women in his office had seen beyond his mask to the real him, the one who knew his patients weren't getting his best effort. The truth was, they hadn't been for some time.

"Penny gone? Shoot. Oh, well, I guess I can get her to do this on Monday." Nicole stopped, peered at him more closely, and frowned. "Is something wrong?"

"Quite a lot, actually." The need to reassert himself, to regain control of his wavering life, took over. "You will be leaving Blessing in a matter of weeks, Dr. Brandt. But this is my home and my practice. I'm the senior partner and the bills are paid out of my pocket. Don't you think it might have been wise, if not courteous, to consult me about the tests you ran on Dermot De Witt?''

He saw her flinch as his words hit home, watched her shoulders straighten, her eyes meet his, and felt a twinge of shame. Had he become the petty bully Penny had all but accused him of?

''I did try to consult with you, Dr. Darling.'' Her low voice flowed out in measured tones. ''Several times. You wouldn't listen to me.''

''So you decided to go around me, insinuate to my patient that I was treating him with the wrong protocol?''

''Don't be ridiculous!'' Her eyes burned. ''There are enough patients in this office to keep three doctors busy. I'm not that hungry, or that devious. Mr. De Witt came in last week while you were out of town at the clinic. He was suffering from a severe allergic reaction. I suspected it was the medication and ordered tests.''

''One of the tests you ordered had nothing to do with the medication he was prescribed.'' He saw the flicker in her eyes, watched her shrug.

''All right. I saw his hospitalization as an opportunity to test out a theory and I took it. What's wrong with that?''

''What's wrong is that I specifically told you I didn't want to try that method. There hasn't been enough information about it, in my opinion.'' Anger flared again as Joshua recalled the conversation he'd heard at lunch at the deli, oozing praise for his temporary doctor. ''You deliberately went against my wishes. I cannot condone that.''

''Can you condone a patient who seems to be recovering because of that method? You know very well that you've begun protocols with less information to go on.'' She shook her head, her face confused. ''I don't understand you, doctor. I'm not against you. I'm not trying to take your practice away. I'm not even here for the long term. I'm trying to help you, and I'm trying to help your patients. Isn't that why I'm here? Isn't a healthy patient what we both want?''

Shame rippled through him. Dermot *was* getting better. And despite the list of side effects the drug info had included, Dermot continued to thrive. Had Joshua sunk so low that he couldn't, or wouldn't, see the benefit of her work?

''I'm sorry, Nicole. I apologize. Of course you're right. The medication does seem to be helping. I guess I'm just worried it could be temporary. Dermot's been a good friend, and with his daughter away, I feel responsible for him. I know you'll keep a close eye on him.'' Joshua turned to leave, wishing he could crawl into a hole.

''Thank you,'' she murmured. ''May I say something else?''

He paused, then turned back. At least he could do her the courtesy of listening this time.

''I'm sorry I didn't try harder to consult with you, Joshua. That was a mistake.'' She sighed. ''It just seems that there are so many things going on here. It's hard to grab a moment lately.''

Joshua stared at his shoes. He'd grabbed a moment. He'd grabbed several this afternoon. While Dr. Nicole Brandt had been booked to her ears, he'd had several openings, something that hadn't happened for as long as Joshua could remember. The experience was humbling.

''The patients like you,'' he muttered, knowing he owed her that much. ''You touch them on a level I don't seem able to.''

She frowned. ''That's not what I understand. I've

heard many tales of how you've listened, cared for their kids when you should have been home with your own, gone the extra mile to ensure their grannies and grandpas are taken care of.''

Not lately he hadn't. Lately he'd measured his life out in parsimonious measures, hoping to ensure that life, or God, or chance, never again threw him a curveball he wasn't prepared to handle. The truth was, he had no business lecturing Penny or Nicole, or anyone. He was a failure, both as a doctor and as a father. Look how the girls had turned to her, asked for Nicole to do things for them even when he was home and could have done it.

''I know we have different styles,'' Nicole continued, blind to his introspection. ''I have a lot to learn about office management and I appreciate what you've taught me. I understand that besides being a life's work, you still have bills to pay and children to feed.''

''Yes, well...'' There was little Joshua wanted to add to that. Nothing should come before a patient's welfare, nothing. He lifted his head, looked her straight in the eye. ''Why didn't you come over last night? You told the girls you'd pitch for them.''

She shook her head. ''No, I said I'd stand in for you if you couldn't do it. You could. Besides, I had some stuff I wanted to read.''

''You spend a lot of time reading.''

She nodded. ''I want to be prepared when I finally start training.''

''Oh.'' He stood there watching her avoid his stare, wondering if she knew the truth and was just pretending to be busy, in order to spare his feelings.

''They wanted you, not me.'' There, he'd said it, blurted it out like a petulant schoolboy with hurt feelings. Joshua barely smothered his disgusted groan.

To his amazement, Nicole laughed. Her blond head waggled from side to side.

"Sure they wanted me. To laugh at. To make fun of." The bright curtain of hair fanned around her head as she shook it. "Uh-uh. Been there, done that, thank you very much. Embarrassing."

His ears perked up. "Embarrassing? What do you mean?"

"Do you know why your daughters want me to pitch, Joshua?" Her emerald eyes danced with amusement when he shook his head. "Neither did I until I heard Ruthie on the telephone with one of her friends. She said I throw like Billy Preston. Do you know Billy Preston?"

Joshua sucked in a breath. He knew serious, uncoordinated Billy Preston very well. Furthermore, he'd seen the boy pitch and understood exactly what Ruthie meant. Joshua tried to quell his smile, simply nodding at Nicole's chagrin, but somehow he couldn't quite mask his mirth.

"Then you know that Billy Preston pitches wildly. The ball goes all over the place. He can't throw to save his life, and your daughters always score on him. They want me to pitch so they get practice at hitting the ball. A lot of practice. No, thank you."

"I'm sorry if they offended you." He searched her face, wondering just how badly her feelings were hurt. Should he speak to his daughters again? "They're kids. They always speak their minds, but they don't mean to hurt you."

"I know." She stared at him, her green eyes solemn. "They're exactly like you."

"Like me?" Was that a good thing? He shook his head. "I don't think so." Surely the girls took after Kyla, all sweetness and innocence?

"Perfect imitations." Nicole kept staring at him.

Joshua couldn't find anything negative in her stare, so he kept probing.

"Why do you think they're like me?" he asked, curiosity nipping at him.

"You're both brutally honest. The difference is, they haven't learned to hide behind a shield yet. You have."

"A shield." He couldn't look away, nor could he end this conversation, though Joshua was certain he didn't want to hear the next part.

"A shield, a barrier between you and others. You use it all the time to stop us from getting too close to you, from seeing the cracks in your armor."

"My armor?" He laughed. "Now you're getting fanciful."

She shook her head, and her lips rose in a faint smile that told him she knew what he was doing.

"Not fanciful, just practicing some of that brutal honesty you favor."

Joshua stepped backward, all defenses going up. But Nicole didn't stop speaking.

"So here's my take on the situation. Sometimes life sucks, Joshua. Sometimes you just don't get what you want. And it isn't because God hates you, or because He's unfair, or even because you did something wrong. Sometimes stuff just happens because that's life. And all you can do is keep dog-paddling along, going with the flow, accepting what He hands you and getting on with it."

Joshua knew he risked alienating her with his next question, but he asked it anyway.

"Is that what you're doing by going into surgery?"

She stared at him for a long time, finally nodding.

"Maybe I am. My father wants me to be what my

mother never could because he didn't have the money for her to finish training and he feels guilty. Who's to say he's wrong?'' She shrugged. ''I've never been that great with people. I think I'd be good as a surgeon.''

''And maybe you can make him see you instead of your mother, is that it?'' Amazed that she couldn't see the truth herself, Joshua smiled at the beautiful woman in front of him. ''You're wrong you know—you're great with people. You have this...I don't know, ability, maybe, to figure out where they're coming from and empathize, while getting them to confide in you. That's a skill that can never really be learned. You either have compassion or you don't.''

''Then I guess I learned it here, from you. Because I sure never had it before. I've always been on the outside looking in when it comes to relationships.'' Her voice dropped. ''I've never had really close friends. I have friends, of course, but they're not the type you confide in.''

He couldn't believe they were having this conversation. She wasn't the type to open up, certainly not to him. Still, he was enjoying learning more about her.

''If you could confide, what would you tell them?''

Suddenly he had to know more about those phone calls from her father, what made the green chips in her eyes darken and cloud over when she hung up, why she stole away to sit in the park square, alone, when she could have shared lunch with a hundred different people.

''I don't know.'' Her fingers twisted together, her brow furrowed. ''Secrets, I guess.''

''Things you wouldn't dare tell another soul because they'd think you were disloyal or horrid to have said it?'' he asked, knowing exactly what she meant. ''My wife was like that. You could tell her anything. She never judged, never reprimanded you, never punished. Kyla had this way of just listening.''

"You must miss her."

He found himself surprised at his own answer. "I do. But I'm learning to cope. I think."

She smiled, but there was no warmth in it. "Are you? I wonder. I think what you're doing is closing yourself off."

Fury rose in him. "You have no right to judge—"

The door swung open with a crash, and a teenage boy ran inside. "Can you please help me? There's been an accident. My dad's caught. I can't get the others free, either."

"I'll go." In seconds Nicole had raced away for her bag, returned and was heading out the door.

"I'm coming with you." He grabbed his pager, his own black bag and his jacket. "Let's go. Jason, you lead. We'll follow."

Nicole already had the motor in her sports car purring. Joshua raised one eyebrow, then gave up proclaiming his authority and climbed inside. Almost before his door had closed, she was moving.

As Joshua fastened his seat belt, he caught her smug little smile.

"What?"

"I'm just surprised you came with me."

"Why? Doesn't your car work?" He stifled his impulse to tell her to slow down, kept his eye on the half-ton truck disappearing in front of them.

"You're about to find out." She smoothly shifted into High. "Relax, Doc. I once dated a Formula One driver. I'm very, very good."

She was good at everything. As far as Joshua was concerned, that was the problem.

* * *

"Don't ever do that again."

Nicole jerked up from her files, shocked by the fury in his voice. They'd gotten along well the past two weeks in a kind of tense cooperation. He'd corrected her on three cases, stupid mistakes that shouldn't have happened, and probably wouldn't if she hadn't been so nervous.

"I'm sorry?" She set down her pen and tried to remember what she'd done.

"I could have saved most of these people a trip out here if you'd shown me their résumés first. Not one of them has the kind of experience or commitment I want for this office."

"I see." She frowned, recalling at least three of the prospective doctors whose impeccable reputations should have suited him very well.

"Next time I'll check through them first, *before* you set up any interviews. Though why you thought I couldn't do it myself is beyond me." He turned and headed for the door.

"Dr. Darling?"

"Yes?" He twisted to glance at her.

"I won't be here for much longer." She saw something cross his face, and rushed to cover her bases. "I thought it would be easier if there was someone in place who already knows the ropes."

"Perhaps. But I want the right person. I don't want to be training twice."

She opened her mouth to say something, but her phone rang. With an apologetic look at him, she answered it.

"Oh, hi," she murmured as her father's dictatorial voice boomed over the line. "How are you?"

"Never mind me. There's a position that's opened up.

I spoke to Adams a few minutes ago. Today's Friday. If you can get here by next week, you can start immediately."

"But—but—"

He ignored her stammered response.

"You're wasting your time in that pokey town. The big boys are in the city. That's where you need to be. Okay, you did your time, you proved you can handle the ordinary stuff. Now it's time to move out of Podunk, Colorado. Unless you've changed your mind?"

The challenge in his voice was unmistakable. Nicole saw Joshua glaring at her and knew he'd heard at least part of her father's words.

"I haven't changed my mind, Daddy," she murmured. "It's just that Dr. Darling hasn't found a new partner yet. A week is hardly enough notice—"

"You're not committed, that's what it is. If you were, you'd jump at the chance. Your mother would have. She would have given anything to get the training you're being offered."

But Nicole wasn't her mother. And she rather liked Blessing. She fit in here—people accepted her. She'd even helped work on some props for the high school musical. In Blessing, folks liked coming to her for advice and help. They had faith in her. But her father would never understand that. Never.

"Are you still there?"

"Yes."

"So when will you arrive?"

She sighed. "I'll have to let you know, Daddy."

By the time she'd hung up, Joshua was standing by the door.

"There's an opening in a class next week. I'd like to take it."

"Go ahead."

"But how will you—" She let the question dangle there, knowing it was better not to ask. "I'm sorry."

"Don't be silly." For a moment the mask dropped away and a lopsided grin transformed his stern features. "You've done everything you promised, and more. You don't owe us anything, Nicole. Get on with your life!"

The halfhearted teasing tugged at her heart. He had to be concerned about the future. Was he pretending this nonchalance to make her feel better?

"Maybe I could stay…."

She watched the mask descend, hiding whatever feelings she thought she'd seen. Tension filled the silence.

"That would be counterproductive." Dr. Darling was back in control. "We'll manage just as we did before you arrived. These are my patients, Dr. Brandt. This is my home. I'll be fine. I always am." He turned on his heel and left.

Nicole bit her lip, her heart aching at the aloof mask he'd chosen. Her going would overburden him. He knew it and so did she. She'd gotten to know him so well, to understand what motivated him. He was genuinely hurt by the confusing turns his life had taken, and she would add to that by walking out on such short notice.

The résumé of the only doctor she hadn't been able to contact for an interview with Joshua Darling sat on the corner of her desk. She picked it up, studied the words once more. Dr. Lucas Lawrence was single and well traveled. He knew small towns, and he was a G.P. He would make an excellent partner, if she could only get Dr. Darling to see that.

Nicole closed the door to her office, then dialed.

"Dr. Lawrence, this is Dr. Nicole Brandt."

They chatted for over half an hour. By the time she

hung up the phone, Dr. Lawrence had promised to be in Blessing on the following Thursday, in time to run through the day with her. At least Dr. Darling would have his partner. Maybe not one who was perfect or permanent, but at least Lucas would be there to step in and fill the gap when she left.

But who would fill the hole in her heart when she said goodbye to those darling girls and their handsome disgruntled father? The ache that thought brought bothered her more than Nicole had expected.

"I'm sorry I have to rush away. But I've waited a long time for this. I can't just let it go. Do you understand?"

Joshua understood perfectly. She was giving up everything she'd built here, to run and do her father's bidding, even though he had a hunch she didn't want to go at all. Still, he'd always known she would leave. Why should he care when it happened? He stared her straight in the eye.

"I hope you'll enjoy your new position."

"I don't want her to go, Daddy. Nici is my bestest friend. We had plans." Ruthie's bottom lip quivered and she hid her face in his pant leg. Rosalyn yanked on the other leg, asking to be picked up.

"I'm sorry, Ruthie. I wish I could stay and make snow angels with you at Christmas. And I'd really like to see you in the Christmas pageant. But I have to go."

He watched her swallow hard, one hand at her throat. Once again clad in those disreputable jeans and a baggy sweater that hid her figure, she had scrunched her hair into some kind of messy topknot. The effect told him she hadn't bothered about her appearance before coming over here. In a way, he was glad. This Nicole was much more approachable than the calm, controlled woman he saw at the office every day.

And yet she was still the most beautiful woman he'd ever seen. She had an inner glow that he hadn't noticed when she'd first arrived. It softened the model-like angles of her face and lent a sheen to her jade-green eyes. Far from the untouchable princess who'd first arrived in Blessing, Nicole Brandt had managed to fit perfectly into their small town.

Now she was leaving.

"When?"

She chewed on her bottom lip, her eyes peeking up at him through her lashes, much as Ruthie did when she knew he wouldn't like the answer.

"I'll stay through the day on Thursday so you can do the clinics, but I'll have to leave immediately after."

"That will be fine." He ordered the girls upstairs, to get ready for bed. "I'm sure you'll do very well in your studies. You certainly seem dedicated."

"I wish—"

"I'm sorry, but I have to get upstairs. The girls need me." It was better not to go into wishes, Joshua decided. It was better to keep your eye on the goal and aim directly for it. That way nothing could sideswipe you.

"Yes, of course." She shoved her hands into her pants pockets. "I guess I'll see you tomorrow at church, then. Good night."

He nodded once, remained where he was. Nicole opened her mouth, as if she wanted to say something more, but then shook her head, turned and walked out the front door. It closed softly behind her.

"Is she really leaving, Daddy?" Ruthie stood behind him on the bottom step, her big blue eyes riveted on the door.

"Yes."

Fat tears plopped onto her cheeks, but she made not a

sound. Simply turned and walked slowly upstairs, her feet methodically moving up and over each step. Ruthie's constant and abundant energy seemed drained away. She brushed her teeth, pulled on her nightgown and lay in her narrow bed, her eyes on the ceiling. Indeed all three girls seemed strangely subdued.

Joshua read a story, prodded for some small talk, but finally gave up when only monosyllabic answers emerged. Finally he snapped off the lights and pulled the door almost closed. Rosie's soft whisper held him glued to the spot.

"I did what you said, Ruthie. I prayed really hard. I asked God to make Nicole stay. Why didn't it work?"

Joshua waited, his heart thudding loudly in the silence.

"I don't know, Rosie. I just don't know."

Quiet blanketed the house, but it wasn't the sweet comfortable quiet of a day finally ended. As he moved to the top of the stairs, Joshua caught the soft aching sniffles of his daughters and felt the old anger swell as he trod the risers down, then stepped into his office.

Why are You doing this, God? He strode into his study, caught a glimpse of his wife's smiling face. In one flash he had the picture in his hand, then he stuffed it into a drawer. The time for mourning was over.

You left me alone to raise those three. I have a practice to run, patients to care for and no help. You've taken everything. What is it You want from me?

Heaven's silence haunted him late into the night.

Chapter Eight

"Thank you again, Miss Winifred. I could never have managed without you." Nicole quashed the quaver in her voice. Tears were for later. "I'm sorry I have to leave like this, but I'll write and we'll keep in touch." Now there were other matters to be attended to. She waved a hand at the man by her side. "Lucas will need a place to stay. Can you help with that?"

"Of course, dear. Don't you worry. I've found a lovely little house."

Winifred wrapped her in a hug that warmed Nicole's heart. Her eyes sparkled with unshed tears.

"I'm going to miss having you here. It's been almost like having a daughter to fuss over." Her softly powdered cheek brushed Nicole's. "Do keep in touch. We all want to hear about your life."

"Thank you." Nicole slammed her trunk closed, waved, then walked to the driver's side of her car. She huddled inside her coat as dark wintry skies blocked the sun's warmth, and the cold breezes of fall whipped dried leaves across the road.

She couldn't help but follow the path of those tumbling leaves to the lonely house across the road. The girls were at school, of course. She knew that. But somehow she imagined their sad faces peering out at her, begging her not to leave. Back at the office she'd slipped a gift with a funny thank-you card attached onto Joshua's desk. She only hoped he understood the message on that little plaque. She'd wasted several minutes staring at the pictures of his precious daughters, her heart aching at the tender funny smiles on each heart-shaped face. Leaving was so hard.

"Dr. Brandt?" Lucas's soft voice drew her back to the present. He thrust out a hand. "I'll work hard to maintain the standard you've set. You don't have to worry about me slacking off or the practice suffering."

She shook his hand, a faint smile tugging at her lips. "I won't worry about that, Lucas," she promised. "I know you'll do just fine. Thanks for coming on such short notice."

There were a hundred things she wanted to say, but there was nothing more Nicole could say. It was time to leave.

Lucas held open her car door. "Goodbye, Dr. Brandt."

"Bye." She twisted to glance at Winifred, saw the faint marks of tears on her pale cheeks. "Goodbye, Miss Winifred."

"Go with God, dear."

With those words ringing in her ears, Nicole shifted into First and drove quickly down the street, glad that school was in and there were no children to watch for. All she wanted was to leave as quickly as she could, before her brain tried to talk her into staying where she wasn't wanted.

Nicole drove straight through town to the highway, barely conscious that a light rain had begun to fall. *Home.* Yes, this time she truly was leaving home. And for what? To take training she was no longer sure she wanted?

"Help me to do Your will," she whispered, then pressed her foot down on the gas pedal as Blessing disappeared behind her and the future loomed ahead.

Before she'd traveled many miles, Nicole had to lift her foot off the gas pedal until her car barely crawled along the interstate. She hadn't passed anyone in ages. Thick ribbons of misty fog now layered the countryside, hiding whatever vista lay around the next corner.

At least concentrating on the road took her mind off leaving Blessing. Was this mist getting thicker, or did it just seem so because of the craggy tree-covered cliffs that loomed over the road? Nicole knew she'd gone less than thirty miles. It would be a long trip back to Boston.

Up ahead, a flash through the milky whiteness in front of her held her attention. What was it? Another car, halted on the shoulder? But no, as she negotiated another curve, got a better look, she thought it came from the middle of the road!

Nicole crept closer, eyes aching with the intensity of peering forward. Suddenly she caught her breath, aghast at the scene of devastation in front of her. The highway, black and shiny with rain, was littered with cars and trucks crushed together in a mass of torn metal and shattered glass. She unrolled her window, caught the sound of a voice begging for help.

"Oh, Lord, help me now," she whispered, getting as close as she could before parking her car in the middle. Once her flashers were activated, Nicole grabbed her cell phone and dialed. "This is Dr. Brandt. I'm about twenty-five miles outside Blessing on the interstate. Eastbound. There's been an accident. At a rough guess, I'd say over a dozen vehicles. I'm about to check patients, but I'll need ambulances, police and maybe some firemen. It's bad.''

Once the emergency response voice had reassured her that help was on the way, Nicole buttoned up her coat, grabbed her bag and headed for the first vehicle. The first few cases were superficial cuts, bruises, contusions. She kept working her way along the road, further into the site, doing what she could, focusing on the job and nothing else.

Perhaps that's why the mangled semitruck, its metal trailer lying across two lanes of traffic, shocked her. She panned her flashlight over the carnage. Something was pinned beneath—a car. She reassured the man whose broken leg she'd just splinted, then moved closer, trying to ascertain whether someone could still be alive amidst such havoc.

Suddenly her knees wobbled, her breathing stopped.

Joshua's car. He was under there.

Lord, we need You now as never before. Show me where to look.

As if in direct response, a whisper-soft groan wavered through the dimness.

''Joshua?'' She stepped over, bent to crawl under a jagged bit of silver metal, until finally she found him, lying on the cold wet asphalt, his face bleeding, his legs pinned under part of the trailer.

''It's me, Joshua. Nicole. Can you hear me?'' She checked for vitals, biting her lip at the thready pulse. His colorless face worried her. How long had he been here? A quick survey told her it had been long enough for hypothermia to begin its deadly work.

Conscious of rescue workers now converging on the scene, Nicole yelled for help. A man appeared, listened as she explained the need to free Joshua's legs, then raced away to bring help.

"Joshua, can you hear me?"

"Cold," he mumbled, his lips barely moving.

"I know. Here. Maybe this will help." She stripped off her coat and laid it over him, glad she'd donned her polar fleece jacket before leaving town. "Can you tell me where it hurts? Joshua? Wake up."

He blinked his eyes open, stared at her, then sighed. "Hurts everywhere."

"Can you move your legs?"

"No." He seemed to waver for a minute, then swallowed. "The girls?"

"The girls are at school, remember? But we have to get you out of here." She gulped, then forced herself to ask the question. "Can you not move your legs because something's on them?" Please God, don't let the nerves be damaged. She checked his blood pressure again, frowning at the reading. "Stay with me, Joshua."

"Trying." He licked his lips. "Don't think my spine's involved, but not sure."

"Just keep thinking about your girls, Joshua. Don't forget, they need you to be there for them, to play with them, to help them with math, to give them away at their weddings."

"Long way away," he muttered, wincing as she probed his body.

"Closer than you think."

He sighed heavily, seemed to lose consciousness. Nicole brushed her hand over his battered face, cupped his cold wet cheek in her palm.

"Stay awake, please. Don't fade out on me. I need you conscious."

"Know that," he mumbled, his lips tilted down in a frown. "I'm a doctor."

"Well, right now I'm in charge and you do what I say."

"You're…bossy." He seemed to drag in a breath.

"You bet." Nicole listened to his chest again, her heart sinking.

"Ma'am, we're going to hoist up the trailer, but it isn't very stable. We'll only have a few minutes to pull him free."

"I don't want to move him until I'm certain of his injuries. Can't you get a crane—winch it off?"

"We can." The fireman nodded. "But it will take at least an hour to get it in here. I'm guessing you don't want to wait."

"No, I don't." Nicole glanced down. Joshua had faded out again. Maybe now was the best time. "All right, I'll show you how to move him. We could have spinal injuries, so we must be careful. I want him airlifted out to Denver as soon as he's free. He needs a specialist."

The fireman nodded, gave an order on his radio, then began directing the operation.

It seemed to take forever to shift the enormous metal trailer. Nicole monitored Joshua's vitals continuously, her lips tightening as his body responses continued to deteriorate. His lungs weren't quite clear. He was on the stretcher now, but it was barely the first in a long list of steps needed to get him the proper treatment. She inspected his legs, gaped at the damage, then treated them as best she could for the trip to Denver. The entire time he never quite regained consciousness.

"You are not letting go, Joshua Darling," she told him

loudly, half praying as she ordered him to wake up. "I promised those girls their daddy would be there for them, and you will be." *Please, God, he will be.* "Look at me, Joshua."

His eyelids flickered. She could tell he was fighting to stay awake. Joshua's fingers tightened around hers a moment later. She glanced at his face, caught the pleading in his dark blue eyes.

"You help the girls," he gasped. "Be there. If something happens."

"Nothing's going to happen. Now be quiet while I prep you for the flight."

But he wouldn't let go of her hand. "Aunt Win's too old. Needs help."

"I'll tell her you said that."

"Promise."

She heard the desperate pleading tone in his voice, saw the concern on his face. He would fuss and worry until he knew they were okay. But would he give up? He'd lost a lot of blood, was bleeding internally, had massive lower body injuries. Would he push his way through, or give up?

"I'll promise on one condition—you don't give up. Not ever. You do what they tell you, you get stronger and you get back home where you belong." Nicole held her stethoscope against his chest. "Breathe, Joshua."

But he wasn't breathing. His chest wasn't moving.

"You will not die on me, Joshua Darling. No way. I'm too good a doctor, and so are you." She grabbed a tube from an outstretched hand, inserted it, then began bagging him. He couldn't die. Not now. Not on her watch. She refused to consider telling the girls she'd let him go.

Up down, up down, his chest moved rhythmically until finally he was breathing again on his own.

"Don't you dare do that again, Joshua Darling. You fight for those girls, for your life together. You fight hard."

His blue eyes flickered open, staring at her.

"You keep your end of the deal, Dr. Darling, or I walk. Got it?"

He blinked his agreement.

"Good." She checked him over one last time, brushed a hank of black hair off his forehead, then smiled. "Okay, load him up. I think he's stable enough to make it."

"You're not coming?" The paramedics fastened the straps, rolled him through a cleared path to a helicopter waiting on the other side.

"I can't. I've got the rest of these people to take care of. You know what to do." She leaned down, brushed his ear with her lips. "You fight with every bit of energy you can scrounge up, Joshua. I don't care how much it hurts. And when you even begin to think about giving up, you just remember Rachel and Rosie and Ruthie. They need a father. They're worth fighting for."

She stepped back and watched him being loaded, her brain whispering a prayer as her hands busied themselves with another victim. Moments later the helicopter disappeared from sight. Automatically she went through the next steps. First of all she'd have to call Miss Winifred. Together they'd pick up the girls. Get to the hospital.

"Doc? Could you look at this man?"

"Yes. Just give me a moment. I have to make a phone call." She dialed Winifred, explained the situation and asked her to prepare the girls. "We'll drive to Denver as soon as I can get away from here."

"We'll pray while we wait." Miss Winifred hesitated a moment, then asked the question Nicole didn't want to answer. "Is he very bad?"

"Yes."

With nothing else to report, Nicole hung up, turned back to face the devastation in front of her. She treated whatever patients they led her to on the other side of the scene. But always her thoughts remained on Joshua Darling.

How could she leave him now?

"Perhaps the children should wait outside?"

Nicole saw fear make the three little girls cower and she shook her head. They'd lost one parent and were afraid they'd lose another. She had to put a stop to that.

"No. They stay here. Joshua is their father. Good or bad, they need to hear the truth. Please tell us."

The specialist shrugged, then explained his findings.

"He'll live and I'm quite certain he will walk again, but it's going to take a lot of hard work. He'll be here for at least a week, probably two. He can go home when I say, but only if the home renovations he'll need are completed. He'll also require constant monitoring and regular physiotherapy. Most of all he'll need grit and determination."

"Daddy wants to get better. I know he does." Rachel blinked away the tears. "He wants to come home and be with us."

"Of course he does, honey." The specialist smiled, squatted down to their level. "But your daddy's going to be in a lot of pain for a while, so he won't be able to hold you—not at first. Later, when he comes home, you can help him get better by doing exactly what Dr. Brandt tells you to do."

The girls nodded. Ruthie threaded her fingers through Nicole's. "And Auntie Win," she added solemnly.

Winifred smiled and nodded. "Good girl."

"Can we see him?" Nicole knew she needed to see for herself, every bit as badly as the girls, that Joshua Darling was going to recover.

Dr. Long frowned. "He won't be awake. The surgery was long and intense." He glanced at the girls, then lowered his voice. "His lung collapsed again. Won't the machines scare them?"

Nicole smiled. "They don't scare easily. They just want to make sure their daddy is alive. I told them he'll be asleep for a long time so his body can get better. They understand."

He nodded. "You seem very close to this family—like a part of it."

"I wish I was."

Only after he'd left and they stood around Joshua's bed, watching his chest rise and fall under the white sheet, did Nicole realize what she'd said. She played with it, tested the sound of it. She wanted to be part of the Darling family? Yes, the idea was very appealing. To be there for the girls, to tuck them in every night, to watch Joshua mend and grow strong, to push him when he was ready to give up, to encourage him and help him and watch him return to life—yes.

She cared about him.

Nicole stared at his battered face as the reality of her feelings washed over her in a wave of blinding truth.

Despite his cranky remarks, his niggling complaints, his lack of compliments and cool reserve, she'd become personally involved in the Darlings' lives. Worse, she'd fallen in love with Joshua Darling.

When had it become so important that he find new

meaning for his life, that he act like the loving father she knew he was? When did it start to matter whether he praised her work or not? When had she let down her guard enough to fall for a man who only wanted her out of the way?

"Nicole?" Miss Winifred touched her arm. "I'm going to take the girls to get something to eat."

She nodded. "All right."

"Are you coming?"

"No. I think I'll stay here. I'm not hungry, but I'm a little tired. I just need a few minutes to regroup."

"Of course you do." Winifred brushed a hand over her hair. "You've had a grueling time. Relax. Sleep if you can. We'll be back in a while."

They were almost out the door when Ruthie returned and patted her hand.

"Thank you for helping my daddy," she whispered.

"Oh, Ruthie." Nicole threw caution to the wind and gathered the little girl into her arms. "You're welcome, honey." She smothered her tears against the bright red wool of Ruthie's jacket. "You're very welcome."

"Only—what will happen now?" Ruthie's smooth forehead pleated in a frown of concentration. "Daddy can't look after the sick people. He's sick, too. You're going away. Who's going to help them?"

Nicole started to explain about Lucas, then stopped. Lucas was one man, and new besides. He couldn't possibly handle all that needed to be done. The decision was simple.

"Who's going to take care of us?"

"We are." Nicole brushed her hand over the golden head, then motioned to the other two girls to join her. "Your daddy is very sick. He's going to get better, but it will take a long time. I'm going to work in his office

while his legs heal. Your aunt Winifred and I will make
sure you three are well taken care of. I don't want you
to worry about that. Do you know what I do want you
all to do?''

They shook their heads.

''I want you to pray. Really hard. Daddy's going to
need his girls to help him get better. Can you do it?''

''Of course.'' Rachel didn't bother to look at the other
two. ''We're big girls.''

''Yes, you are.'' Nicole smiled at them, amazed by
their quiet acceptance of her orders. ''Now off you go
and have some dinner. I'll be right here with your
daddy.''

They grinned, then Rachel and Rosie walked to the
door. Rosie slipped her hand into Winifred's. But Ruthie
lingered beside Nicole's knee.

''You won't go to your school now?'' she whispered,
blue eyes huge. ''You won't leave us?''

''Not until your daddy tells me it's time to go.''

Ruthie threw her arms around Nicole's neck and
hugged for all she was worth.

''I love you, Nici,'' she whispered.

''I love you, too,'' she told the little girl. And meant
it.

But once they'd gone, she faced the reality of her
promise. Keeping this one meant breaking another. But
what else could she do? Reluctantly Nicole walked to the
ICU ward's central desk, picked up the phone and dialed.

''Hi, Daddy. It's Nicole.''

''Are you in town?'' Did those blustering tones hold
just a hint of joy?

''No. No, I'm not. I'm afraid I can't come.''

''What?''

Before he could berate her, Nicole explained the accident.

"That's not your problem. You've got a spot, girl, a chance to have your dream. Are you willing to blow it again?"

"He's got three little girls to support. He'll need months of treatment. What will happen to his practice in the meantime? It's not something that will just sit and wait for him to come back to. Somebody's got to keep it going."

"Why you? What about the other guy you found?"

"Lucas? He'll be a help, but he's brand-new. Today was his first day! Besides, there's no way he can handle the office and the clinics." She tried to make him appreciate the desperateness of the situation. "Please understand. I can't just walk away, Daddy. This town has become like a family to me. They treated me very well, welcomed me into their homes and their lives. I can't run away now, when they need my help."

"What do you want from me?"

"I don't know." She swallowed. "I was hoping you'd…come down, help us out, maybe?"

"Are you insane?" His voice chipped away like a hammer on cement. "I have no intention of helping you throw away your life. How long do you suppose it will be until you'll finally be free of the place, free to resume your training?"

"I don't know," she whispered, tears welling at the anger in his voice.

"I'll tell you when. Never. You'll get yourself so enmeshed in this hokey little town that you'll start to think it's your duty to stay there, buried in the back of nowhere."

She heard something snap in the background and knew he was furious.

"I've paid every one of your bills, Nicole. Doctor usually leave school owing thousands of dollars, bu you'll walk away free and clear because this was some thing you told me you had to do. But I'm warning you if you allow this opportunity to slip away, I'm finished covering the expense. You'll have to find a way to pay for your own mistakes. Do you hear me?"

"I hear you." Nicole stared through the ICU's glass wall into Josh's room, tears welling as she gazed at the silent man lying in the hospital bed. "I'm sorry you can't understand, Daddy. I'm sorry you can't see that I have to do this."

"What I see is a waste of a whole lot of money. You're throwing away a chance for a career that will propel you to the top, offer you more money than you can imagine. A qualified surgeon can write his own ticket in Boston. Once you're finished training, that's the time to do your charity work. You'll have enough money to waste then."

Nicole sighed, and her shoulders slumped.

"But surgery was never about the money, Dad," she whispered, allowing the tears to fall. "At least for me." Her throat blocked up, refusing to allow out the words that would tell him the reason she'd pursued the training in the first place, the only reason.

"Money is the bottom line for everyone. Try and see how far you'll get without me bankrolling you."

"Bye, Daddy."

Nicole cradled the phone, then realized that she hadn't left her father the number of the hospital so he could call her back after he'd cooled off.

Despair surged inside. She was all alone now. She'd

taken on the entire running of Joshua's office, of the care for his children, of the satellite clinics he operated. And it was probably the last thing he wanted.

"Help me now, Lord," she whispered. "They're counting on me. And I can't fail."

Back in Joshua's room, she sat silent, head bowed, while the monitors whooshed and beeped their life-giving rhythm. Miss Winifred had once spoken of God's genuine concern for His children. She'd said He never left them alone to handle things, but walked right beside them, supporting and strengthening.

Nicole was going to need that support. Joshua's future depended on it. She pulled a small pad and a pen from her bag and began planning while her heart mourned this latest chance lost to prove to her father that she was worthy of his love.

Chapter Nine

"November first. This is a red-letter day." Nicole paid the parking fee, then drove out of the hospital parking lot. "You finally get to go home. The girls are very excited."

Joshua grunted, easing himself into a more comfortable position. At least she hadn't tried to squeeze him into that tin can she drove. The back seat of the van she'd brought had a lot of room to support his legs, and he could recline at will. And it wasn't an ambulance. He should be grateful.

"What's happening at the office?" Joshua asked as soon as they were cruising down the highway.

"Everything's fine. Lucas has been a wonderful addition. He's the most willing person I've ever met. Just pitches in without a word. He's been great." She tossed him a smile, then concentrated on passing several Sunday drivers. "I didn't mean to make you wait, but we just couldn't get things done in time."

"What things?" he demanded suspiciously, his tension clicking up a notch at the way she studiously avoided looking at him. "Who's we?"

"I've ordered a few modifications at your house," she murmured.

"What?" He started to jerk forward, caught his breath at the pinch of pain reminding him that his ribs were still healing, and drew a deep breath of calm. "You'd better explain, Dr. Brandt."

"Oh, get off your high horse. It's Nicole." She glared at him, her fingers tightening on the wheel. "You heard the specialist as well as I did. It was either modify or leave you in the hospital. I thought you'd want to get home."

Joshua sighed, called himself an idiot. What was it about her that immediately raised his hackles? She was a good doctor—he'd seen that firsthand. In a little over a month she'd become closer than any friend he'd ever had, ferrying his kids back and forth to visit him, pitching in with Aunt Win to keep things on an even keel at home, managing his practice. Nicole Brandt had obviously canceled her plans to leave, though she'd never said a word. Neither had he. He didn't want to question his good fortune.

So why did he deliberately bait her?

Patience, Lord. Teach me patience. And hurry.

"I'm sorry. I know you've gone above and beyond and I appreciate it. I guess I'm just…nervous." It cost him to say that, to admit his weakness to her.

"Understandable. Your body is healing. You need to concentrate on that and leave the rest of it to us."

Joshua frowned, checked his watch for the date, then sagged against his seat.

"I missed Rosie's birthday," he muttered, depressed

by the swift passage of days and weeks he could barely recall and then only through pain-hazed memories.

"She loves the dollhouse you gave her." Nicole grinned. "She's got her little family all carefully arranged and each night she tucks them all in. She's a real mommy, that girl."

"I gave her a dollhouse?" He caught the glint of fun in her eyes and nodded. "Thank you for doing that. I'll pay you back." He checked his pockets, grimaced and sighed. "As soon as I find my wallet, that is."

"Oh, you're going to pay me back, all right, Dr. Darling," she cooed. Her blond head nodded once. "Big time."

"It was pretty expensive?" He wondered why she'd bought the thing if it was so much. Lord knew what his finances were like, but being laid up like this certainly couldn't be helping his bank account.

"More expensive than you know." She giggled at his frown. "You know, I think I'd make a top-notch surgeon, but building things is not my forte."

"It came unassembled," he guessed. "Kyla used to do that to me on Christmas Eve. We'd get the kids tucked up in bed, then she'd bring out some monstrosity that needed putting together before Santa left. I never got any sleep." Funny, it didn't hurt to remember that. Joshua half smiled at the thought.

"Nice memories, Doc." She was silent for a while, steering carefully down the highway.

"Yes, they are," he agreed, and let himself drift back in time. He was startled from his thinking when her soft voice broke the silence.

"Just for future reference, I'm going to tell you a secret, Dr. Darling. And you'd better not let on that I told you."

"Oh?" He felt a frisson of worry twitch at him and leaned forward. "What is it?"

"Dr. Lucas Lawrence is the worst carpenter I've ever known. He tried to help me one night. It was not a success. I put four stitches in his thumb and he has a bad bruise from a misguided hammer."

Joshua couldn't help it—the chuckle tumbled out. He'd never met the man, but suddenly he felt a kinship for him.

"That must have been embarrassing."

"Which is why we will never speak of it again. Just keep him away from your power tools." She slanted him a look, then resumed her stare out the windshield.

"I've been warned."

"Good. Now maybe you'd better rest a bit. The girls are going to wear you out with questions, I guarantee it."

"I don't mind. At least I'll be home." *Home.* The word had such a wealth of meaning in it, he realized. Familiarity. Comfort. A place to regroup. He closed his eyes, conjured up a picture of it and promptly fell asleep, to dream of his daughters waiting for him on the doorstep, cuddling that odious dog. Why did he also see Nicole standing behind them, a welcoming smile on her lips?

"Joshua?"

"Huh?" He jerked awake, glanced around and shifted upright. "We're here already?"

"You slept quite a while. Are you feeling okay?" She took the familiar road into town.

He gave himself a mental once-over, then nodded. "I'm fine. You never did explain about the alterations."

"No, I didn't." She offered nothing more, simply kept driving.

They were on his street now. Everything looked so strange. The gorgeous autumn colors were gone, and skiffs of snow covered the lawns and gardens his neighbors were so proud of. Even the trees that lined the avenue were bare gray sticks against a dull metal sky.

"Why are there so many cars here? What's going on?" He tried to peer out the windows, recognized vehicles. "That's Gordon McIvor's truck."

"Uh-huh."

"Pete Grant owns that van. He uses it for deliveries."

She didn't answer. A moment later they were steering up his drive, which was now filled with people.

"What on earth are they all doing here?" he demanded. "Waiting to catch a glimpse of the cripple?"

She slammed the gearshift home, swiveled in her seat and fixed him with a glare.

"Your *friends*," she enunciated loudly, "are here to welcome you home. They want to lend a hand any way they can. They've been here all along, pitching in whenever and wherever they were needed. You owe them a lot."

Having said her piece, Nicole climbed out, slammed the door shut and left him there. Shame suffused him. She was right. He was a jerk of the worst kind, ungrateful, lugging around a chip the size of a mountain and just waiting for someone to try to knock it off.

Joshua had a hunch Nicole Brandt wouldn't give a second thought to tackling that particular job. He sighed. His emotions were all over the place these days. The effects of pain, pills and trying to adjust to life without the complete use of his legs. But he was alive. That counted.

"Joshua?" The side door slid open. Aunt Win peered inside, found him and grinned. "Thank goodness you're home. We'll have you out of here in a jiffy, dear. Just be patient.''

Ah, patience. Hadn't he prayed for that a thousand times over since the accident?

"Hey, Doc. How're you doing?'' Herbert Johnson grinned, his freckles faded now that summer was past. "Pete and me are gonna lift you out of this thing. Dr. Nici's got a wheelchair ready to roll you right into the house.''

"Dr. Nici. Oh.'' Joshua stared at his temporary partner, noticing the familiarity between her and the group. Then he bit his lip and endured the shifting necessary to get him out of the van. Seated in the wheelchair, he heaved a sigh of relief. "Thanks, guys.''

"Didn't hurt you too much, did we?'' Pete asked, his eyes brimming with compassion. "It's just that you've got so many sore places, it's hard to know where to lift.''

Pete was a big, red-faced plumber with the softest heart in the world. He never spoke two words he didn't have to, especially not with anyone else around. And there were hordes of people—on the lawn, on the driveway, right up the walk and into the house. Joshua reached out, grabbed his hand and pumped it.

"Didn't hurt at all, Pete. And you're right. I have a lot of sore spots. Figured if I was gonna get any time at all off, I'd better make it worthwhile.''

Pete's face mirrored his shock at the joke from the doctor he obviously remembered as serious and dull. They both heard Nicole's giggle in the background. A second later Pete's face wrinkled with his trademark ear-splitting grin.

"Took it a little far this time, didn't you, Doc?'' he teased.

"Overdoing. Bad habit of mine." Joshua smiled. "Thanks a lot, Pete."

Pete blushed again.

"Okay, inside. It's too cold out here to be lollygagging." Dermot De Witt grabbed the handles of the wheelchair and began steering it up the brand-new ramp someone had installed on top of the steps.

Joshua saw concern on so many faces as they caught sight of his blanketed legs. They were there, crowded around in the cold, to welcome *him* home. These were his patients, people he'd treated for years. But they were also his friends, and it was clear they were worried by the gashes, bruises and bandages they saw covering him. He had to do something.

"Just a minute, Dermot." Joshua twisted, looking around at the crowd. "I want to thank you, all of you, for being so kind to my family. I'll never be able to tell you how much it means to me to know that the girls were in such good hands."

"Aw, Doc." Dermot's hand rested on his shoulder. "We didn't do anything special, nothing any friend wouldn't have done for another. Now quit blithering and get inside, before Dr. Nici sends you back to Denver."

Joshua blinked, then grinned at his patient.

"Sorry, folks, but you heard Dermot. I was wrong with his treatment, you see, and now he can hardly wait to get his revenge." Strangely enough, it didn't hurt to say that. He'd made a mistake with Dermot, but clearly the man didn't hold a grudge.

They all laughed at his joke, Dermot made a threatening gesture and the tension was broken. Joshua caught a look of pure pride on Nicole's face and felt a rush of warmth suffuse him from the inside. Apparently she approved. At least he'd done one thing right.

"I have to rest now," he called. "But come for a visit. I'll check you out while we talk." Laughter followed him into the house as Dermot rolled him inside, set the brake and then made his farewells, brushing off Joshua's thanks.

"You just get back to normal, Doc. That's all the thanks I need." After leaving behind foil-wrapped candies for each of the girls, Dermot was gone.

"I'm afraid I have to put a nix on the work thing, Dr. Darling. No work. Not a finger lifted." Nicole glared down at him with that no-nonsense look she favored.

"Now just a—"

"Daddy!" Three bodies hurtled down the stairs, then jerked to an abrupt halt beside his chair.

"Hi, Daddy." Only Rachel dared to lean against his arm, her cheek brushing his sleeve with a featherlight caress.

"Hi, sweetie. How are you?" He brushed his hand over the silky curls and sighed. Now he was home.

"I'm sad." Her big blue eyes swam with unshed tears. "Do you hurt very bad, Daddy?"

"Not so bad I couldn't use a hug. Just be careful not to bump my legs. They're not quite all better yet." Each of them hugged him long and hard, as if they'd been very afraid they might never get the chance again.

It was Rosie who clung the longest.

"Boy, that's a good hug." When she didn't release him, Joshua lowered his voice to a soothing murmur. "It's okay, sweetie." He eased her tight hold just a fraction. "I'm here, don't worry."

A shaky sigh whispered from her lips. "Are you going away again, Daddy?"

"No, sweetheart. I'm home. It will take me a while to get better, to start walking again." He glanced up at Nicole. "And when I get better, I'll go back to work. But that won't be for a while."

She hesitated, as if she didn't quite believe him. Her eyes went straight to Ruthie, who shifted from one foot to the other.

"What's wrong, Ruthie?"

Her eyes darkened to a serious navy. She stood on her very tiptoes so her lips grazed his ear.

"I love Nici and Auntie Win lots and lots, Daddy. And they took good care of us while you were away."

"I'm glad to hear that." He let one finger brush the tear off her golden lashes. Ruthie gulped, then spoke again.

"But don't go away again, okay, Daddy? Not ever. I get too scared."

Joshua stared, unable to understand what she wasn't saying.

"You get scared?" He glanced at the others. "You, too?" They nodded solemnly. "But why? You know I'd never leave you."

Ruthie's fingers threaded through his. Her voice was filled with unspoken fears that had obviously plagued her since his accident.

"I think it's like you felt the day Nici came—remember I hurted my arm that day?"

He nodded.

"You were really scared and you were yelling. That's how scared I get when you go away, Daddy."

The words resonated inside him, their full impact blasting into his stomach like a fist. They were worried about *him*. Joshua rushed to reassure them.

"You don't have to be scared anymore, honey. None of you. I'm right here and I'm fine. I'm not going away."

Ruthie didn't look satisfied by the mere words he'd spoken. He frowned.

"Don't you believe me?"

Rachel, at least, slowly nodded. Ruthie wasn't so easily pacified.

"Mommy did," she blurted out. "She said good-night and then she was gone and I didn't see her no more."

Joshua closed his eyes, his heart breaking as he realized the pain his daughters' tender hearts had endured simply because he'd failed to explain properly. But what could he say? How could he tell them the same thing wouldn't happen to him one day, when, though he'd buried it deep, he carried the exact same fear?

Nicole's hand on his shoulder alerted him to her presence. Just for a moment he'd let her take over, shoulder this burden, too. Just until he found the right words.

"Sweetheart, your mommy didn't leave you because she wanted to. You know that, right?" Nicole's soft voice urged the little girl to think about it.

Ruthie frowned, thought for a moment, then nodded.

"She got sick and nobody could make her better unless she went to heaven."

"To be with God," Rosie chimed in.

"That's right, darling." Nicole gathered the little girl against her crouching form. "Your mommy didn't want to leave. She wanted to be right here with you, just as your daddy wants to be here." She glanced up at him, a question in her eyes, as if she wondered about overstepping some imaginary boundary.

Joshua nodded his permission. Let her say it. He couldn't find the words right now.

"Daddy had a bad accident. He didn't want to stay away, but the doctors had to fix his legs and he couldn't come home until they did."

Ruthie looked at Rachel, who nudged her in the side. Rosie stared at them both. Finally, after a whispered conversation with her sister, Ruthie turned to stare at both Nicole and Joshua.

"But what if God wants our daddy in heaven, too?" Her voice hiccuped in a sob. "What will happen to us then?"

Nicole stared at Joshua, her green eyes dark and lustrous, imploring him to reassure his daughters. The herculean effort of facing his own fear paled in comparison to the stark dread he saw in their eyes.

"Ruthie, Rachel, I want you to listen to me. You, too, Rosie." He took a deep breath and told them the same thing he'd told himself a thousand times before. Only this time he desperately wanted it to be true.

"I think God wants me right here with my girls," he murmured, studying their dear little faces. "He wants you three to grow up, and He wants me to be right here to help you if you need it. That's why He helped me get better."

"Are you sure?" Ruthie blinked. Her fear wasn't completely appeased, but she appeared to be willing to reconsider.

Joshua stared at her, only then realizing that the doubts had been building in those little minds for some time. The accident hadn't caused their instability. The origins stemmed from those times after Kyla's death when he'd buried himself in work and left their uncertainties and questions to someone else. Was the accident God's way of forcing him to understand his daughters' needs?

"I'm sure," he whispered.

"Ruthie, your daddy's going to be right here while he gets better. You can check on him every day when you get home from school. But right now I think he needs to rest.'' Nicole smiled, and her hand brushed over the fair head.

As he watched his daughters, Joshua saw their faces light up with excitement.

''We've got a surprise for you, Daddy.''

''A surprise?'' He frowned, then chided himself for doing it. Why was he always waiting for the ax to fall? Why couldn't he anticipate good things, instead of bad? He was here, wasn't he—alive, to walk again, God willing. That was a good thing.

His gaze roamed the room, then halted as he took a fresh look at the hardwood flooring, only then realizing the tired old carpet had been removed.

''What on earth—''

''That's one of them.'' The girls giggled, their eyes flashing with excitement as they danced from one foot to the other.

Nicole grinned at them, then explained.

''Some of your friends came in and did that for you after they found out you would be able to use a wheelchair. They felt you'd be more mobile if you could get around easier.''

''My friends did this?'' He stared at the gleaming wood and swallowed. Someone had come in and resurfaced the main floor of his home, just so he could move around more easily?

''Yes.'' Aunt Win motioned Nicole to steer his chair into the guest bedroom directly off his study. ''They've been pretty busy while you've been away.''

Joshua blinked at the transformation someone had created in the tired old pink spare room. Here, too, the floors were hardwood. Someone had painted the walls a soft creamy taupe that was picked up and embossed in the textured duvet lying on the bed. Slubbed-silk pillows in cream and brown lay tossed in front of the headboard, offering comfort and relaxation. A reading lamp waited beside the bed and beside it, a vase of soft white roses.

Nicole drew open satin striped drapes. Joshua stared at the set of garden doors that opened up the south wall of the room to a small paving-stone deck and the backyard. The sun peeked through the clouds and flowed into the room, warming it.

"They wanted you to be able to see the girls playing and still be able to relax." Nicole's voice whispered in his ear. "They just wanted to help."

He stared at her, stunned by the extent of the work.

"I don't know what to say. I never expected anything—"

"They know that." Nicole smiled. "They did it because they care about you. Nobody could have stopped them once they made their plans. I don't think the town's seen such excitement in years. Everybody pitched in."

Rosie snuggled up on his left side, her hand patting his knee.

"Do you like your new room, Daddy?" she asked, her eyes huge.

"You can't ask that yet, Roz," Ruthie chided. "He hasn't see the bathroom."

"The bathroom?" Joshua swallowed. The alterations that had been made to his home hadn't come cheaply. He and Kyla had once spoken of new flooring, but he'd said they had to wait—until his practice was doing better.

He winced, trying to mentally prepare himself as Nicole rolled his chair to the bathroom door.

"They made the opening larger, so your chair will go through. Everything has been fitted to fill the needs of someone who's physically handicapped. Pete said it was a good investment. When you sell, a couple could make this a mother-in-law suite.'' Aunt Win began enumerating the assets the local plumber had insisted the bathroom required.

''They knew you'd want to feel independent.'' Nicole's eyes darkened with worry as she stared down at him. ''They weren't meddling, Joshua. They just wanted to help.''

''But it's too much!'' He could only guess at the cost of that special shower. His mouth dropped when he saw the whirlpool tub. ''Way too much.''

''It's just some small things we could do, Doc. You've been taking care of us for a long time. Finally we got a chance to reciprocate without you telling us no. We couldn't resist.'' Pete stood in the bedroom doorway, his cap crushed in one hand as he shuffled his feet. ''I hope you don't mind.''

''Mind?'' Humbled by the gentle man's generosity, Joshua could only shake his head. ''How could I mind, Pete?'' he asked, stunned by this gift so freely given. ''But you've done so much, gone to so much expense.''

''Everybody chipped in, did what they could. We've all been on the other end, Doc. We know what you've done for us and our kids. Why, you drove out to my mother's place every day last fall when she hurt her leg.'' Pete leaned against a wall. ''That was way beyond what you get paid for. We don't want you taking off for some big city, Doc. You belong in Blessing.'' He glanced at Nicole. ''Just wish we could convince your partner of that.''

''She's not—'' Joshua swallowed his own words.

This wasn't the time. And anyway, it wasn't true. Nicole Brandt *was* his partner. In fact, she'd done more than any partner would have to keep his business running, his home functioning and his girls worry free.

Though he felt dreadfully uncomfortable being so needy, having someone else minister to him, Joshua refused to show it. They'd gone out of their way to help. So had Nicole. The least he could do was offer his gratitude. He glanced at the little grouping around him, heart thudding.

"Thank you, Pete. Aunt Win, and girls. And Dr. Brandt. I don't know what else to say."

"Seeing you get healthy is all the thanks we need, Doc. You take care, now."

Before Joshua could say another word, Pete disappeared. Aunt Win allowed the girls to kiss him, then they, too, were shepherded out. Only a tall, lean man waited by the door.

"Joshua, I wanted you to meet Dr. Lucas Lawrence. He's been a great help these past few weeks. I thought you'd like to speak face-to-face." Nicole motioned the man forward.

Joshua studied him as thoroughly as the pain and tiredness swamping his body allowed. After a moment he thrust out a hand.

"Thank you," he said quietly.

Lucas shook his hand, but only for a second.

"Forget it. I'm glad I could be here." He let go, his shrewd eyes completing an intense assessment. He frowned.

"You're in pain, aren't you?"

"Some." Joshua flushed under the discerning stare. "Okay, I hurt like the dickens."

"I told you he was stubborn, Luc. I should have paid more attention." Nicole removed a syringe from the bag she carried and filled it with something from a small vial.

"I don't need a shot—" Joshua saved his breath. Dr. Lawrence already had his sleeve rolled up, his arm swabbed.

"We're in charge now, Joshua. You do what we say." She emptied the contents into his vein, discarded the needle and unrolled his sleeve before smiling at him smugly.

"How long have you waited to say that?" he demanded crankily.

"Long enough that it gives me great satisfaction," she snapped back, green eyes sparkling as she took his pulse without missing a beat. "Okay, Luc."

"Hang on just a bit longer now." Lucas half lifted him out of the chair and set him on the bed, then eased his damaged legs under the blankets.

"Now close your eyes and relax," Nicole ordered. "Your body wants to sleep, so let it. Luc and I will take care of everything else."

"She's very bossy," Joshua told Luc. "You have to—" He had to stop and yawn.

Lucas Lawrence had the nerve to laugh at him. "Go to sleep, Doc. You're in good hands. Your partner knows how to manage guys like us with one hand tied behind her back."

Joshua nodded, tried to open his eyes, managed just a quick peek at Nicole's face as it loomed above his. She was very beautiful, even when she was bossy.

"I wanted to tell you something," he mumbled, trying to remember what that was.

"Probably more directions," he heard Nicole mutter. "You wait, Luc. I'll bet he's up at the crack of dawn tomorrow morning, trying to get to the office. We'll probably have to drug him to keep him in bed." Her fingers grazed his forehead.

Using every morsel of fuzzy concentration, Joshua raised his hand and covered hers.

"Good job, Doctor," he mumbled, squeezing her fingers.

Her hand froze, blazing a warm spot where it lay against his skin.

"Now I know he's sick," she whispered. "It's the first real compliment he's ever paid me."

Joshua tried to argue, to remind her that he'd told her many times how much he appreciated her help. But his tongue wouldn't work and he just couldn't summon the strength. So he leaned against the soft support of the pillows and let his body float away into pain-free oblivion as he dreamed of Nicole's glittery green eyes daring him to try something new.

Chapter Ten

"That's most of them." Nicole flipped the last file closed and tucked it into her briefcase. "I'm sorry it took so long, but I wanted to keep you apprised. Are you dead?" She flinched. "I mean—"

"I know what you mean. Not dead yet. But thanks for asking. I don't wear down quite as easily as I did a few weeks ago." Joshua kept his eyes closed. "Though I still say it's taking too long to get as mobile as I should be."

Nicole was certain that in spite of his words, he was mentally reviewing the cases she'd just discussed with him. Looking for something she'd missed, of course. Well, let him look. She knew her job. Her head jerked up at his next words.

"Sounds like you've got things under control. You might want to get another panel done on Mrs. Eldridge. Her blood pressure skews things sometimes."

"Already ordered." She let a flicker of satisfaction wiggle inside. It wasn't easy, she was run off her feet, but she *was* managing. "The Parker baby has the chicken pox."

"She'll get over it. She's as healthy as any kid I've ever seen." He shrugged, clearly uninterested in chicken pox.

"Did you do your exercises today?" she asked, eyeing the apparatus that stood next to the bed.

"This morning." His glare dared her to question that. "Are the billings done for this month?"

"Yes." She glared right back. "The specialist said you're to do them three times per day. Your upper-body mobility is as important as your lower." She waited, and when he didn't reach for the machine, she moved to shift it so it hung suspended over his bed. "Now would be a good time to make up one session."

"You are not the boss here. I am not your patient."

A wide grin of delight spread across her face, a trill of satisfaction rushing through her.

"Yes, Dr. Darling. Right now I'm afraid you are."

He tried to outglare her, but when Nicole wouldn't look away, he grabbed the bar and began the slow, painful process of levering himself upright.

"Satisfied?" he grunted, his knuckles white with effort.

She ignored that. Beads of moisture formed on his forehead after just a few minutes. Nicole watched carefully, ensuring he didn't overdo.

"Still pretty painful?"

"Not as bad," he admitted, pulling upright for the fifth time. "The spinal swelling's gone down."

"That's enough." She waited until he relaxed a bit, then eased the grip out of his hands. "You don't have to overdo. Just keep at it regularly. Slow and steady."

"I've been in this condition long enough to realize those words are far easier to say than to actually put into practice. It's a phrase I intend never to use with any of my patients again.'' His eyes warned her to take care.

''Good. Then we've all gained something from this.'' She took his pulse again, then glanced into his eyes. ''You do realize how fortunate you are, don't you?''

''Fortunate?'' He huffed out a laugh. ''I don't feel very fortunate.''

''You should. You've got a window of opportunity here, Doc. A little space carved out when you can't do anything but lie there and heal, and consider that God has given you some precious time to spend with those girls.''

His gaze held hers.

''I wanted to talk to you about that. I've begun to realize how concerned they were about losing me. Ruthie said you told them I'd never go away.''

''Isn't it the truth?''

''Yes. But I don't know that I'd hammered it out in my mind so clearly before this, and made sure they knew it. I appreciate what you've done.''

She said nothing, content to let him explain. But then his face altered, and he changed somehow. One hand waved across his legs.

''Every day that Svengali physiotherapist arrives to torture me, I think of how cavalier I've always been about good health. I feel like I've had a wake-up call.''

''You're doing very well. I don't think anyone expected the progress you've managed to make in these few short weeks.'' She frowned. ''Are you pushing yourself so hard because you think I'm doing something wrong?'' Nicole found herself holding her breath, waiting for his answer. Suddenly his opinion mattered very much.

''I'm hardly in any position to criticize you.'' He

shrugged. "You could do anything you wanted and I wouldn't know unless you told me."

It was not the ringing endorsement she wanted to hear. A stab to the heart couldn't have hurt more. Nicole blinked, hard.

"I'm sorry if you think I haven't been doing things properly. I had to make some changes, but I only did what I thought would profit you. If I'd been trying to steal from you, I wouldn't have brought the case files for your consultation." She grabbed her bag and headed toward the door, wondering if she'd ever get it right.

"But I didn't mean—I was just—Dr. Brandt. Nicole!"

She stopped in the doorway, but refused to turn around. "Yes?"

"I need you to look at me."

To watch her squirm. She sucked in a deep breath, schooled her features into a mask of blandness and swiveled on her heel.

"Yes, Dr. Darling?"

"It's not much, I realize. But would you accept my apology?"

Apology? From him? She frowned.

"I wasn't casting aspersions on your skills, believe me. I know exactly what you've given up to stay here and help out. I've seen you with the patients, remember? I know that they like and trust you." He looked directly at her, not over her head, or at the thin gold chain around her neck, but right into her eyes.

"I've also read the financial reports my accountant sent over. I don't know all the changes you've made, but whatever you're doing, it's succeeding. Thank you very much. For everything."

"I didn't do that much. The girls at the office helped out. And of course, your friends and neighbors. I just kind of organized them. I only wanted to make sure everything was still running smoothly when you come back." She shrugged. "It wasn't much."

"It was a great deal. And I appreciate it." He hesitated a minute, then frowned. "And the training? Is there another spot coming up that you can enroll in?"

She avoided his stare.

"Truth to tell, I don't know. I've been too busy to check. Anyway, you won't be back to work for several weeks. I'm not going anywhere. At least not till after Christmas."

Nicole crossed her fingers. He had to let her stay that long. He had to. She was going to need every dime of meager savings she could stash. Besides, she'd dreamed of spending Christmas with the girls, of watching their faces when they took part in the Sunday-school play, went caroling, opened their gifts. She wanted to make it special, a Christmas they wouldn't forget, no matter if they never saw her again.

"I don't think it will be necessary to remain that long." Dr. Darling frowned. "That's too long to ask of anyone. I'm sure I can get back in harness before that."

"I'm staying."

He sighed, then nodded, a funny look—was it relief?—crossing his face.

"Very well, then. Stay until after Christmas. Thank you. I appreciate your willingness to put your life on hold. But the minute I'm back, you're to get on with it. I don't want to be responsible for killing a dream."

Killing a dream. Yes, but was it hers or her father's?

"I make my own decisions, Joshua. I'll decide when it's time for me to leave Blessing." And it would be the hardest decision she'd ever made. "You concentrate on taking those first steps to freedom. Your work will still be there when you're ready to come back."

She reached out to grasp the water glass, intending to hand it to him, but he ignored her and forced himself to stretch far enough to get it himself. It was symbolic of his attitude toward her, of the many times over the past few days when he'd brushed away her help and insisted on doing things for himself. Joshua Darling would not be beholden to anyone.

But as she studied him, Nicole knew he was still hiding, still trying to get by without becoming fully involved. He'd opened up, but not nearly enough.

"You know, there's no reason for you to spend so much time in this bed. I know the room is lovely and the girls have done a wonderful job making their snow sculptures for you to see in the backyard. But they'd far prefer to have you join them at the table for dinner, listen to their chatter."

His face reddened and he opened his mouth to speak, but Nicole cut him off.

"After all, you're supposed to be getting back to normal. If you want the girls to stop being afraid, it might be an idea to stop acting like an invalid. This is your second chance. Take it, grab it. Do all the things with them that you never had time for before." She saw one black eyebrow tilt, and backtracked. "Okay, not all the things. But if you could be part of their everyday world, if they could see you dressed and waiting for them after school, it would go a long way toward easing their fears about the future."

Having had her say, Nicole retraced her steps to the door.

"I better go."

"I'll see you after dinner," he called. "You promised the girls a game of Chutes and Ladders."

"Don't think I'll be able to make it," she told him, her step never wavering. "I guess you'll have to take my place."

Let him get off his duff and play the game himself. It would do Dr. Darling good to see the world through the eyes of a child. His child.

Joshua eased himself back onto the pillows, grimacing at the tiredness that swamped him now that he was certain Nicole was gone. How could he have grown so weak in such a short time?

"Meddling busybody," he muttered, flopping his head against the pillow. "I've damaged more parts of my body than I knew I had. What does she know about getting up?"

"Quite a lot, I should think." Aunt Win leaned against the doorjamb, her arms crossed over her chest. "Nicole has followed your progress very carefully. She's been on the phone to your specialist many times since you've come home, always checking to be sure she's handling everything to his satisfaction."

"She has?" He frowned. "That just proves my point. She's meddling."

"She's concerned." His aunt snapped the covers up to his neck and settled them there with a firmness that told him she was ticked.

"That girl has bent over backward to help you out, Joshua Darling. And you're too busy wallowing in your own pity to notice she's worn herself to a frazzle."

"I know you're all tired, Aunt Win. I'm sorry. And I truly am grateful. It's just that it gets me down not to be able to do even the simplest things without passing out at the pain. Why did this have to happen? And why now?''

"I'm not God. I don't know. But I do know that if He hadn't wanted to work something through it, He wouldn't have allowed it. Just because you don't know the reason doesn't mean there isn't one.''

"It just seems so pointless. Go through all of this— for what? To go back to doing what I was doing before?'' He caught sight of the worry washing through her eyes and knew he'd upset her. "Sorry. I'm just tired, I guess.''

"What you are is jealous." Aunt Win plopped her bottom onto the side of the bed and glared at him.

"Me? Jealous?" He laughed. "Of what?"

"Of whom, you mean. Of Nicole Brandt, of course."

"Jealous of—I suppose you think you know why?" He really wanted to hear this, Joshua told himself. His aunt was being utterly ridiculous.

"Of course I know why. You're jealous because she's looking forward to the future. And in her case, it's filled with possibilities." Her pale hand covered his. "You're jealous of all her hopes and dreams, of the empty page she's getting ready to write the rest of her life on.''

"Huh?" He shook his head, confused by her description, then refocused. "No, Aunt Win. I'm not jealous of Dr. Brandt.''

"Really? Aren't you the tiniest bit frustrated by the thought of returning to those long hours you used to keep? Isn't thinking of her leaving Blessing for a future that isn't already mapped out just the littlest bit enticing?''

He wanted to deny it, but the truth was, he couldn't think of anything more restful than forgetting about the clinics, the office, his patients, his duties—for just a week or two. To be able to drive along the highway with the wind blowing and relax, knowing there was no one depending on you to care for them, no one whose livelihood depended on you—that would be wonderful.

"You've got to admit she's had it pretty easy."

"Has she?" Aunt Win's eyes intensified to a bright electric-blue.

"Sure she has," he continued, brushing off the warning implicit in her glance. "Nicole Brandt is a poor little rich kid. Never worried about anything but pleasing Daddy. She can afford to hang around here as long as she wants. When she's ready, Daddy will open up a spot for her surgical training. No sweat."

"You're my nephew and I love you. But you're an idiot. After your accident, when she told him she had to stay here, her father withdrew his support. She's scrimping to save enough to go back once you're better. Still think she's a poor little rich girl?" Aunt Win stood, smoothed down her skirt and stomped out of the room.

Then she poked her head back in just long enough to hand him one of her bakery boxes and offer some advice.

"You have the same shot at the future that Nicole does, Joshua. It all depends on what you make of it. Chew on this for a while."

He stared at the white box with its familiar red script, stifling his groan. Aunt Win was a dear soul, but why must she always insist God sent *her* the answers in the form of her heart-shaped love cookies? Even supposing heaven did poof down those little sayings that she studiously piped across the top in red icing, as far as he could remember, they'd never been much help. At least, not to him.

He waited till the sound of her marching heels dissipated in the silence of the old house, then muttered his frustration.

"The same shot as little Miss Daddy's Girl? Ha! As long as I keep it all going, don't drop a ball while I juggle everything. Maybe." He closed his eyes and let himself drift on the wings of make-believe—escape reality, he promised himself. Just for a few minutes. But there was no escape.

He opened the white box.

"A hole is nothing, yet you can break your neck in it."

Implying that he was letting himself sink into an abyss of jealous oblivion by envying Nicole her future? Joshua made a face. Tact had never been Aunt Win's strong point. Besides, she was wrong. He didn't want to leave Blessing or his girls or his work.

He just wanted—what?

Joshua broke off a bit of the cookie, savored its rich buttery flavor and tried to envision a perfect future, but no matter how many scenarios he tried, one small blond doctor kept reappearing, jade eyes flickering with a thousand lights.

Joshua was grateful when a sound in the next room drove the uncomfortable daydreams away.

"Why doesn't your daddy come and see you, Nici?"

That was Ruthie. How did she dream up those incessant questions? Joshua wondered, then chided himself for being glad he didn't have to answer them all.

"Well, I guess my dad is busy with his own life. I'm all grown up now. Grown-ups don't get to have their parents with them all the time."

They were in the study. He guessed Nicole had gone there for a moment's peace and had been routed.

"But he's your daddy. Doesn't he want to come and see you?"

Silence. Joshua wished he could see his temporary

partner's face right now. Perhaps he'd have a better idea why Nicole so seldom discussed her father.

"He's kind of mad at me right now."

"Oh. I'm sorry."

"It's okay." A pause. "He's—uh, he's not like your daddy, Ruthie."

"You mean he looks different?"

Nicole chuckled.

"Well, yes. He's older, for one thing. But I meant that he's very busy with his work. He doesn't really have time to come way out here. Blessing is a very long way from where he lives."

"I know about that," Ruthie enthused. "Daddy says Blessing is the back of beyond." A moment's silence. "But doesn't he get lonely? Don't you?"

"Sometimes. He loved my mother very much. I'm sure he misses her every day." Nicole stopped, then continued in a quieter voice. "He's the one who wants me to be a surgeon, to learn how to operate on people. My mother wanted to do that, too. My dad thinks I should be like her, that I should do the things she didn't get to do."

"He wants you to be like your mommy? Instead of being your own self, you mean?"

Joshua smiled. Ruthie clearly didn't identify. At least he'd done that right. The girls were their own little personalities, not imitations of Kyla.

"I think he wishes my mother was still alive, that she hadn't died. That someone else had—"

She swallowed the last word, but Joshua heard it just the same.

That someone else had died. Like you? The inward whisper shook him to the core. Was that why Nicole sounded so forlorn? She believed her father resented her very existence? He'd assumed she didn't want a closer relationship with her father, that the man pushed her too hard, or demanded too much from her. If she wanted his affection, why hadn't she stayed in Boston? Surely there were other clinics she could have chosen, closer to the city? Did earning her father's love mean forcing herself into something she wouldn't otherwise have chosen?

The questions wouldn't die. In the background he heard Ruthie musing about her own situation.

"My daddy didn't want my mommy to die, either. He got very mad."

"He did?"

"Uh-huh. I heard him smashing stuff one night. I was scared."

Joshua almost groaned aloud. They'd heard him and never said a word. What had those little minds thought—that he was angry with them?

"After Mommy died, Daddy got very busy. I think he was trying to make sure bad things didn't happen again, but I'm afraid they will. I'm afraid if I do something wrong, and a bad thing happens, Daddy will get really mad again. Like he did after Mommy went away to heaven."

"But people get mad all the time, honey. It doesn't mean they don't love you. It just means they're upset."

"Sometimes I'm upset."

The forlorn tone in Ruthie's voice stabbed deep into Joshua's heart.

"You are? Why, Ruthie?" Nicole's gentle tones elicited a prompt response.

"I'm scared I'll forget all the important stuff about my mom. Like the way she'd tickle, or her funny prayers. She was good at prayers. I wish my daddy would remind me. But Daddy doesn't talk about Mommy. Not anymore.''

"Do you think you're forgetting her, Ruthie?"

"I'm trying not to. But sometimes I have to come in here and look at her picture just so I can remember her face. Sometimes I forget what her voice sounded like, too. I just can't remember it all,'' she wailed, her voice breaking.

Joshua sat up straight. This was what Nicole had meant by using this time to get to know his girls. She was next door, listening, asking the very questions he should have been asking, allowing out the very fears and worries that he should have aired long ago.

He drew himself up. He might be useless at a lot of things, but this he could handle.

"Ruthie? Nicole? Can you two come in here for a moment?" he called.

Silence. Then they walked through the door, Ruthie gripping Nicole's hand in hers, worry darkening her eyes.

"I'm sorry, Daddy. We didn't mean to disturb you."

She looked afraid—of him. His own daughter was scared to bother him with her deepest fears. How sad was that?

"You're not disturbing me. I asked you to come. Climb up and sit with me, Ruthie. I heard you talking to Nicole. I think maybe you and I should talk." He patted the bedside.

"I'll check on the others." Nicole lifted her up, then turned to leave.

"No, please. Stay." He let his eyes do the talking. "Please?"

"All right." She sank onto a chair.

"Ruthie, you know that your mommy loved you very much, don't you?"

"Uh-huh." Her little face squinched up tight, hiding her expression.

"And you know that she couldn't help going away, that she was too sick to stay with us?"

She nodded, her eyes suddenly wide with worry. Joshua couldn't remember the last time he'd discussed Kyla with the girls. Shame rippled through him.

"When someone dies, it hurts us very badly. At first we get angry. We don't understand, and we wish they were here. At first we remember everything about them. But after they've been gone for a while, we forget some things. That's all right, because we have to go on living. There are things you have to do like go to school, and learn addition and subtraction, and practice your gymnastics. When you're doing all those things, your mind gets busy and it forgets things. And then it doesn't hurt so bad to think about the person who is gone and you like to remember the happy times."

"Is that how you feel about Mommy?" Ruthie's big blue eyes refused to let him off the hook.

Joshua swallowed. He'd initiated this conversation—now it was up to him to follow through. He glanced at Nicole, caught her smile, the nod of encouragement, and sighed.

"Sort of. I remember the happy times we had, when we got married, when you girls were born, the day she tried to ride a horse." He heard Ruthie's giggle and joined in, his fingers threading through hers. "It feels good to remember that, because I loved your mommy and she has a special place in my heart."

"Mine, too."

"The thing is, Ruthie, God made us with lots of room in our hearts for loving a lot of people. Just because we love someone else, it doesn't mean we love your mommy less. Our hearts kind of grow to make room for all kinds of love.''

Ruthie's head bent, her eyes fixed downward.

''What's wrong, sweetie?''

''I wish I could see her again, hug her. I can't remember what the hugs were like. If I could remember, maybe it wouldn't hurt so much when the other kids talk about their moms.'' She blinked up at him, the tears trembling on her lashes. ''Sometimes it's scary not to have a mom.''

He reached out and grasped her chin. ''Ruthie, you've always got me.''

''But you're sick and...''

''I'm your dad, and I love you very much.'' The lump in his throat wouldn't move, so Joshua spoke around it. Mental health was every bit as important as physical health and he would not permit his daughters to suffer in silence any longer. ''Sometimes I wish I could get a hug, too, Ruthie. Do you think we could share one?''

She peered at him like a curious baby sparrow checking out its parent.

''You and Mommy used to hug lots. But now you haven't got anyone to hug, have you, Daddy?'' Her eyes widened at the discovery.

''No, sweetie. Nobody but you and Rosie and Rachel.'' He felt the tears on his cheeks, knew that Nicole would see them. But it didn't matter. Nothing mattered as much as his sweet child's broken heart. ''Would you hug me, Ruthie?''

''But won't I hurt you?'' She frowned at his elevated leg.

''Let's try and see.''

She edged herself carefully into position, lining up her

tiny body against his chest so her arms would reach around his neck.

"Is this okay?"

"Tighter," he demanded softly, lips pressed against her shiny head.

She nestled her face into his neck, her arms straining to hold him close. "Better?"

"Perfect," he whispered, closing his eyes. "Absolutely perfect."

When had he lost this? How had he forgotten how precious his own flesh and blood was?

A sound on the other side of the room drew his attention. Joshua opened his eyes, saw Nicole standing in the doorway, openly weeping. She gave him a thumbs-up and a teary smile, then hurried from the room.

For the first time, Joshua found himself wondering what it would be like to be hugged by the prim and proper Dr. Brandt. He rolled his eyes at the thought. She'd given up her career goal, but only temporarily, and only because she felt duty bound to stay. Now wasn't the time to be daydreaming about her. Once he was up and around, she'd leave faster than a seagull after a fish.

And well she should. No way did he have anything to offer that could compare to what she could get for herself as a top-notch surgeon.

As he lay there holding his daughter close, Joshua realized that Dr. Nicole Brandt had a lot that he wanted in a partner. She had spunk, originality and drive. She wasn't afraid to express her opinion, or to challenge him when she thought he was wrong. She was capable of far more than he'd imagined when he'd stupidly labeled her a spoiled little rich girl. Caring, compassionate, determined to make a difference, Nicole was perfect for Blessing. She was the perfect foil to his need for control.

But it doesn't change a thing. She has her life, a future to look forward to. Staying here would not be a step up. Her father wouldn't be pleased.

"Daddy, you're squishing Auntie Win's cookie." Ruthie wiggled away, held up the broken box and grinned at the remaining crumbs. "Can I have some?"

"We'll share. Are Rachel and Rosalyn home yet?"

She shook her head.

"Rach has ballet and Roz is at the birthday party. Don't you remember, Daddy?"

"No, honey, I don't. I forget a lot of things. How about if you go in my desk and get out the big brown photo album? Maybe that will help me remember. What was your name again?" He wiggled his eyebrows.

"Oh, Daddy!" Ruthie wiggled free, dropped to the floor and grinned. "You know very well I'm Ruthie. Daddies don't forget their kids."

"No, honey. They never do."

"We can remember Mommy together, can't we, Daddy?" She dashed from the room, feet flying.

They could remember the past, all right. That wasn't a problem.

But what about the future?

Chapter Eleven

"**A**nother red-letter day. First of December, first day at church. You're doing very well, Doc. I hate to say it, but—how time flies." Nicole grinned at him, delighted that he'd finally agreed to attend the Sunday-morning service, though her heart gave a pang at the tension she saw in his taut shoulders.

"At least you didn't say 'when you're having fun,'" he grumbled, undoing his seat belt with a snap.

"Just relax," she ordered.

"Easy for you to say." He managed to escape the confines of the vehicle and maneuver upright onto his crutches. "You're not the one everyone is staring at. I feel like they're waiting to watch me land on my butt."

"Daddy!" Rachel giggled. "Nobody's watching you."

"Well, actually, some people are. They're staring." Ruthie grinned. "But they're nice stares. I think."

"Run to your classes, girls," Joshua ordered, his tone bordering on exasperation. "I'll be fine."

They glanced back. Each girl gave Nicole the once-over, then nodded. Clearly they felt he was in capable hands. Joshua stood where he was, watching them skip up the stairs and disappear inside the church. As far as he could tell, some of their worry had dissipated. Their lives seemed on track, though his wasn't.

As if a switch flicked, his mind refocused, reality intruded and he cast an angry glance at those who stood watching. Waiting.

"I wish they'd stop staring at me like hawks after a mouse," he mumbled, head bent as he carefully edged up the steps. "I don't need an audience to kiss the ground."

"No one is waiting for that, Joshua."

He gave her the look, the one he'd practiced in the little handheld mirror Aunt Win had lent him—the arrogant look with one eyebrow quirked upward—the one that told her he knew there had been times during her employment when she'd waited for exactly that. Her cheeks burned, and the fiery glint he was coming to know flashed through her eyes.

"You think I'd get some perverse pleasure out of seeing you take a fall?"

"Take a fall," he repeated. Then grinned. "Nicely put, Doctor. But yes, in your shoes, I imagine I'd get just a twitch of satisfaction from exactly that." He winked, just to show there were no hard feelings. "Of course, it's not as though I don't deserve it. I've been less than kind to you at times. In your place, I'm sure I'd relish the prospect of watching me dive into the dust."

"Well, I am not you!" She glared at him, her fingernails white against the wooden door. "Wanting such a thing would be counterproductive. Don't you remember? The sooner you're back to work, the sooner I can leave."

No sooner had he manipulated his way through the

vestibule doorway than Nicole let the door close and strode away, her temper zipping straight to high.

Why had she said that? She didn't want to leave, didn't relish the opportunity of leaving behind the friends she'd made here. She certainly didn't look forward to leaving the girls.

Or *him*.

Which was absolutely ridiculous, when you thought about it. She sniffed her disgust at the ridiculous infatuation with a doctor who couldn't have cared less that she dreamed about him.

"I'm sorry." Joshua's hand held out a big white handkerchief. "It's a truce flag. I seem to have this innate ability to always say the wrong thing. I don't know why."

She glanced up, caught his frown as he tried to puzzle something out.

"For some reason, whenever I talk to you, the words never come out the right way," he muttered. "I'm sorry."

He was apologizing? Nicole blinked, searched for some sign that he was teasing. But for all intents and purposes, Joshua Darling seemed perfectly serious. She felt a fool for reacting so badly.

"It's my fault. I guess I'm just too ready to attribute the worst intentions. Let's forget it."

"Agreed." He seemed relieved. A minute later he caught sight of his aunt. "I thought you said Aunt Win wasn't feeling well, that she wouldn't be coming this morning."

"That's what she said. Why?" Nicole twisted around, saw the older woman giggling in the corner with Furly Bowes, her assistant. "Hmm. She doesn't look the least bit ill to me. In fact, she looks positively glowing."

"She's up to something." Joshua's low-voiced hiss of irritation made Nicole stare.

"Why would you think that?" she demanded.

"Avoiding us. Pretending she's sick. Hiding in corners and whispering. All the signs are there."

"Signs? Of what? Look, Joshua, we've just talked about attributing something to someone else that isn't necessarily true. Let's not go there again. Besides, the class will begin in a couple of minutes and I don't want to miss any of it. This series on grace is so good. I've never heard God's grace to us explained in exactly that way. It's—stimulating."

She hustled him down the aisle and into a seat before he could protest any further. Thankfully, the speaker called for order a few seconds later, so there was no time for Joshua to hassle her about her bossiness.

And she didn't have to tell him the truth.

A tiny flicker of guilt wiggled its way into her mind, but Nicole shoved it down with a resoluteness she'd honed over the past few months. He didn't need to know about the chicken pox outbreak. There was nothing Dr. Darling could do anyway. He should be concentrating on his own healing.

The virus had made its way from the Parker baby through the elementary school in record speed until almost every nonimmune child in town had experienced some strain of the infection. The Darling girls had weathered chicken pox years earlier and, thankfully, were not suffering. But yesterday the local day care had closed its doors when three of its workers displayed the red spots. Still, it was the tiniest babes and the elderly who suffered the most. And it was they who kept her and Luc Lawrence busier than usual as worried caregivers kept calling.

Nicole and Luc had almost weathered that epidemic when a virulent case of flu had begun attacking already weakened systems. Seniors were severely hit, many had to be hospitalized and the few vacant beds in the nursing home were also filled. With so many struck by the virus, Winifred Blessing, her friend Furly and the doctors seemed the only ones who had remained immune. The two bakers were now trying to organize some kind of home care for the overburdened nurses, but it was a mammoth task for two women who already had a business to run.

To add to the misery, unseasonably cold Arctic air had drifted down into Colorado, forcing Nicole to battle snowstorms and icy-cold winds to make it to the clinics last week. She had her work cut out just getting to the houses of those seniors who still lived in the rural areas. Luc had slaved right along with her, taking double and triple shifts at the hospital and nursing home with nary a complaint. But they were both tired and in need of a break. But when, and how?

She closed her eyes and whispered a plea for heavenly help. Much as she loved general practice, times like this caused her to look upon surgery with new eyes.

Nicole suddenly noticed everyone was standing. The class was over. And she'd missed every word. She knew Joshua was staring at her, so she dragged out her doctor face and pretended all was well. It would be, too, if she could just get some sleep this afternoon.

"Really enjoyed it, did you?" He picked up his crutches and wobbled to his feet. "One of the best sessions Ned's ever given."

"Mmm." She pretended to search for the gloves she knew were in her coat sleeve. Obvious maybe, but at least she could avoid his knowing stare.

"You might as well tell me what's wrong, Nicole. I'll find out anyway. I always do." Dr. Darling's blue eyes darkened until they glowed almost navy. "Spill it."

"I can't imagine what you're talking about. First you accuse Miss Winifred of some nefarious scheme, now it's my turn." She fixed her reprimanding look in place. "Perhaps some therapy would be in order?"

He didn't answer, but the flicker of a smile just twitching the corner of his mouth told Nicole everything she needed to know. He *would* find out. She didn't doubt that. Just not yet.

"Sunday school is over. I'm going to find the girls," she murmured. "Don't bother moving. I'll bring them back here."

"There's someone I need to talk to."

"But—"

"I don't see Dermot here today. I can't help wondering—"

"He's at home." She tried to cover the rush of words, knowing very well that he'd homed in on it. "Please don't overdo, Joshua. This is your first time out. I don't want you gallivanting all over the church. You're liable to trip on the carpet and do some damage."

He ignored the warning.

"What's wrong with Dermot?"

"Fever, chills." Nicole shrugged, hoping he'd see it as nonchalant. "I think he's got the flu. I told him to stay home, in bed, and get plenty of rest."

"But what about his horses? Someone's got to care for them. If he's ill—"

"Joshua." She waited until he looked directly at her. "It's handled, okay? Gray MacGonigle offered to do whatever needed doing."

"I should—"

"Sit down. Or go home. Whatever. But you are absolutely not going out to the Double D. No way. I forbid it." She crossed her arms, planted her feet and glared him down.

"You forbid it?" Joshua's eyes were huge. "How dare you forbid me anything! Who do you think you are?"

"Your doctor. And I'm trying to make you see sense. You're healing. Great. But you are not yet ready to return to work. And you're certainly not ready to handle horses!"

"And I suppose you think you'll decide when I am?" Red spots dotted his cheekbones, emphasizing the hollows beneath.

"In consultation with your other doctors, yes. I will." It was the first time she'd dared to stand up to him so directly, in public, with others around. Nicole's knees knocked together, and her heart thudded well out of its usual resting pulse. She held her breath, waiting for him to flatten her bragging.

Joshua glared at her for a good five seconds, harrumphed twice, thumped his crutch on the floor once and tapped his fingers against the pew in a methodical, irritating pattern. His eyes were bright, sparkling.

Wait a minute. Nicole stared.

He was laughing—big boisterous guffaws that wouldn't be silenced, but rang to the rafters. All around the sanctuary, people turned to stare, glanced at Nicole, then smiled at them both.

Nicole's breath whooshed out in a sigh of relief. He wasn't mad. He even seemed…proud? Of her?

"Dr. Brandt, I believe we've made an autocrat out of you. Power obviously goes to your head."

She stumbled for a response.

"Yes. Well, flattery doesn't. So just sit there and relax while I get the girls."

"Is talking allowed?" Dr. Darling looked the picture of demureness with his hands folded in his lap. "I promise I'll just sit here and only use my jaws. I don't think I'll strain them."

For once it seemed he was going to do as she asked. And she'd never loved him more. But he couldn't know that.

"There's always a comedian in the group. Unfortunately, you are not funny." She turned her back and marched out, ignoring his muffled snicker.

Though he pretended to laugh, Joshua had never been more surprised in his life. Nicole Brandt was a fireball beyond anything he'd imagined. Passionate, determined, caring. She was all of those, but there was so much more to his temporary partner than that. She was also independent, bossy, sensitive, but most of all, determined to do her best by him.

A flicker of something warm and soft blossomed in his heart. For all her harsh words and blustering manner toward him, Nicole Brandt was a marshmallow. She was the best kind of doctor—one who gave from the heart, no matter what it cost her.

He'd seen the pallor of her skin, knew from one tidbit or another that the girls dropped that she was overworking, running flat out because of his office. She was turning into exactly what he'd been before he'd been sideswiped, knocked for a loop.

Joshua twisted in his seat, caught sight of her speaking to a patient in the foyer. She smiled, said a few words, then wrapped the elderly lady in a hug to reassure her that everything would be fine. He remembered, with a pang, that he hadn't hugged a patient in ages. If ever. Until she'd come here, he'd have wagered Nicole Brandt hadn't, either. But somehow all the stiffness in her had been reshaped, molded, reworked until she fit Blessing like worn denim jeans. Why hadn't adversity affected him like that?

"That was one of God's best moves," a voice behind him proclaimed.

Joshua turned, saw Gray MacGonigle watching Nicole.

"That woman has done more for this town than I'd thought possible. She sure whipped you into shape." Gray chuckled at the chagrin he saw. "No point in denying it, Doc. She's got you pegged and you'll toe her line or answer why. It's very…er, interesting." His eyes danced with mirth.

"She's a bully," Joshua mumbled, trying to hide his embarrassment.

"That sweet thing wouldn't hurt a thieving coyote. But give her a few minutes with that animal, and Dr. Nici would have him singing a different song. There's something about her—a certain presence. Kind of makes you want to try a little harder, make sure she's not disappointed." He scratched his head, then glanced down at Joshua. "Don't you think?"

Joshua shrugged. He didn't want to talk about how wonderful Dr. Nici was, but he knew exactly what the other man meant. He'd felt the same emotion a hundred times over. Every day she walked through the door at home, he wanted her to see the progress he'd made, waited for that beaming smile that told him he'd met her standard.

"Too bad she's so set on leaving. She'd make a perfect partner."

The words hit Joshua hard. Nicole Brandt *was* perfect. She was certainly a far better doctor than he. And truthfully, he wouldn't have minded one bit if she decided to stay. But he wouldn't, he couldn't hold her back.

"She's got big plans," he told Gray. "She's not the kind to stick around a place like Blessing."

"Given the right incentive, she might change her mind." Gray tilted back on his heels, his eyes speculative. "Ever gone down a path because you didn't think you had any other choice?" He watched Joshua for a moment, then nodded. "Yeah. Me, too. Not my finest hour."

"She has something to prove to her father, Gray. It's between them, and I certainly wouldn't interfere. Besides, I think she's looking forward to that surgical training. I'm sure she'd be good at it." His voice dropped. "She seems to be good at everything," he muttered, watching as Nicole shepherded his daughters through the foyer and toward him, a smile on her face as she shared their joy.

"Think maybe you're jealous, Doc?"

"What?" He jerked around to stare at Gray, nearly wrenching his back in the process, but the other man had loped away in his long, measured stride. "No," he sputtered indignantly. But no one heard.

"Are you hurting, Daddy?" Rosie whispered, pressing her rose-blossom cheek against his as she knelt on the pew.

"No, honey, I'm fine. Why do you ask?" He snuggled against her, breathing in the soft scent of her delicate hair.

"Because your face is all wrinkled and mad looking. Are you mad?" Honest Ruthie. Trust her to get to the heart of the subject.

He laughed.

"Not mad, Ruthie. Just thinking."

"About Christmas?" Ruthie's hushed voice echoed the looks on the other faces as their big blue eyes stared into his.

"Ruthie." Nicole's quiet voice withheld...something.

Joshua watched the interplay between them, knew the exact moment that Ruthie understood what was going on. She nodded, sat down and folded her hands in her pocket. He found no clue in Nicole's green eyes, so he switched his attention to his daughter.

"What about Christmas, honey?" he probed.

Ruthie blinked, checked with Nicole, then smiled at him.

"Christmas is about secrets," she told him. "Teacher says it's better to give than to receive, but that we have to know how to do both. I'm going to be a giver." She wiggled in her seat, excitement adding a glow to her already shining face. "You'll see, Daddy."

"Okay, Ruthie. The service is about to begin. No more talking."

Nicole was a little too quick to shush his daughter, Joshua decided. There was definitely something going on. But what?

There were a thousand questions he wanted to ask, but the triumphant chords of the organ prevented his asking them and Joshua had to be content to sit and listen as the choir opened the service. Then Pastor Jones rose.

"Welcome to Blessing Church on this first Sunday of Advent. We're delighted to welcome in the season of Christ's birth and doubly excited that this morning the Darling girls will lead us in lighting the first Advent candle. Girls."

Joshua gulped as his daughters stood, glanced once at

Nicole for reassurance, then took their places at the front of the church, their faces beaming as they noted his surprise. Rachel stood on one side, microphone grasped in one hand, a small sheet of paper in the other. Rosalyn stood in the middle, hands behind her back, grinning her delight at being on show. Ruthie waited on the far side, her face impassive. Clearly she was concentrating.

Rachel began to speak.

"Christmas is about getting ready for Jesus' birth. Advent means 'the coming.' It is a time to celebrate light in the midst of darkness, symbolized by candles on the Advent wreath. The wreath is made of a circle of evergreen branches laid flat to sym—" Rachel glanced up, found Nicole with her eyes and nodded. "Symbolize the endless nature of God's love for His people." She smiled happily, then handed the microphone to Ruthie.

Joshua almost smiled as his middle daughter's chest puffed out with pride. She needed no notes. It was clear that Ruthie had memorized every word.

"Four candles stand in the circle of the wreath. The three blue candles are the candles of hope that God's promise to send a Savior will be fulfilled in the coming of Jesus. The fourth candle is pink. It is the joy candle to celebrate the son of God who came to earth."

Ruthie grinned, then thrust the microphone in front of Rosie. His baby took a huge breath and said her piece.

"Today we light the candle of waiting to remind us not to get too busy to remember Jesus."

The microphone plopped to the floor with a loud thud. Joshua winced, watching breathlessly as Rachel carefully lit the long match. She waited for Ruthie and Rosie to close their fingers around the stick. Almost in slow motion they all tilted forward to light the first blue candle.

Once that was done, all three lustily blew out the match, then turned to face their audience.

Pastor Jones moved to the pulpit.

"Well done, girls. Now I'm going to ask everyone to stand. We're delighted to have Dr. Darling with us today. Joshua, would you lead us in this first Advent prayer?"

Joshua shifted awkwardly to his feet, wishing desperately that someone had prepared him for this. How could he pray aloud, knowing how shabbily he'd treated God over these past few months? How could he lead in prayer when he had no answers of his own? He could feel Nicole's presence next to him, knew she was waiting. The same old questions swirled around his brain, tying his tongue in a thousand knots.

He was no spiritual leader to be speaking to God for all these people. And yet, wasn't that whom Jesus had esteemed most—those who had no one else but Him to depend upon, those who called out when they needed Him most?

Joshua took a deep breath, closed his eyes and spoke.

"Father, this is the Sunday of preparation. And yet we are so busy, trapped in our routines, too busy to hear Your voice. Our spirits are weary and we sometimes feel You are far away." Once started, the heartfelt words flowed from his heart in words he didn't remember composing.

"How can we hear Your voice today? Speak to our hearts during this season of grace, just as You spoke to Your prophets and saints. Remind us of the true journey we are on and the work You would have us do. We are Your servants, Father. In this holy season, turn our eyes to watch for Your blessed coming. Amen."

A resounding *amen* completed the prayer.

The girls strolled back to their seats, happy grins on

their faces. In the hush of the moment, Ruthie's voice carried across the sanctuary.

"That was good, Daddy."

Everyone laughed.

"Indeed it was," their pastor agreed.

The service continued. For Joshua, the words spoken and sung held new meaning. He puzzled over it, hesitant to believe what seemed so obvious. The hard decisions, the details, the endless questions about tomorrow, next week, next year—none of that was up to him. He was here now, in this hour. God expected no more than that he handle what he was given today.

Overwhelmed by the freedom of suddenly accepting his inability to control the future, Joshua allowed himself to soak in the peace he felt descending on him. If there were odd moments, he didn't notice them. Every word of the sermon, every song seemed to turn on that one word—today. He had today. He could fuss it away, drive himself until he collapsed from the stress, or he could take today and make it wonderful. Not only for himself, but for the girls, as well.

"Joshua?" Nicole peered down at him, a tiny frown lending lines to the corners of her vivid eyes. "Are you all right? Have you overdone things?"

"I'm fine." He noticed that people were filing out of the sanctuary. His own daughters brushed past him, anxious to speak to their friends. The service was over. How strange that he'd missed the benediction. He levered himself to his feet. "Shall we?"

Nicole didn't say a word, but he could feel her eyes on his back the entire length of the aisle. He stopped several times, greeted patients, asked about new babies who'd been born while he was ill. It seemed terribly important to know that Mrs. Featherby was happy with the new hip he'd suggested she get. And that Zachary Spenser, far from being diminished by his cancer treatments, had taken a new hold on life.

These were his people, his friends. His work wasn't simply a business with a positive and negative cash flow. The people in Blessing had become an integral part of his life, the true measure of his time spent in this small town. There would be serious problems next month, next year, but today things were good. Life was full.

As he made his way toward the foyer, Joshua realized his mistake in believing that his work in Blessing was a job. It wasn't. It was a partnership. Everything he'd done, from his role on town council to the committees he'd sat on, including the advice he'd offered senior students at career day, was the sum total of what he'd learned about life. That's what he was supposed to share. In return, these people, these friends, gave back from their own knowledge. And the return on his investment was proving far greater than anything he could have imagined.

Nicole helped him into his coat, then waited while he spoke to Pastor Jones. Then, together, they walked toward the car, her arm firmly linked through his, though no one would guess that it was because she supported him.

"You're quiet."

He waited until he'd made it to the car, then turned to look, really look at her. She was beautiful. The black coat hugged her slim figure and emphasized her green eyes. The fur collar caressed her rosy cheek, wound sinuously around her slim neck. The sun sparkled diamonds off her shining hair. Nicole Brandt was a diamond, a pearl beyond price. He owed his life to her.

She half smiled, eyes curious.

"Why are you staring at me?"

"Why not? You're very beautiful. I'm sure I'm not the first man to notice." He watched her duck her head, saw her cheeks flush in a color that wasn't caused by the cold. "You coached the girls for this morning, didn't you?"

She nodded. "They wanted to surprise you."

"They did. I was very impressed."

"And proud?"

Her eyes asked the question, too, and for once Joshua didn't even try to ignore it.

"Prouder than I've a right to be," he agreed quietly. "I had nothing to do with their performance and yet I felt like my buttons would pop. To think those smart little girls are my daughters is...scary. I know it isn't enough, but...thank you."

Nicole turned away to open the car door. "It's enough."

The words were soft, barely whispered, and Joshua might have thought he'd dreamed them if he hadn't glimpsed the look in her eyes. She was crying.

"Nicole, I—" He stepped forward, reached up to brush the crystal drop away from her cheek. "I'm sorry," he whispered, shamed that in all the months she'd been here he'd never really considered what he'd asked of her.

"You haven't anything to be sorry for." She did look at him then. A smile quivered across her lips.

"Then why are you crying? It must have been something I said. I seem to have a knack for saying the wrong thing."

"It wasn't that." She shook her head, pale hair flying around her shoulders. "It was just...everything."

"Huh?" He studied her, trying to understand.

"The emotion of the moment," she whispered. "I

think I finally realized how proud you must feel sometimes. For a minute, it was almost as if they were my
daughters and we'd—'' Her voice jerked to a stop. She
blinked at him, a shocked look washing over her face.

"Nicole?" Why didn't she finish? Why was she
avoiding looking at him?

"Never mind. You'd better get in the car, Joshua. I'll
go look for the girls."

Before he could say a word, she scurried away like a
scared rabbit. "Yes, I definitely have the knack," he
muttered, edging himself closer to the car so he could
lean against it. "Too bad I don't know how to get rid of
it. I suppose next I'll scare away dogs. Which might not
be too bad if it was Ladybug." That brought a tiny smile.

"You keep talking to yourself, you'll scare away all
the sane people."

Joshua jerked his head up to locate the owner of that
voice. A man stood at the front fender of the car. He was
clearly out of place. He wore a black pinstriped suit that
fit his tall, rangy body as if it had been made for it. Over
that he wore a black wool coat. Kid leather gloves covered his broad hands.

He looked like a misplaced oil baron.

"I suppose now you've gone into some kind of
trance." Disgust laced the low gruff voice.

"No, no trance. It's too cold for that. Are you lost?"

"I don't get lost."

That, Joshua decided, he could well believe. If he was
any judge of character, and he was, this man knew exactly what he wanted from life, and he got it.

"My name is Shane Brandt. I'm looking for my
daughter. I assume you know her. After all, you're the
reason she's stuck around this backwater so long."

Joshua suffered through the disparaging glance around

his town. So this was Nicole's father. The rich man. You could see the signs of wealth in everything the man wore. But it was more than that. He had a certain aura, an arrogance, a savoir faire that told the world he was used to getting his own way and expected nothing different today.

Joshua completed a second assessment and frowned. Shane Brandt was a man on a mission.

"Nicole is around here some—"

"Daddy?"

He twisted, saw the shock cover Nicole's face. She hurried forward, her eyes riveted on her father, three girls trailing behind.

"Nicole, why is your cell phone always either busy or shut off?"

No hug, Joshua noted. They stood staring at each other like two distant acquaintances, wary of further involvement.

"I—I've been very busy. I guess I didn't notice it was off." She fiddled with the strap of her purse, eyes darting between her father and Joshua. "Why—why are you here?"

"Why? To take you back, of course." He glared at Joshua, then turned his attention back to Nicole. "It's your last chance. There's an opening. You have to be there tomorrow morning. At 9:00 a.m. No excuses."

Joshua frowned. Surely the man couldn't be serious. But one look told him Shane Brandt was indeed determined that his daughter attend this session. He'd probably pulled a few strings to get her there. It was understandable. He was her father. He wanted her to continue on the path she'd chosen.

But for Nicole to leave?

Though his voice remained silent, Joshua's entire being cried out in protest.

No! She couldn't go!

Chapter Twelve

Nicole knew her mouth was hanging open. She couldn't seem to help it. Her brain was stuck on her father's words.

Nine o'clock tomorrow morning. Last chance. Was that why he was here? To make sure she did as she was told?

In the blink of an eye she was a little girl again, desperate for her father's approval, needing to feel his arms around her, assuring her that she was loved, cared for, esteemed.

The cajoling words hadn't changed in all those years.

"Either you are serious about this or you're not, Nicole. I've tried to be understanding. You had to stay. Fine. You've been here several months. The man is up and around."

"He's not completely healed yet, Daddy."

"Doesn't look like it will be long." Shane scanned Joshua's lean body and nodded. "This is your chance to do what your mother never could, Nicole. This is your chance." His voice changed, beguiled her with the same old reminders. "She would have wanted that for you, to fulfill her dreams. It was so dear to her heart. I know you'd like to make your mother proud."

She longed to scream, "Stop it!" But the words wouldn't be said. Instead, they went on and on, reminding her that she'd always failed to make the grade, never managed to quite master what her mother had.

I just wanted you to be proud, Daddy. Her heart cried the remembered words to him, but she could see from the growing frustration wrinkling his forehead that he wouldn't understand. In his world you didn't quit, or you got stepped on and knocked out of the game. Practicing medicine wasn't the same as running a business, but Shane had never quite understood that.

"It may be your last opportunity, Nicole. They've held your name on the list far longer than they should have, as it is. You can't expect them to wait forever."

Her attention wavered, slipped to the movement she caught in the corner of her eye, dimming her father's words. Joshua's head drooped, his shoulders slumped and he pressed himself against the car. In a moment she fully expected he'd be telling her to leave.

"So we might as well go pack your bags. I know these people will understand."

"Will they?" She shook her head. Drawing upon the strength she'd only recently learned to tap into, Nicole remembered Miss Winifred's words and sent a prayer heavenward.

Then she drew herself up and faced her father in a way she should have done years ago.

"How could they understand? I don't."

"But—"

"I'm sorry, Daddy, but I'm not going anywhere. There is no possible way I can leave Blessing right now."

Her father's face tightened. His eyes flashed a signal that warned her of his rising temper. How she hated that temper. She wasn't one of his employees—she was his daughter. Why didn't he treat her like one?

"You said six months, Nicole. It's gone far beyond that now. There is a substitute doctor in place. I checked. Let him handle things until—" Shane paused, cast a disgusted look at Joshua before addressing him. "I suppose you will be returning to work. Eventually?"

"Of course Joshua will be back. As soon as he's fit. Which isn't quite yet." Nicole's blazing glance dared her patient to argue. "But that is totally irrelevant. Right now we're in the middle of one of the worst flu epidemics the area's seen in years. We need every hand we can get to manage. I will not walk out on my patients. I won't."

She realized two things then—that she'd just told Joshua about the flu problem, and that the girls had been watching the entire event with growing consternation. Rosie was smothering little muffled hiccups that shook her tiny body. She hiccuped only when she was upset.

"Come along, children. Get into the car. Joshua, you, too. It's time you were out of this cold and at home."

"I am not an invalid, Nicole," he muttered, but he did get inside.

Probably because he knew she would have stuffed him there if he hadn't, she decided grimly. Why was he so interested in her father? A minute later he stuck his head out, nodded to Shane.

"Why not join us? You can share our lunch. My aunt made a casserole. There's plenty for everyone."

Nicole almost laughed. The great Shane Brandt in the back of a stodgy old station wagon with three little girls? It was unthinkable. Besides, if she knew her father, and she did, he'd already rented the biggest sedan he could find in order to make the trip to Blessing. She wasted a moment wondering where he'd flown into and how long he'd spent driving to reach her.

Shane nodded.

"Good idea. I'll follow you. I'm not finished talking to my daughter. Not by a long shot." Shane stalked away, his heels hitting hard against the walk.

"That man is mad." Ruthie did up her seat belt, but her sad eyes were on Nicole. "I don't like him."

Nicole read a reflection of that sentiment on Joshua's face, but he was gracious enough not to say it.

"He'll get over it, Ruthie," she muttered, and lurched out of the parking lot toward home. *I hope.*

Shane waited while they unloaded from the vehicle, then grasped Joshua's elbow and manhandled him toward the house. To be fair, Joshua tried hard to ignore his blustering bossiness and took it as a sign that the man thought he was helping.

"We weren't introduced. I'm Dr. Darling," he offered, puffing a little as he leaned against the wall while the girls, then Nicole, filed inside. "Joshua Darling. I'm very glad to meet you."

"Yeah." Shane didn't take his hand, merely waited for him to lumber inside.

Nicole felt his gaze home in on her. She drew in a breath of courage. When he got that look, Shane was harder to sway than a bull in full rampage. His eyes blazed with fury. She decided to ignore it until she got him alone.

"Joshua, perhaps it would be best if my father and I went elsewhere to settle this. I think we're upsetting the girls and there's really no need to burden you with our discussion."

"You're not burdening us. And the girls understand

when people have things they need to talk through. Don't you, girls?'' He smiled at them and they nodded uncertainly. "Let's have lunch first. You can talk after that."

There were a thousand responses Nicole could have made, but she wasn't offered a chance. Winifred sailed through the front door at that precise moment, a tray of rolls in one hand, the familiar white box with red script in the other.

"Not started yet? Good. I brought a few extra things." She glanced around, then stepped directly in front of Shane. "I'm Winifred Blessing, Dr. Darling's aunt. And you're Nicole's father. I would have recognized those eyes anywhere." She studied him for several moments, then twisted to smile at Nicole. "I can tell he's just as stubborn as you."

Nicole concentrated on removing her coat, then lifted the packages away from Miss Winifred.

"I'm sorry, Miss Winifred, I should have introduced you to my father, Shane Brandt. Daddy, this is Miss Win." She glanced at them, then turned. "I'll get things started in the kitchen," she murmured, hoping she could escape the debacle she knew would follow.

"We'll all help. Come along, Joshua. There's no need for you to retire just now. You looked perfectly strong at church. I'm sure you can remain upright long enough to enjoy lunch with us."

Nicole smothered a smile at Joshua's resigned response.

"Yes, Aunt Win."

"Good. Hang your coat in there, Mr. Brandt. May I call you Shane?"

Nicole left them behind and scurried into the kitchen. She set her packages down and wondered if she could sneak a look inside the box.

"It's another of her bits of advice," Joshua muttered, leaning against the door frame, watching her. "Ordinarily I'd tell you to ignore it. But given the glint in her eye, maybe we'd better see what it says." He hobbled over beside her and lifted the lid.

Nicole stared at the heart-shaped cookie.

"A wish changes nothing. A decision changes everything."

"Well, I suppose that's true," she muttered, wondering what Miss Winifred's intention was this time. Joshua's warm breath feathered across the skin on the back of her neck. His arm brushed hers as he adjusted the box so he could peer into it.

"The question is, what decision does she want you to make?" His eyes met and held hers, a different question lurking in their depths.

"I should think that would be obvious, nephew." Winifred pulled a stack of plates from the cupboard and handed them to Shane. "We all have to make the best decisions we can with whatever information we have available." She handed Joshua the cutlery and directed the girls to gather glasses and juice.

When Joshua fumbled with his crutch and dropped a fork on the floor, Nicole reached out to take the utensils from him, but Miss Winifred's voice stopped her.

"He's not an invalid, girl. He can help out a little. It won't kill him. Joshua is a strong man in the prime of his life. Pitching in once in a while is the least he can do." The look on her face dared them to reply. Satisfied with their silence, she turned to Shane. "You can help the girls wash up now. We'll have lunch set out in a minute."

He stood there, staring at her. Nicole caught Joshua's

grin and smiled back, enjoying the picture of her non-plussed father finally at a loss for words.

"Go on then, Shane."

He pivoted on his heel, walked through the door. A moment later they heard the low rumble of his voice in response to Ruthie's.

"I'm not mad, so stop asking."

"Well, you look mad, and I don't like it!" Clearly Ruthie was determined to have the last word.

Having laid the last of the cutlery in place, Joshua flopped into a chair. He winked at Nicole.

"Bet he hasn't obeyed anyone in a very long time."

He was smiling.

How could that simple lift of those full lips alter his face so drastically? He was no longer the grumpy doctor or angry patient, and his chiseled good looks held her attention. Was he flirting with her?

"No, I don't imagine he has," she murmured, moving her gaze to the plate in front of her. "He's used to giving, not taking orders."

"Exactly like his daughter." This time the teasing was unmistakable.

Nicole would have sat there like a lovesick teenager, gaping at him, if it hadn't been for the arrival of her father. He carried Rosie in one arm, but most of his attention was focused on Ruthie.

"I never thought of it as selfish, Ruthie. Having my own airplane makes it much easier for me to get a lot of jobs done in a short time. Otherwise, I'd have to spend a lot more time getting there, and less time on doing the job."

They sat down as Miss Winifred urged everyone to allow her and Rachel to serve.

"But Nici isn't a job." Ruthie wasn't giving up yet.

"She's your daughter. And she's been here a long time. Why didn't you come to visit her before? Didn't your plane work?"

"Nici." Ignoring her question, Shane rolled the word over his tongue, his eyes glazing over.

Nicole knew what he was thinking. She could see the memories washing over him.

"It's my special name for her," Ruthie explained, grinning at Nicole. "We're friends."

"Nici." Shane peered down at the little girl. "Her mother used to call her that. I haven't heard it in a long time."

"You should have come to visit her." Rosie wasn't yet into forgive and forget.

"But don't you call her a special name?" Clearly Ruthie understood the marring frown that crossed his brow. "Like my daddy calls me Ruthie sometimes."

"But that's your name." Shane glared at her as if she were trying to trick him, but Ruthie took no offense. Her usual sunny smile bounced right back.

"Uh-uh. My real name is Ruth Ann Elizabeth. But my daddy calls me Ruthie. 'Cept when he's mad. Then he says all my names."

"I see." Shane helped himself to the roast beef casserole without saying another word. But every so often his gaze slipped down to the little girl, then across to his daughter.

"Anyways, I think you should'a come to see Nici before. I bet she got lonely." Ruthie chewed on her bread, her face thoughtful. "But maybe it's good you didn't. She's been awful busy doing Daddy's job."

"Are you mad 'cause Nici's helping Daddy?" Rachel studied him with the intense scrutiny children use to ferret out every detail. "Is that why you want to take her away?"

"I don't want to take her away." Shane's lips pursed. "And I told you I wasn't mad!"

Nicole raised one eyebrow at him in warning. She would not allow him to browbeat these children. Shane rolled his eyes at her, sighed, then recanted.

"Actually, I came to help her move. Nicole is supposed to be in Boston to take some special training. It starts Monday. I thought she might need me to get her stuff moved."

"But Nicole can't go now!" Rosie's face crumpled in horror. "Daddy's not better yet. Who will help us practice our Christmas words if Nici's not here?"

"Who's going to sew my angel costume?" Rachel looked outraged.

"Nici's not going." Ruthie was angry. "She said she'd come to my school play. I'm going to be Mary."

Nicole caught Joshua's look. He, too, looked sad. Was it possible that he would miss her? Her heart shattered. Why had her father chosen now to come? Christmas wasn't so much to ask, was it? A few days of a special season to share with the girls? A few stolen moments of happiness before she plunged into a new phase of her career?

Then she remembered. The flu. She couldn't leave now. There were too many patients who needed her. She latched onto the reprieve.

"My leaving isn't something we're going to have to worry about just yet, girls," she murmured, breaking in to the silence that had descended on the table. "I'm not going anywhere." She faced her father. "I've got patients, a lot of very sick patients, who need me. I intend to see this thing through. I won't let them down."

Shane stared at her in disbelief.

"You can't mean that!" His eyes locked on Joshua. "She doesn't understand. This could be her last chance. Can't you see that?"

Nicole held her breath, waited to see what her boss would say. Did he want her gone so badly he'd side with Shane?

"Your daughter has to make her own decisions. It's not up to me."

The words lent her some much-needed strength. She straightened her backbone, faced her father down.

"It's not Dr. Darling's fault, Daddy. This is my decision. And I'm not leaving. Not now." Nicole watched her father absorb that and softened her tone. "I understand what you've tried to do for me. I know you're only trying to help me." She tried to soften the blow, knowing he couldn't understand. "But I took on responsibilities here. What kind of doctor would I be if I just walked away?"

"They're not your responsibilities," Shane yelled, his face red and flushed. "You don't owe these people a thing. You don't even know them."

Nicole smiled, her eyes moving to each person gathered around the table.

"Oh, I know them, Daddy. There's a woman whose husband died, leaving her with four children under six years old. She's hanging on by her fingertips, trying to keep her family together. Last week she learned she's going to need surgery. I referred her to the specialist. She's my patient." She waited, let him absorb that. Her eyes on Rosie's golden head, she spoke again.

"I have another patient who's not much more than seven. She was involved in a farm accident a while ago. It was bad, but I've been watching her, trying to make sure we don't miss anything that could cause problems later on. She has a baby brother she wants to teach how to ride. For that she needs full use of both arms.'' She paused, met his stare. ''I know her, Daddy. I know her very well. She's my patient.''

''That's Lizabeth.'' Ruthie's whisper drew Shane's attention. ''She cut her arm in a big machine.''

''But surely—'' Shane stopped short at Rachel's frown. ''Sorry.''

''I've gotten to know the folks in Blessing very well, you see. And as I did, a funny thing happened. They became more than patients. They're my friends. They helped me understand what being a doctor is all about. They've welcomed me, listened to me and encouraged me. I am part of this community now. I can't just walk away, any more than my mother would have walked away from her clinics. Nor would you have wanted her to.''

Nicole waited, watched him closely.

''You would never have asked that of her.''

The words hit home. She could see him mulling over what she'd said. For now, that would be enough.

Shane spent the rest of the day watching the interplay between his daughter and the family who seemed to gather her in as one of their own. He'd made a tactical mistake, come on too hard, too overbearing. But that could be rectified. Except for the aunt. He didn't particularly care for the aunt. She was too bossy and far too domineering, and he had a feeling she could see through his placating words to his real intent to get Nicole out of here. But he tolerated Winifred Blessing because he sensed Nicole wanted it that way. And for now, that was enough.

Not that his daughter had paid him much heed. She'd been called to the phone on and off all afternoon. Several times she'd had to leave, to check on someone. Each time she returned, she and Joshua Darling held a mini conference. Shane had been surprised both by what he'd seen and overheard. Nicole updated the man, told him her prescribed therapy. Dr. Darling made no attempt to correct or modify her line of treatment. Once or twice he'd offered his own suggestion, but left her free to agree or disagree. To Shane's view, they operated like a team, pulling together to find a solution. There was a bond between them. One that went deeper than a medical relationship. His concern grew.

His daughter was different now. She'd changed, grown up, learned to shield her inner thoughts from him. She became more reserved whenever Dr. Darling was around, though her tones were always friendly. It was clear she admired him, but was there something more? Shane thought so. He found himself noting her sidelong glances, the furtive way she had of peeking at Joshua when she thought no one else was looking.

The truth hit him like a red-hot poker when Nicole ordered Joshua to rest during the afternoon. A tender discipline softened her words, made her eyes glow. She carefully tucked up her patient in bed, easing his legs into a comfortable position before she drew the coverlet up to his neck and tucked it against his body. He almost expected to see her bend and brush a kiss against the man's cheek.

Then Shane knew. His little girl had fallen in love. Was that why she wouldn't leave this town?

Fear gripped him and hung on tight. For he saw something in the quiet exchange of words between them that he was certain his daughter had not. This man cared about her. On each occasion, he went out of his way to soothe her, to reassure her that she had made the right decision. He patted her hand, smoothed her fingers and gentled her with a touch on the arm when she fussed about a patient. And his daughter, that strong proud doctor, loved it.

Shane suddenly realized that, with just a few well-chosen words, Dr. Joshua Darling could take his daughter away from him, if he wished. The question was, did he want to? Shane didn't know. But it was no wonder Nicole had put himself and surgery on the back burner. She'd found a new life here, one in which she'd grown into a new person. Three tiny girls who adored her, an elderly woman who trumpeted her every success, a distinguished man who encouraged her—why wouldn't she want to stay? What had he ever offered that could compare?

He felt his shortcomings many times through that long afternoon. So it was with relief that he cornered her after dinner, while Joshua played checkers with the girls.

"Nicole?"

She turned, smiled at him. "Had enough, Daddy?"

The comment made him angry.

"Why do you say that? I had a great time with those girls this afternoon, even if they did chase me all over the park."

Nicole chuckled.

"I know. They never seem to stop."

"Is that why you want to stay? To see them grow up?"

A white look drained away her pleasure.

"Wh-what do you mean? We're friends and I care about them. But that's it."

He backed off. "You know, they make me think about

grandchildren. What it would be like to have grandchildren. It's not the detestable idea I'd anticipated.''

She blinked, a wariness in her eyes. "Really?"

He nodded.

"Those girls rejuvenate me, make me realize I've been stuck in a rut. The middle one, Ruthie, questions everything. I've discovered I have no answers for a lot of what I do. It's eerie."

"You do understand that I can't leave, don't you, Daddy? I couldn't just walk away. Joshua would go back to work and do himself more harm than good.''

"Perhaps." He glanced over at the doctor. "He could handle some of the work, though. Maybe see a few patients?" He saw the mutinous look flood Nicole's face and hurried on. "Just think about it. The days must be very long for him with everyone else so busy. Maybe he's even getting a little depressed that his healing isn't happening faster. Give him something to think about, and I'm guessing he'd be an easier patient.''

"He's bored. Is that what you mean?" Her eyes softened as she watched Joshua teasing Rachel. "I suppose he is. And it might help if he saw some of the regular patients, ordered a few meds, that kind of thing. Maybe for a couple of hours in the morning." Then she shook her head. "But one of the girls in the office is out sick. The others couldn't possibly manage with three doctors.''

"I'll help."

"You?"

He knew she was staring, but Shane pretended to be tying his shoe. By the time he straightened, he was certain she'd agree. Maybe by tomorrow at this time, he'd know the extent of the attraction between these two.

"I can show people into the waiting rooms, hand out

files. Maybe I'm not trained, but it looks to me like you guys could use extra help.''

''Yes, we could.'' Nicole peered up at him. ''Are you sure? You don't have to be in New York or at some board meeting?''

''I'm sure.'' He wanted to bellow his delight. For the first time in as long as he could remember, Nicole was going to let him be part of her life. He could watch her in action, gain a firsthand perspective of her work. It was more than he'd dreamed of when he'd flown here. Suddenly the surgical opening didn't seem nearly as important. There would be another one. He'd make sure of that.

For a chance to get close to his daughter, he'd do a lot more than buy her a place in some hotshot training hospital.

Chapter Thirteen

"He's like a proud peacock." Joshua's breath flickered against Nicole's hair as he stood behind her, watching Shane work his charm on the entire waiting room. "And they love it."

"Everyone loves my father." A wry grin twitched her lips as Shane gave his impersonation of a very famous politician. "He's a charmer."

"He's a hard worker. Penny says he's very efficient at weeding out the malingerers. We've gone through three times the usual number of cases, thanks to him. Talk about time management!" He grinned at her. "He could give me lessons."

"Never mind." She shook her head. "I just don't understand why he wants to do this. He's never been interested in my work before. At least, not to this extent." She turned, automatically checked Joshua's face for the usual signs of strain. Since he'd just checked his own image in the mirror, Joshua knew there was nothing for her to see.

"I think he's looking for a chance to be near you and

he'll take whatever he can get. Ruthie was right, Nicole. He does miss you.''

''Ruthie said that?'' Nicole shook her head. ''It's hard to believe. My father's always been so—''

''Involved in his own life?'' Joshua nodded. ''That's natural. Men often feel compelled to make sure their children will be taken care of if anything happens to them. That kind of thing can get carried away, make you a workaholic.''

She peered up at him.

''It sounds like you're speaking from experience.''

''You know I am.'' He shrugged. ''Perhaps that's why I can understand your father's perspective. He's finally realized what he's given up—you. The chance to see you grow, change.'' He smiled at her. ''Don't look so surprised. It is, after all, what you accused me of doing, focusing on my work to the exclusion of my kids. And you were right.''

''I was?'' Nicole swallowed, forced her brain to digest this new side of her boss. ''That's a first.''

''Cut the act. You know how self-centered I'd become. I missed out on a lot that I should have shared with the girls. I don't intend to do that again. Life is too short. You have to make every day count.''

''That sounds like it should be on one of your aunt's cookies,'' she teased.

He grinned.

''It was. I just adopted it. Why not? It's true.''

''I'm very glad to hear it. The girls love you.''

His quiet response sent her heart into overdrive.

''They love you, too, Nicole. You're a remarkable woman.'' His eyes searched hers. ''Not everyone would have sacrificed themselves the way you did, taken so much abuse, just to make me see the truth. I appreciate it. And I won't forget.''

"I didn't do anything you wouldn't have figured out for yourself. Sooner or later.'' Her eyes twinkled. "I hope.''

"It's the later that bothers me.'' He eased down into the chair, still watching her. "Once we get this epidemic under control, what will you do?''

"Move on to surgery, I suppose.'' She shrugged, pretended it didn't matter. "You'll be back full-time before too much longer. You won't need me here.''

"So you've decided to do it.''

There was something in his voice—disappointment? Nicole thrust the glimmer of hope away and told herself to deal in reality. More like delight. Joshua Darling would be glad to see the end of her. She knew that.

"It's the next logical step.''

"I thought perhaps, after your work here…'' His voice trailed away.

"What?'' She waited, but Joshua was not inclined to continue down that road.

"Very well, then.'' He stood, moved toward the door. "If you want help to go over some of the material, I'd be glad to assist. I took some surgical training myself.''

"I didn't know that.'' She stared at him, wondering what else she'd missed. "When was this?''

"Before Kyla and I married.'' A red tinge stained his cheekbones. "I was interested in the monetary side of things, and everyone knows surgeons get top dollar.''

"But marrying Kyla changed that.'' It wasn't a question. In Nicole's mind, Joshua's wife had become some kind of angel. All she'd heard of the woman told her that Kyla Darling had been perfect. At everything.

But Joshua was shaking his head.

"No. Coming back to Blessing changed that. I came to help out one summer and never left. I'm still here."

Shane stuck his head in the door, informed Joshua that he had two more patients to see before he would be escorted home. Joshua winked at Nicole, and headed for the door.

"Yes, boss," he grumbled. "On my way, boss."

After dealing with her last patient of the morning, Nicole pretended to fill out files while she mentally readjusted her picture of the small-town doctor. So Joshua had once had aspirations of his own. And they'd been altered by his experiences here in Blessing. It was surprising, yet oddly reassuring to know that they shared this common denominator.

Of course, that would be as far as it went. She couldn't stay here, even if she wanted to. Luc was here, more than pulling his weight. He'd settled in nicely and even if Joshua encouraged her to stay, which he hadn't, Nicole knew she couldn't ask Luc to uproot himself and move on. It wouldn't be fair.

"Nicole, there's a man on the phone." Shane consulted the paper in his hand. "Gray something. He says you have to get out to the Double D right away. It's an emergency."

Thank goodness Joshua had already left the office. If he'd heard Dermot De Witt was ill, he'd have insisted on treating him. And there was no way Nicole could have prepared Joshua for the shrunken, pasty man the blustering rancher had become.

"Do you realize this is the first evening in weeks that you've spent here and the phone hasn't called you away?" Joshua took in every detail of Nicole's relaxed pose in the big armchair. "You look exactly like a contented cat."

"I am. I'm toasty warm, comfortably full from that delicious dinner and just the tiniest bit drowsy." She stretched, the electric-blue velour moving with her like a second skin. "I believe I may live to see tomorrow."

"That's good. Christmas is only two weeks away." He wondered if she'd still be here then. How easy it had become to grow accustomed to having Nicole around.

The three of them, Luc, Nicole and himself, worked as a unit in the office now. Each seemed to anticipate the other and thankfully, much of their previous tensions had dissipated. Joshua enjoyed working with Luc and found him to be a great asset. But it was to Nicole that he turned to discuss a case, or just to share his ideas. She looked at things differently, and her perspective gave him a chance to reexamine his own position. Who would he share his jokes with when she left?

Shane had found himself a job at the Double D, helping with the horses. The girls spent more and more time with him, learning about ranch life firsthand. Joshua suspected there was more behind his decision to visit the ranch so often, but he didn't ask. Maybe Shane just wanted to be around—for Nicole.

"Friday nights are wonderful things," Nicole mumbled, half smothering a yawn. "It's as if, just for a tiny window of time, everything fades away and all the possibilities in life seem doable."

A loud burst of laughter from the kitchen had them both grinning.

"Your father is very good with the girls. He never talks down to them, never tries to avoid their questions. And they treat him like a grandfather." He watched the sting of red color her cheeks and wondered what caused it. "It's good for them, you know. They've only ever had Aunt Win and she's had to fill in more times than enough. Your father seems to enjoy being with them."

"Speaking of your aunt, where is she tonight?" Nicole frowned at him. "In fact, she's been conspicuously absent from your house for the past two days. Is there something you need to tell me?"

He debated the wisdom of letting the cat out of the bag, then decided it didn't matter.

"She's organizing a birthday party for your father."

"She's what?" Nicole sat up straight, all traces of sleepiness gone. "Why?"

"Why?" He stared at her. "Because the community was looking for a way to thank him for his help, because she wanted to surprise him, because it's his birthday. All of the above, and several other reasons, I suppose."

Nicole chewed her bottom lip.

"Joshua," she began, searching for her words.

He liked the fact that she'd grown so comfortable with him, he decided. The strain between them had almost vanished, except for the odd little moment when she caught him staring at her, or when he got a little too close and she backed away. That wariness was taking a long time to cure.

"Yes?" He waited for her to share her thoughts.

"I'm not sure how this will go over with him. He's not—well, let's say he doesn't respond to surprises very well."

"Really? I'd say he handled every surprise we threw at him last week with more composure than I've seen from medical people trained to handle them. He's a regular guy, Nicole. Not some god on a pedestal."

"I didn't mean that, but—regular?" Disbelief filled

her face. "My father is a regular guy?" She burst out laughing. "Hardly."

"But he is. He wants what every man wants—to see his kid happy, to make sure she's doing okay. To be there if she needs him."

"We are talking about my father?" She gaped at him in disbelief. "The same guy I haven't seen for months? The one whose motto is 'my way or the highway'?"

"You're too hard on him. Everybody messes up, wasn't that what you told me? He worries. Maybe he's a little overprotective, but—"

"Maybe?" She stared at him, her forehead furrowed. "Like maybe the Pacific is a big lake? What planet are you on, Dr. Darling? I've known the man for my entire life. He charms when he needs to, gets what he wants, then he walks away. That's the way he's made his fortune. It's no different in our relationship."

Why did she refuse to see the truth? Joshua held his temper in check.

"Yes, it is different, and you know it. He isn't here to manipulate you. He thinks you truly want surgery and he's determined to get it for you."

"By pushing me into it?" She shook her head. "That's not love."

Intent on making her see the truth, Joshua got up and moved to stand in front of her. But it was awkward peering down on the top of her head, so he manipulated himself until he was sitting on the footstool in front of her.

"Of course it's love. What do you think brought him here, made him stay when he could have been much more comfortable in a big hotel in the city?" He lowered his voice, his heart aching at the sadness on her face. "Shane loves you, Nici. Just as you love him. The two of you just aren't very good at showing each other."

"If he does love me, it's only because he sees me as some kind of reflection of my mother. That's why he wants me to get into that training. It was what she wanted and he couldn't get it for her. It was the one thing he couldn't manipulate." She blinked at him, diamond teardrops hanging on the ends of her silver lashes. "But I can't be my mother, Joshua. I'm me. I can't pretend anymore."

The words rushed out on a sob of pain.

"Why can't he love me as I am? Why do I have to be a mirror image of her?"

"Oh, Nicole." Seeing her so distressed hurt. Would she let him touch her? Praying for direction, Joshua reached out and gathered her shaking body into his arms. He murmured something nonsensical, one hand smoothing over her gilt hair.

"What's wrong with me, Joshua?"

Her tears were soaking the front of his shirt, but at that moment Joshua couldn't have cared less. Pain and pleasure combined as he held her and prayed for the right words to ease her hurt.

"Nothing's wrong with you. You're smart and efficient, a great doctor. You care about people and you do your best to help them. There's nothing wrong with you, Nici."

"Then why can't he love me?" Her arms were around his back, holding on as if he were her lifeline.

Joshua tilted her head back, stared into her eyes and spoke the truth as he knew it.

"Your father does love you, Nici." He brushed away a tear. "Anyone who sees him watching you knows that. He loves you very much."

"He's right."

Shane's quiet voice almost made Joshua pull back. But

Nicole didn't ease away. If anything, her grip tightened, as if she needed his strength. He gave it gladly.

"I do love you, Nicole." Shane's voice wobbled, but he kept speaking. "I love you more than anything in this world. You're my entire life. I only want the very best for you." He hunkered down beside them, his eyes riveted on hers. "I want to protect you and comfort you. I want to give you only good things. Most of all, I want you to be happy."

"Oh."

Nicole snuffled the word against Joshua's shoulder. He smiled at the little-girl sound and shifted, trying to give father and daughter space. But still she clung to him. So he held her as she listened to her father's explanations.

"Nicole, it's true that after your mother died, I was devastated. I'd loved her dearly and it hurt terribly to lose her. I felt guilty that she hadn't achieved her dream. It was my fault, I know. I channeled everything we owned into the business. I was too self-centered to even consider that we didn't have forever. Then she was gone and I never got a second chance."

The tremor was back in his voice, but Shane didn't give up. His face grew even more intent as he tried to explain his decisions to the girl who thought she had to earn his love.

"But that didn't mean I loved you less, Nicole. You were all I had left of her and I couldn't bear to think that anything I might do would cause you pain. I knew you weren't happy at home and I thought being with other children would be good for you." His eyes grew moist with the memories. "I spent months planning our Christmases. I had lists of things we were going to do together. But that first time you came home and hid in your room, I believed the memories were too much, that you were still angry at me for denying your mother her dream. Then you stopped coming home.''

"I wasn't angry. I thought you sent me away because I reminded you of her. I thought you couldn't stand to look at me and know she was gone." Nicole's tears tumbled down her cheeks. "I didn't know about your plans, Daddy. If only I'd known."

"They don't matter, Nicole. That's in the past. But I think it's time we got it all out so we can face the future.''

Joshua sat silent, watched the hope flicker across her father's face and knew how much it cost him to ask the next question.

"Did you go into medicine because you thought I wanted it? Did I pressure you into that?" Shane's vivid green gaze, sharp jade shards, probed for the truth.

Joshua was certain his business partners must hate that look. It did away with pretense, probed and dug until the truth must come out.

"Answer me, Nicole."

She blinked at the steel in his voice.

"I don't know when I decided to be a doctor, Daddy. I loved going with her to the clinics." The green irises grew cloudy as she remembered. "I loved the way those people looked at her when she made them better. I wanted to be looked at like that. I wanted to have the power to make a difference, just as she did. I chose it to be able to help."

"And now? Is medicine still what you want?"

The tension in Shane's face was evident. He needed to know that he hadn't done more damage. For his sake, Joshua hoped Nicole could ease his mind. Trying to infuse some of his strength into her, he brushed a hand down her back, felt the tremor of nerves that had been stretched too long.

"Is being a doctor what you want, honey?"

"Oh, yes." Her face shone as she spoke, eyes clear now, glittering with animation. "To be able to help fix things, to make the pain go away—it's what I always dreamed of, Daddy." Her hands fluttered between them as she tried to express herself. "To be able to practice here has been wonderful. I love it here. Everyone knows everyone else in Blessing. It's like a big extended family." Suddenly she stole a glance at Joshua, and the words died away. She edged out of his embrace, leaned back in her chair, away from him.

With a pang of regret, Joshua let her go. So she'd reverted into her shell again. Drawn away. Why was that? She said she liked it here, and she didn't sound anxious to leave. So what was the problem? Why didn't she offer to stay?

Frustration nipped at him, but he refused to indulge. Father and daughter needed this time to hash things out. It wasn't the moment to horn in and selfishly demand a response from her that she wasn't prepared to give.

Reluctantly he admitted the truth. He'd done what he could to help them mend the breach, but the simple truth was, Nicole was still afraid. Of him, of closeness—he wasn't sure which. And it really didn't matter, because sooner or later she'd leave. There was nothing to hold her here, especially now that she and her father had begun to come to terms with their past.

"And the training?" Shane was relentless in his pursuit of the truth. "Is it true that I've pushed you into that?" He scratched his head. "I haven't meant to. I thought it was important to you and I didn't want you to get sidetracked and then regret not following through."

His voice dropped. "That was my one sorrow with your mother. If we hadn't married so soon, if I'd just waited to expand my work, then maybe she'd have found a way to finish her training. Heaven knows, I was no help to her."

Nicole reached out and squeezed his big hand. Joshua gulped at the sight of this delicate woman comforting her father—a man who'd lost the woman he loved, then missed out on his own daughter's childhood.

"It's okay, Daddy. Mom wouldn't have regretted a thing. She was doing what she loved."

He glanced up at her, pressed a kiss against her forehead. "Thanks."

"You're welcome." They stared at each other for a moment, then Nicole leaned into her father's embrace, sighing as his arms drew her close.

Joshua was in the way. They should be alone—they needed privacy. But his crutches were on the floor behind Shane and he couldn't reach them. So he sat silent. Watching.

Finally Shane drew back, a sheen of moisture covering his cheeks.

"Honey, if surgery isn't what you want, don't do it. I don't need you to prove anything to me. I love you as you are. I don't care if you go or not, only that you get what you want. You're already a great doctor. I've seen that with my own eyes. Whether or not you continue— it's your decision."

"I know it is." Nicole sat back in her chair, wiped her face with her father's handkerchief. "You did push, just a little." She grinned at him. "But I guess fathers are allowed. Don't worry, I'll make my choice. Soon. But not until after Christmas. Okay?"

Shane nodded. "It's up to you."

"I can't explain it. I just have to pray about it some more. I have to be very sure before I take the next step."

Did she glance at him? Joshua frowned, unable to imagine what part he had to play in this, other than as a sounding board.

"Take all the time you need, Nici. I'll be around. You can count on that." Shane brushed her cheek with his hand, then turned to get up. His glance homed in on Joshua. "Young man, you look very uncomfortable. Is something wrong?"

"It's just—I need my crutches."

Shane glanced around, found them and handed them to him.

"Sorry. Must have kicked them there." He watched Joshua stand up, then grinned. "Looks like you need a new shirt. My daughter bawled all over that one."

"Daddy!" The daughter in question blushed a very bright pink.

"Well, you did. Still, I expect it was worth it."

Whatever that meant. Joshua frowned, then turned to look at Nicole, hoping he'd find the key to understanding the interplay between father and daughter. But her face was tilted down and her eyes wouldn't meet his. He shrugged. Sometimes escape was the better part of valor.

"I'll go change. I would have left earlier, but—"

They weren't paying any attention to him. Shane, one hand on his daughter's shoulder, kissed her gently, said good-night, then let himself out. Nicole stayed where she was, frowning after him, a curious glint in her eyes as if she couldn't fit together all the pieces of a puzzle.

Leave it to Aunt Win to burst through the front door, her face alight with pleasure.

"It's all set, my dears. Tomorrow evening in the church hall. All we have to do is get him there."

Considering the work the town, and especially Aunt Winifred, had put into this birthday celebration, Joshua sincerely hoped that the trepidation on Nicole's face was misplaced. But some electronic transmission snapping in his brain told him that a whole lot more was going on with Dr. Nicole Brandt than simply worry about her father's reaction to a birthday party.

Otherwise, why did she keep staring at him, as if she were waiting for…something?

Chapter Fourteen

"I think you can stop worrying now. Your father's having a ball."

Nicole's fingers automatically tightened around the plate of birthday cake that she'd been passing around.

"What makes you think I'm worrying, Joshua?"

"These." He lifted his fingers, brushed them over the furrows lining her forehead. "He's a hit, Nici. Everybody loves him. He's one of their own now. Probably because he's your father, but whatever the reason, Shane Brandt is doing just fine with the locals."

She laughed.

"They do seem to go all out to welcome you, don't they? Winifred's cake message was certainly appropriate, don't you think? 'Compromise: the art of dividing a cake so everybody thinks he got the biggest piece.'" She grinned. "I thought she was limited to those cookies, but it seems your aunt has a saying for everything."

"It fits the occasion, though. Your father's compromise in coming to town has reaped big rewards." He stood there studying her for several moments.

She knew what was coming.

"Have you made up your mind yet?"

"I've hardly had time." Why did he keep asking? Didn't he want her to spend Christmas here? "You have to admit that things have been a little hectic."

"Understatement. You're getting good at that." He seemed about to say something else, but Rosie came running up and involved him in tying her shoe.

Nicole took the opportunity to move away, passing the cake as she tried to savor the memory of this night, burn it into her brain. If only Joshua could care for her, if only he understood how much it meant to her that she finally fitted in, was part of this town. That she wanted to be part of his work, of his life. Surely he must know how much she loved the girls?

"Come along, Dr. Nici. We've been waiting for a piece of that." Dermot De Witt beckoned her over, his looks much improved after the shot she'd administered this afternoon. "Your father is quite a man. We're glad to have him here."

"He wants you to raise some horses for him, Dermot. He's very interested in the breeding you do. And the girls have loved visiting your place." Dermot seemed more lively, she decided. The change in medication was working, though very slowly. If only he weren't so worried about whatever he was worried about. She'd tried to probe, but he refused to tell her what was causing the stress in his life.

"They're welcome anytime. I'd like to have some time with your dad, one-on-one, though. He's a whiz when it comes to financial things. Might give him a problem to chew on." Dermot licked the icing off his finger, his eyes focused across the room. "Maybe he can find a solution for me." He wandered away.

Gray MacGonigle accepted a piece of cake, also. But though his attention was focused on Dermot, he never said a word when the man walked directly in front of him. There was something going on between them. Nicole didn't know what, and really, it was none of her business. But it bothered her just the same.

Shrugging, she turned, then noticed Millicent Maple squished onto a bench just inside the doorway leading to the hall and the church offices.

"Did you get some cake, Millicent?" she asked, then held out the plate. "It's very good."

"Don't eat much refined sugar or white flour. Not good for the system." Still, she took the largest piece on the plate. "Can you wait here a minute? I want to give this to Candy. Then mebbe I'll try it meself."

Knowing that her dog was the closest thing to Millicent's heart, Nicole nodded and stepped backward into the hall, out of the line of traffic, while she waited for the woman to return from outside. She scanned the crowd, looking for her father, but didn't see him immediately. Then his familiar voice rumbled through the echoing hall behind her, followed by Joshua's quiet response. They must be in the pastor's office. She edged farther into the hall.

"She'll be going soon, Shane, and I can't put off finding a replacement. She's had to stick around here long enough. I don't want to hold her up. I know that surgical opening has been on her mind."

"Has she said that?"

No! Nicole wanted to yell. She'd said nothing about the opening to Joshua because she didn't want to contemplate leaving him or the girls. The past few weeks she'd begun to wonder if perhaps he might be growing fond of her. There was no sign of fondness in his voice now.

"Didn't need to tell me. She's preparing for it, Shane. Every spare minute she gets, she's into the texts, trying to bone up." His voice changed, hardened. "I've got to start looking for someone permanent. I want to be prepared when she gives notice. I don't want her hanging around here out of some duty or obligation. I need a partner who—"

"Ah, yes. Your perfect partner. I think Nici mentioned that."

There was a hint of laughter in her father's voice. But Nicole didn't share it. Her brain got stuck on one thing. Joshua wanted her gone. He was getting ready to take up the reins of his life and he didn't need her hanging around anymore. Or he wouldn't, as soon as he found someone to replace her.

"What about Luc?"

She'd wondered the same thing.

"I talked to him. In my books he's a welcome addition, but Luc says he's not ready to commit to a partnership yet. And I'm not sure how quickly I'll get back to full gear. I'm happy to have him as long as he wants, but if I can find someone who's committed to the work, I'll hire him immediately."

Choose me! Nicole wanted to holler. *I'm committed. Haven't I proven that over and over?*

But it was clear that Joshua Darling did not consider her in that light. She was simply a temporary doctor. Obviously he didn't see her as that perfect partner he was looking for. The knowledge seared straight to her soul. Her heart ached as she accepted the truth.

She loved Joshua, loved the girls, loved Blessing. She'd tried to follow the path God had set her upon. But she'd obviously made a mistake somewhere in believing that she might remain here, might find stability and peace with the one man she could imagine spending her future beside. As she watched Millicent stagger out of the swirling snow and in through the back door, Nicole knew what to do.

Blessing had been only a temporary stopping point. She'd been blessed here, learned to love as she'd never believed she could, enjoyed three little girls and a community that gave far more than it took. Here, in Blessing, her father and his love had been restored to her. But the one thing she'd hoped for more than any other simply hadn't happened. Joshua didn't want her to stay.

It was time to leave.

"Candy sure loves that stuff. I'll taste a bit, if you don't mind. Might as well see what all the fuss is about." Millicent took the square of cake and nibbled at a corner. Her beady brown eyes peered into Nicole's. "You hanging around Blessing a while longer, Doc?"

There was no time like the present.

"Just until after Christmas. By then Dr. Darling should be well enough to resume most of his duties. Perhaps he'll have a partner by then." She smiled, edged away. "I guess I'd better get passing around this cake. Take care, Millicent."

"Not me who needs the caring," the old lady muttered, her face drawn into a scowl. "It's that doctor. He needs—" She shook her head. "Winifred will know what to do about him."

Nicole left her muttering to herself and hurried back to the kitchen. Years of strict discipline at hiding her feelings allowed her to get through the next half hour. By the time her father made his speech of thanks and shook hands with almost everyone present, she was more than ready to leave.

Snowflakes drifted down from a darkened sky as they trudged back to Miss Winifred's. True to form, Shane had rented a hotel room, but Nicole had remained at the baker's house. It seemed like home. Now she'd have to leave home. Again.

"Daddy?"

"Uh-huh." He grinned down at her, obviously content with his world.

"I want you to contact your insider and see if you can get me into the program in January."

"What?" He jerked to a stop, his hand on hers halting her progress, as well. "Why? Why now?"

"It's time," she murmured, swallowing back the tears.

"But you love it here. And the people love you. I've seen the look on your face when you're up to your neck in patients, Nicole. You love the people in this town."

"Yes, I do." She shuffled her feet in the white powdery fluff barely covering the ground and wondered why winter had waited so long to make an appearance. Hopefully the snow would stay. The girls wanted a white Christmas.

"Then why leave?" He stared at her for a long time, saw the determination in her eyes and sighed. "Have you told Joshua?"

"I'll tell him tomorrow. I'd like to give him a specific date for my departure, so the sooner we can nail that surgical placement down, the better."

"I'll make some phone calls in the morning." Shane's step had lost some of its zip. He walked slowly beside her, climbed the steps and waited as she unlocked the front door.

"Good night, Daddy." She brushed her lips against

his cheek, relishing the closeness they'd finally achieved. "Sleep well."

"You, too," he murmured absently. "Nicole, are you sure this is what you want?"

No, she wanted to shout. *It's not what I want at all.*

"I thought you'd appreciate my decision. You seemed to want it before." She forced herself to keep out the bitterness. It wasn't his fault Joshua didn't care.

"I want whatever you want, honey. If surgery will make you happy, then I'm all for it. I just want you to be certain. There's no need to rush into anything."

"I know." She faked a yawn. "I'm tired, Daddy. I'll see you tomorrow."

"Yes, you will. We're taking those little pixies for a sleigh ride after church, remember?" He grinned, rubbed his hands together. "It's a while since I was around a little girl, but I'm revising some of those plans I made years ago. It's going to be a fun Christmas, isn't it, Nici?"

She nodded, forced a smile, while her heart ached for the one gift she would not receive.

"Think it over, sweetheart. Don't make your decisions too quickly. After all, there's no rush." He brushed his lips over the top of her head, then turned, stomped down the steps and with his long-legged power stride he was soon disappearing around the corner.

Back to the church, no doubt. Maybe he'd take Dermot home and they'd have that discussion. Shane was thrilled that Blessing folks didn't seem to care a whit that he had tons of money, loads of influence and a bark meant to scare people away. As they'd done with her, they simply scooped him up and included him as one of them. He seemed to delight in the friendships he'd made here. For a moment Nicole wondered if he'd leave when she did.

But it didn't matter. Not really. She could be here or a thousand miles away. Her heart would still do that little two-step whenever she thought of Joshua.

She'd have to learn to get over that.

"You have to do something, Aunt Win!"

"I do?" Winifred Blessing stared at her nephew in surprise.

"Yes. You made no bones about trying to pair us up when she first came here. Now she's ready to leave the moment Christmas is over and you're not doing a thing." Sick of the ever-present crutches, Joshua dropped them over the sofa and called up every morsel of strength to walk on his own. "Look at me! I can barely toddle over to a chair and she's hightailing it out of here."

"You don't think Nicole will make a good surgeon?" Winifred calmly sipped her tea, her eyes wide, thoughtful. "I think she's most competent."

"Of course she's competent. Why do you think I hired her?" What was wrong with the women in his life? he wondered. First Nicole, up and resigning like that, before she'd even gone in to work this morning. And now his aunt, acting as if she *wanted* the woman to leave. "I have no doubt she'll make a fine surgeon."

"Then what is the problem, nephew? You seem to be managing fairly well. Nicole has Christmas in the Darling household well organized, Mrs. Tyndall has everything else under control. You haven't had to exert a muscle or put yourself out one iota. Except to write out the checks." She tilted one eyebrow at him. "I don't think you have grounds to complain, Joshua."

"I'm not complaining." Yes, he was. "I'm just saying that I'm not yet one hundred percent. I'm getting better with the morning clinics, but I'm not strong enough to handle a full day." Like today. He'd had to leave at noon before he could speak to Nicole again. It was leave gracefully or fall down.

"You're healing more every day. Besides, once she's gone, you can change things back to the way you like them. I should think you'd be glad."

Joshua stared at her. For the first time in her life, Winifred Blessing wasn't making sense.

"I don't want to change anything," he muttered, teeth clenched at her unreasonable behavior.

"What was that, dear?"

"I said I don't want to change anything. We work well together. Our styles complement each other. We've built up a trust. It's going to be hard to find that with someone else." He would never do it. There couldn't be anyone who could take Nicole's place. Her smile, that quirky way she had of holding her head and eyeballing him, her faith and encouragement—how could he hope to find another partner like that?

"Joshua, I'm beginning to think you don't want Nicole to leave." Winifred set down her teacup and fixed him with her sternest look. "Am I right?"

He glared at her and his mouth dropped open in protest, then closed as the truth of her words hit home.

"I—I—" He sank into a chair, dropped his head into his hands and sighed. "I can't ask her to stay, Aunt Win. Not now. Not when she's on the verge of achieving a dream. It wouldn't be fair."

"Oh?" Winifred resumed her tea sipping. "Are you certain you know what Nicole's dreams are?"

He nodded. They'd talked about it one night, after she and her father had reconciled.

"She told me that since the pressure was off, when her father stopped bullying and let her decide for herself, she wasn't at all opposed to the training. Her resentment stemmed from his insistence that she do it on his time-table.'' He thought about her words that morning and felt the frustration rise again. ''And if I had any doubts, she made things pretty clear this morning.''

''Really?'' Winifred nodded. ''I'm listening.''

''She said that it was time she got on with her life and that she'd be leaving in January. She said she felt as if she'd put things on hold when she came here and that it was time to move on. She was glad she'd been able to help out and enjoyed meeting the townsfolk, et cetera, et cetera.'' He frowned. ''I didn't hear most of the rest of it.''

''I wonder if you heard any of it.''

''Pardon?'' What on earth was wrong with the woman? Hadn't he just repeated Nicole's words?

''Sometimes, in the course of your life, you are given an opportunity to change your future. You've been granted that opportunity, Joshua. The accident forced you to rethink your life, to reevaluate your priorities and make some changes. You've done very well. The girls know you love them and feel confident that they can come to you at any time.'' Winifred set her cup down, then stood. She stared down at him for several moments before she spoke again.

''Your little girls will grow up and leave home, Joshua. They'll build careers of their own, start families, mold lives that don't center around you. Someday you'll retire from medicine. Then what?''

His mind followed her words, picturing each stage as she mentioned it. But when it came to retirement, it blanked and he could see nothing but long empty spaces of time. Alone.

Winifred bent, brushed her lips against his cheek and patted his head.

"Think carefully, Joshua. Will that life be enough for you? Or will you wish you'd taken a risk, gone for something more? Your life was cold and narrow after Kyla died because you made it that way. Now you have the chance to fill it with love and generosity and caring. Think about the future before you, and make your decision carefully. Perhaps this will help."

From beside her chair, Winifred lifted a small white box. He knew immediately that it contained one of her love cookies and almost groaned aloud. He didn't need advice now. He needed help, wisdom, action. But Aunt Win prided herself on her "messages from God." She would be hurt if he didn't accept this one.

"Thanks," he mumbled, taking the box and resting it in his lap.

"I'll be praying, Joshua." She walked toward the foyer, tugging on her coat as she went.

Joshua thought he was alone, but Winifred returned just for a minute. Her face was impassive, her words quiet.

"Not all risk is bad, Joshua. Your parents took risks all the time."

"And ended up drowning at sea." This was one argument she wouldn't win.

Winifred smiled.

"Would you rather they'd never known the joys sailing gave them? If they'd stayed here, never ventured out, would that have made their deaths more meaningful for you?" Her bright eyes blazed with an inner fire before she turned on her heel and left the house.

Joshua stayed where he was, his mind twisting and

turning with questions. What did his parents and sailing have to do with Nicole leaving?

The small white box begged to be opened. He lifted the lid and glanced down at the fine red icing script. Another message.

"Don't listen to what is said, but to what is meant."

He puzzled over those words for a long time, until a light suddenly illuminated the puzzle of his aunt's words.

At that precise moment the telephone rang.

"Joshua, it's Nicole. I've sent someone to bring you to the hospital immediately. It's Dermot. As you suspected, the treatments have lost their potency. He's losing ground fast. He doesn't have long."

"I'm coming."

Joshua hung up the phone, grabbed for his crutches and tried to stand, all at the same moment. The white box with the cookie inside dropped to the floor. The delicate dough shattered into a thousand pieces, the words disintegrating into bits of red that meant nothing.

Was that a symbol of what his life would be if he didn't take matters in hand?

Please, God, help me know the way You want me to go.

The doorbell rang. He gathered his courage and walked toward it. Right now a patient needed him and he intended to be there for Dermot. But somehow he'd find a quiet moment to talk to Nicole, to learn for himself just how much she wanted to be a surgeon.

"Get Dani."

Nicole pressed her palm against the white forehead and tried to soothe him as he called for his daughter.

"We're trying, Dermot. You just relax." His jagged breathing told her the pain was getting worse and she nodded at the nurse to inject the second morphine shot into his IV bag. "Dr. Darling will be here in a minute."

Relief swamped her when Joshua actually walked through the door. She scanned his features with a loving eye, aware that only a few hours ago he'd been furious at her resignation.

But something had changed. His eyes were clear, his smile without malice. He seemed genuinely glad to see her.

"Nici." The name was almost a caress. "How is he?"

She shook her head and handed him the chart. He scanned it, then laid it and his crutches aside to lean over his longtime patient.

"Dermot, it's Joshua."

Weary eyelids flickered upward. The trace of a smile lit the gray, pain-filled features.

"Finally."

"Well, don't make it sound like I was sunning myself on a beach, man. It takes me a little longer to get around these days, remember."

With the faintest nod, Dermot showed his understanding.

"Something to tell you," he whispered.

Nicole saw Joshua turn, looking for the oxygen mask.

"He won't use it. He insists on saying whatever's on his mind."

"Okay." He reached out to squeeze her hand. "We'll let him do this his way."

She nodded her understanding. No unnecessary measures. She knew the drill, knew how adamant Dermot had been on that point. Still, it was hard to watch him labor over the words, fighting to say...what?

"Don't...waste time. Too short." His eyes were open

now, their scrutiny intense. "Live every day." He panted for enough breath to continue.

"It's okay. Take it easy. We're here. We'll listen." Joshua glanced at her, asking for her agreement.

Nicole nodded.

"Whenever you're ready, we're listening." He dragged a chair near the bed and sat down.

"Wasted too much time on the ranch. Not enough time on Dani."

"Dani loves you," Joshua murmured. "You know that."

"Should have told her the truth. Most wonderful daughter a man could have." Dermot closed his eyes, wheezed for several long moments.

"Maybe—" Nicole caught her breath at Joshua's look and fell silent.

"Should have let Dani help me. So many problems. But the land's hers. Can't take that away. Fancy Dancer settled that." Dermot closed his eyes, regrouped. After several moments had passed, his breathing seemed to drop into a steady, even rhythm that told them he was unconscious.

"Poor guy, he's been fussing about that ranch for so long." Joshua lifted the weathered hand into his, squeezed it. "I should have been there for him. He was the first friend I made in this town and he's stuck by me like glue, no matter how many mistakes I've made. Some friend I am. I didn't even know he had a horse called Fancy Dancer."

She'd never seen him so emotional over a patient. Not wanting to disturb him, she stood and silently watched him wait for death to claim a man he cared for.

"Go home, Nici," he whispered a long while later. "There's nothing you can do here."

"But what about you?"

She saw him shake his head, saw the faint, sad smile that tilted his mouth.

"I'll stay," he whispered. "I owe him at least that much." He glanced up at her. "You've been running on overdrive for a long time. Go home and get some rest. Let me shoulder some of the burden. It's about time I did."

"If that's what you want." The words crushed her. He didn't even want her here, beside him, when he lost his friend. It was clear that she had no place in Joshua's life. He didn't want her.

She slipped from the room, strode down the hall to the doctor's lounge. Winifred came scurrying toward her.

"Oh, Nicole, I'm so glad to see you. This has been the worst day."

"What's wrong, Miss Blessing?" She stretched her neck tiredly and waited.

"It's those blasted ovens. They failed again and I had to wait for the gas man. Now I've got a hundred pumpkin pies waiting to be baked to go with the Christmas baskets. I can't possibly sit in for Mrs. Tyndall tonight."

"I'll go. Don't give it another thought." It would be her last really private time with the girls, a time to remember, to hide away in her heart and take out in the bleak lonely months ahead.

"You're so kind. I just knew you'd help out." Winifred frowned as she caught a glance at Nicole's face. "Why, my dear, whatever is wrong?"

"Dermot De Witt. I'm afraid he's very ill. Joshua is sitting with him until the daughter arrives. I just hope she makes it in time."

"Dermot?" Winifred shook her head. "Oh, no. He and Joshua are so close. I hope—"

"You go check on him, if you like, Miss Blessing. I'll go to the girls."

"You do that, dear. It might be your last chance, since you're leaving so soon. You are still leaving, aren't you? You haven't changed your mind?" Why was Winifred suddenly so curious?

"No, I haven't changed my mind." *I don't have any reason to.*

Miss Winifred got that chagrined look she sometimes wore when things weren't moving as she wished.

"I see. Well, I must go to Dermot. See you later, dear."

Nicole was delayed at the hospital by two emergencies, so it was well after eight by the time she arrived at the Darling home. Mrs. Tyndall was bundled up, ready to leave. The girls were in their pajamas, sprawled on the floor, playing Chutes and Ladders.

"Hi, Nici." Ruthie rushed over and hugged her around the waist. "Want to play?"

The others looked at her expectantly, but Nicole shook her head.

"I'm sorry, girls, but tonight I'm just too tired. I'll just sit here and watch."

"Not these three, you won't. It's bedtime." Mrs. Tyndall ordered them all upstairs and would leave only after they'd obeyed. "I never do like to be early for the ladies' meeting," she explained. "Too much gossiping."

Twenty minutes later the house was completely quiet. Nicole wandered from room to room on the main floor, gathering memories and storing them deep inside her heart. When they became too much, she grabbed one of the surgical texts from her bag, flopped onto the sofa and began reading. But the weariness of her soul, the tiredness of her body and the grief in her heart combined, making it almost impossible to concentrate.

And yet she had to. In less than one month she'd be up to her neck in this stuff. It was better to be prepared.

A rueful smile flickered across her mouth.

Too bad she hadn't thought of that before falling in love with Joshua Darling.

Chapter Fifteen

Joshua let himself in the front door as quietly as he could, given the thud of his crutches. Once he'd divested himself of his coat and gloves, he checked the house—first the kitchen, then the den. He found Nicole in the living room, sprawled across the sofa, a huge medical tome lying across her stomach.

What would it be like to come home to her every night? To share the quiet moments after the girls were sleeping, to plot birthdays and plan Christmas gifts in front of the fire? What would it be like to know she'd never go away?

He had to find out. It didn't matter that he was going out on a limb, didn't matter that she might care nothing at all for him. Joshua knew he loved her with a sure steady fire that wasn't going to flicker and wane just because she wasn't here. It would take an eternity for this love to die.

He wanted her to be happy, oh, yes, he did. But couldn't she be happy with him and the girls? Hadn't she been happy when they'd decorated the Christmas tree?

Hadn't she laughed right along with him at the girls' school play? Hadn't she been there through all the tough parts of his recovery?

She couldn't leave now. Not until he knew for certain that there was no hope for him. Winifred's cookie had intimated something. Joshua believed his aunt's message was meant to tell him that Nicole had upped the date of her departure in the hope that he would act. He still wasn't entirely sure Winifred was right, but he did intend to find out. Now.

"Nicole?" He lifted the book and set it aside. Still her chest moved in that same rhythmic pattern, and her eyelids never wavered. "Nici?"

Easing onto his knees, Joshua set his crutches out of the way and concentrated on her, here, in his home. He brushed his fingers through her soft, silky hair the way he'd longed to so many times over past weeks. She was gorgeous. What did his Nicole need of makeup and haute couture? Dressed in ratty sweats and a bulky sweater, her face tearstained, she was the most beautiful sight in the world.

He'd tried to talk to her so many times, to feel her out, to discern her thoughts. But she'd brushed aside his reminders of how well they worked together, ignored his hints about the future. Again and again she'd pretended she didn't hear him. Well, she couldn't pretend now.

"Nicole. Wake up."

She blinked, her green eyes dark and shimmering, as if she'd just emerged from some fairy tale. A funny little smile wobbled to her lips and danced there.

"Joshua," she whispered.

The gladness he read in her eyes—that was what did it.

Joshua leaned down, pressed his lips against hers and

kissed her as he'd longed to. To his absolute delight, her arms fluttered around his neck and settled there as she held him close, returning his embrace wholeheartedly.

Certain she'd listen to him now, Joshua dotted tiny kisses along her jaw. Nicole arched her neck, then directed his lips back to hers. A second later he heard the words he was waiting for.

"I love you, Dr. Darling."

"Oh, Nici." Delighted by her confession, he slid his arms under her supine body and gathered her to him, burying his face in her hair.

It was the wrong move.

For three seconds she froze, her shocked eyes wide. Then she jerked up from the sofa, away from him.

"Nicole, I—"

"I have to go now. There's a lot to do before I leave. I've moved the date up. I'll still be here for Christmas, but I'm leaving the following day. I have to get back to Boston. I'm anxious to get started on my new career."

A hiccup on the last word marred the jovial voice she employed. He thought he saw a tiny tear escape, and he struggled to find his crutches and get out of his awkward position.

"I've enjoyed my time here, but Blessing was only ever a temporary stop for me. You've improved so much. It's time for me to get on with my plans."

"But Nicole, you said—"

"You were right, you know." She searched the room for her jacket, found it and thrust in her arms. "I'm not the right doctor for Blessing. Lucas is far better at running things your way. I'm sure he'll make the perfect partner, but if not, there are plenty of candidates. It's just a matter of deciding on one." Out of breath and red cheeked, she stopped, but only for a moment. "I'm sorry about Dermot. He was a nice man. Goodbye."

Stunned by her words, Joshua wasted valuable moments. Before he could maneuver his way across the room, she was out the door. It thudded closed, echoing the emptiness he felt.

Not what she says, what she means.

The thoughts from Aunt Win's latest love cookie echoed in his mind. Then he heard Nicole's words again. *Plenty of candidates. Not the right doctor.*

Could it be that self-assured, big-city rich girl Nicole Brandt was afraid? Did she think he wanted her to stay only because of the clinic? Or as some kind of mother substitute for the girls? Had he ever done anything to make her believe that he needed her in his life because she was the only one who could fill the void?

The answer kept him from following her.

He'd done nothing. Oh, he had used her, abominably at first, and shamefully after the accident. He'd impinged upon her good nature, her selflessness, her rigid adherence to duty and her genuine love for the girls. But he'd given nothing back, nothing to earn the love she'd freely given.

Was it any wonder Nicole was afraid to trust that he might want her for something more than her medical ability?

He'd been so eager to have control of his life, so determined to keep things on track, make sure life went exactly the way he wanted. The very idea was laughable. Life sure wasn't moving in the direction he'd hoped. He wasn't even in control of his own heart! In one fell swoop, that slim blond doctor had laid bare his pathetically selfish life and shown him how needy he truly was. His head dropped to his chest.

"Okay, God. I finally, *finally* get the point. Not my way, Your way. So be it. I believe You sent her here for a reason. I believe You've given me a gift beyond anything I could ever deserve. I promise You'll be the center of my life."

It felt good to say it, to give up and let go. But what came next?

He closed his eyes again, thought of Dermot and his words about grabbing life. *Don't waste time. Live every day.*

Good advice. Words to live by. But how? Once more he bowed his head.

"Please help."

Christmas Eve.

Nicole dreaded the evening ahead of her. Not that she wanted to be anywhere else. She didn't. But it was painful to go through the motions knowing that Blessing, the girls, Winifred, Joshua would all be a part of her past very soon.

She'd made it through the day by working flat out, clearing up every odd and end she could think of to make things easier for Joshua. He'd been in and out of the office all day. She assumed he was still trying to contact Dermot's daughter, Dani. In a way, Nicole hoped the girl spent a happy Christmas before she learned of her father's death. There was nothing she could do for him now.

"Your father's here, Nicole," Winifred murmured after tapping lightly on the door of her room. "You'll have to get going if you want a good seat. The church is always full on this night."

Nicole opened the door, smiled at her hostess and preceded her down the stairs. She had dressed up for a change. The black velvet was warm without being heavy. Black stockings and heels were probably a little formal for Christmas Eve in Blessing, as were her diamond earrings, but she didn't care. She would leave them all with a good memory. Because she'd told only Joshua and her father that she was leaving the day after tomorrow, no one would speculate on why she'd chosen to dress up tonight. Just the Christmas spirit at work, they'd say.

"Are you ready, honey?" Shane brushed his lips against her cheek. "You look beautiful."

"Thanks, Daddy."

They offered Miss Winifred a ride, but she had her own transportation and would see them at the church. Once they arrived, Shane helped her with her coat, then disappeared. He returned with the three Darling girls in tow.

"Hope you don't mind. You and I are in charge tonight."

It was on the tip of her tongue to ask about Joshua, but Nicole turned her attention to the girls, complimenting them on their matching red velvet dresses and white satin sashes.

"Daddy's coming," Ruthie told her. "He's just taking an extra long time. He's got stuff to do."

"Yeah, stuff," Rosie agreed.

Rachel intervened and all three rehearsed their parts in the program. The entire service went off without a hitch. The girls performed beautifully. It was almost too much for Nicole. Christmas had never been more meaningful, more perfect. She steeled herself to keep her emotions in check and tried to worship as best she could.

When the last note of "Silent Night" had died away, the congregation began to wish each other a Merry

Christmas. Nicole murmured the words over and over, trying to store a memory of each dear face.

"My dear, I've a bit of a favor to ask you. I've prepared a special treat for Christmas dinner tomorrow. I promised Joshua I wouldn't forget and I've gone and left the thing at the bakery. I wonder if you and your father would give me a ride there."

Nicole stared at her. "But you brought your own car, remember?"

Winifred frowned. "No, dear. I caught a ride with Furly. We sang carols all the way here. But she's taking Millicent home. I don't want to intrude."

Uncertain she'd heard correctly, Nicole tried to puzzle it out, then gave up. What difference did it make?

"I'm sure we can give you a ride," she agreed. "I'm just wondering who will take care of the girls. I haven't seen Joshua all evening and they'll need to get home."

"All taken care of, honey. Now, shall we go?" Shane held her coat ready, his smile wide.

"Er, yes. Of course." She slid her arms into the sleeves, threaded her scarf around her neck and fastened the buttons. "I'm ready." She wanted to ask about Joshua, about his daughters, but that was asking for pain. She kept her lips clamped together.

The night was crisp and clear. Every movement seemed to cause another crackle that echoed across the countryside. They drew up outside the bakery.

"I do hate to enter dark buildings at night. Would you come with me, Nicole?"

Surely Shane would be better protection, Nicole thought, though it seemed unlikely that anyone would be breaking in to a bakery on Christmas Eve. Nevertheless, Nicole opened her car door and climbed out. It was the least she could do to repay the hospitality she'd enjoyed these past months.

In fact, the bakery wasn't dark. Showcase lights provided a glow that made it easy to move around.

"Now, just wait here, dear. I won't be a moment." Winifred bustled through the door into the back room. When, after many minutes, she didn't return, Nicole called out.

"Is everything all right, Winifred?"

"Oh, everything is fine, dear. Just fine. Won't be a moment."

Shrugging, Nicole moved to stand in front of the big picture window, staring into the night. Only a few vehicles traversed the main street tonight. Everyone was at home, with friends and family. Celebrating.

"Nicole?"

She twisted, stared at Joshua's smiling face and almost groaned. Oh, no. Why had Winifred chosen tonight to do her matchmaking? It was too much.

"I think there's been a mistake. I'm—"

"Leaving. I know. Are you completely set on becoming a surgeon?"

"What?"

He leaned on his crutches, his face shadowed so that she couldn't read the expression there.

"I mean, is it an absolute? You're determined and there's no way to talk you out of it?" He edged a little closer.

With the window behind her, there was nowhere for Nicole to go. She thrust her chin out, glared at him.

"Why? What difference does it make to you?"

"Quite a bit, actually. As senior doctor in the practice, and your boss, I'm required to assess your abilities and notify the college as to your suitability for such an undertaking. I thought you might like to hear my thoughts on the subject, so that you won't be surprised when you read the report.''

Nicole frowned, opened her mouth to tell him she didn't care what he would say, then hesitated.

"Do you really think I should keep Lucas Lawrence on?''

At least she was sure about this.

"Yes, of course you should. He'd make a perfect partner.'' She glared at him, tired of trying to understand. "That is what you wanted, isn't it? A perfect partner?'' How she hated those words. They only made her feel more inadequate.

Joshua nodded.

"Yes, I did. But Luc isn't the partner I need. Oh, he's a fine doctor, does a good job, but he doesn't meet all my specifications.''

She couldn't believe her ears. What else was he looking for? But he didn't give her the chance to ask.

"But that's beside the point. I can't recommend you to the surgical board, Nicole. Would you like to hear my report so you'll understand why?''

"You would dare to malign me…'' Chagrined, Nicole could only glare at him. Her eyes widened even farther when he let his crutches go and leaned forward, wrapping his arms around her waist.

"You see, I can't possibly recommend you when I think that what you're really good at is making me forget my own stupid agenda and concentrate on serving the people who most need my help.''

She froze, not knowing how to extricate herself.

"Luc would be an asset to the office, of course. But he isn't my perfect partner.''

"But he—''

"A perfect partner would be someone who could share my workload in the office and at home. My perfect partner is a woman who makes the days fun and brings laughter where there was gloom. My perfect partner is *you,* Dr. Nicole Brandt."

"Me?" She couldn't believe it. "But—"

"You," he whispered, one finger tracing her bottom lip. "I love you, Nicole. And even though you probably ought to be using your talents as a famous surgeon, I can't recommend that you leave because I think you belong here in Blessing. With me. As my wife."

"Joshua, what are you saying?"

"I'm saying that I love you enough to agree to whatever you want, as long as you say you'll marry me. If you truly want to pursue surgery, we'll pack up the girls and head to Boston. Or Timbuktu. I don't care where we go, or what you dream, as long as you always include me and the girls."

Nicole ordered her brain to rationally reason this out, but it wouldn't cooperate. She was ecstatic. And fearful. Delighted. And scared. Did she dare believe?

"I'm not sure that I'm the kind of person you need in your life, Joshua. I like my own way. I'm independent. I don't know anything about raising a family. And I make a lot of mistakes."

He cupped her face in his hands.

"The other night you said you loved me. Was that true?"

She nodded.

"Yes, but—"

He kissed her, long and satisfyingly, so that her knees wobbled and her heart sang.

"None of the rest matters, Nici. We'll learn it as we go."

"But I'll mess up and you'll get angry and the girls will hate me."

He shook his head, his smile tender, then reached out one hand and grasped a small box from the counter.

"Do you remember this?" He lifted the lid, held it so that she could see. "You left it for me the morning of the accident. Your farewell gift."

She nodded, fingered the plaque she'd had engraved.

"I didn't want to go that day, you know," she whispered. "I felt as if you'd locked yourself away and that the girls were losing you. I felt there was more I should have done. Your aunt suggested the words."

"I might have known such wisdom came from a cookie." He grinned.

The words she'd had inscribed leaped out. "The ship is safer in the harbor, but it is not meant for that."

"Joshua, I—"

"It's as true for you, Nici. You reached out, refused to become an imitation of your mother. You took a chance on your dad and found a wonderful relationship." His face begged her to think again. "Can't you reach out again, see the possibilities we could have—as a team? I love you. *You,* Nicole Brandt. Not what I tried to make you. Not what you wanted to become. I'm in love with you, right here, right now."

She sighed, her heart overflowing at those wonderful words.

"I want you to be happy, Nici, but I don't ever want you to try to be anything other than the beautiful woman you are."

"And the girls?"

"You already know the girls love you. Surely you don't doubt that?"

She smiled, shook her head. "No. I love them, too."

"And me?" A flicker of worry wavered through his blue eyes.

Out of the corner of her eye she saw a muscle twitch in his neck and knew he was afraid. That amazed and confounded her. Joshua Darling was afraid she wouldn't love him? The very idea was laughable.

"I love you, Joshua. So much it makes my breath catch and my heart shift into overdrive."

"Thank you, God."

He tugged her close and kissed her so thoroughly, Nicole had to finally pull away to draw new breath into her lungs. But his hands never left her, clinging as if he couldn't believe her words.

"And you'll be my partner? My perfect partner."

"I'm not perfect. Far from it." She grinned. "And neither are you. But I promise to love you anyway. No matter what."

"We'll continue negotiations later." He kissed her nose. "Right now I think there are some people we ought to share our news with." Taking her hand, he haltingly led her, without using his crutches, to the back of the bakery where Winifred sat perched on a stool, the girls in their Christmas finery waiting by her side.

"Did she say yes?" Ruthie demanded.

Nicole searched Joshua's face. "You told them?"

"Of course. If you wouldn't accept my pledge that I love you and want to marry you, I was going to sic these four on you." He bent, hugged his girls. "She said yes," he confirmed with a grin.

"Thank heavens." Rachel huffed out a breath that destroyed her perfectly combed bangs. "I thought you'd never decide, Nici."

Nicole laughed, delighted by their easy acceptance of

her new role. Then she caught sight of Ruthie's little face scrunched up into a frown.

"What's the matter, sweetie?"

In answer, Ruthie held out a crumpled page from a magazine.

"What's this?" Nicole took the sheet, smoothed it and blinked at what she saw.

"It's a fairy princess dress. Me 'n Rach 'n Rosie wanna wear them when the minister makes you our new mom. But Auntie Win says you might not like them." Her stormy face showed her unhappiness with that.

Nicole looked at Joshua, saw his smile and knew it was up to her. Just as he'd promised, she would be her own woman, free to be herself.

"Auntie Win was being very cautious, dear. You see, she knows a lot about weddings. I think she's helped plan a few."

"Perhaps just a few," Winifred murmured, fanning herself, a faint smile curving her lips.

"So I think what we should do is have a meeting and get everybody's opinion. Then when we go shopping for the dresses, you girls will be able to help me pick out my wedding gown."

"Thank you." The love in Joshua's eyes shone on her.

Nicole shook her head. "No. Thank you. This is the best Christmas I could have imagined."

"Me, too. But this is Christmas Eve. I think we should go home and celebrate our blessings."

"What blessings, Daddy?" Three little girls peered up at him.

Joshua crouched down and gathered them into the circle of his arms, then motioned for Shane, who'd sneaked in the back door, to join them.

"I think I'll celebrate my accident."

Ruthie frowned. "That wasn't a blessing."

"Wasn't it?" Joshua rose and brushed his lips against Nicole's cheek. "I think it was a blessing in disguise. Because of it, I found that God had already sent my perfect partner."

As he bent to seal their partnership, Joshua heard his aunt whisper, "Come along, girls. It's time you were home in bed, dreaming. Maybe tomorrow your wishes will come true."

They hurried out the door, but Nicole heard a noise and turned her head to look. She nudged Joshua.

"I already have my wish. And it's a blessing, too," Ruthie whispered, then blew them a kiss before she disappeared.

"So is mine." Nicole stood on tiptoe and brushed her lips against Joshua's chin. "Funny how God works, isn't it?"

As it happened, Ruthie chose all the dresses. Her sisters, suffering from a severe dose of the measles, were unable to travel to Boston in Shane's airplane, so Ruthie picked out three fairy princess dresses in white, with tiny red satin hearts scattered all over the skirts. She also helped Nicole find a gorgeous silk gown that everyone said made her look like a queen.

The Valentine wedding was by no means a small affair. No invitations were sent out, but everyone showed up. After all, Blessing was a friendly place. Everyone knew the doctors and wanted to see them wed. It was good their beloved Dr. Darling had found love again, and with such a perfect partner. And why shouldn't they have a honeymoon? Wasn't Lucas Lawrence on hand to deal with whatever maladies might appear?

The whole town had really cottoned on to the newest

doctor. The relationship was cemented right after Millicent Maple claimed she heard Luc talking to Winifred Blessing. Seems he'd taken a liking to the town and got to thinking about staying on. If there was room.

Everyone knew what Winifred had said.

There's always room for another blessing in disguise.

* * * * *

*Look for Luc's story in HEAVEN'S KISS,
the second book in Lois Richer's
BLESSINGS IN DISGUISE series,
on sale January 2004.*

Dear Reader,

Hello again! I'm delighted you've chosen to join me in my journey to a small Colorado town that I call Blessing. It's a perfectly normal town, where heavenly blessings aren't always easy to spot. In fact, when Dr. Joshua Darling suffers a terrible accident, the word *blessing* just doesn't seem to fit! But looks can be deceiving, as God uses pain to bring joy and love to hurting souls—with a little assistance from the town baker and her delicious love cookies. Isn't it just like God to send his blessings in disguise?

I hope you'll watch for my next book in the BLESSINGS IN DISGUISE series. Dani DeWitt thought she had the perfect life until her father died and she was forced to return home to the legacy of a ranch steeped in debt. Torn between trying to make the ranch pay and her dreams of becoming a playwright, Dani finds a friend in the town's newest doctor, Luc Lawrence. But Luc wants to settle down, while Dani knows that staying means revealing the awful secret she's uncovered. How can giving up her father's ranch possibly be a blessing in disguise?

I wish for you the greatest love, the strongest faith and the richest blessings from God's own hand.

Take 2 inspirational love stories FREE!

PLUS get a FREE surprise gift!

Mail to Steeple Hill Reader Service

In U.S.
3010 Walden Ave.
P.O. Box 1867
Buffalo, NY 14240-1867

In Canada
P.O. Box 609
Fort Erie, Ontario
L2A 5X3

YES! Please send me 2 free Love Inspired® novels and my free surprise gift. After receiving them, if I don't wish to receive anymore, I can return the shipping statement marked cancel. If I don't cancel, I will receive 4 brand-new novels every month, before they're available in stores! Bill me at the low price of $3.99 each in the U.S. and $4.49 each in Canada, plus 25¢ shipping and handling and applicable sales tax, if any*. That's the complete price and a saving of over 10% off the cover prices—quite a bargain! I understand that accepting the books and gift places me under no obligation ever to buy any books. I can always return a shipment and cancel at any time. Even if I never buy another book from Steeple Hill, the 2 free books and the surprise gift are mine to keep forever.

113 IDN DU9F
313 IDN DU9G

Name	(PLEASE PRINT)	
Address	Apt. No.	
City	State/Prov.	Zip/Postal Code

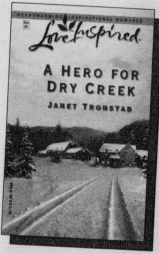